T0326134

HOW
FAR
WE'VE
COME

PRAISE FOR
HOW FAR WE'VE COME

'One of the most impressive young adult debuts of the year.
This gripping novel takes a nuanced look at the legacy of
slavery, injustice and inequality in today's world'
Observer

'Both hopeful and heartbreaking, this gripping book turns a
searchlight on the changing faces of injustice through time'
Guardian

'A brilliant idea and a powerful debut'
***The Times*, Children's Book of the Week**

'A seriously impressive debut. Read it now'
Irish Times

'A powerful exploration of racism, solidarity,
friendship, freedom and hope'
**Laura Bates, author of *Everyday Sexism*
and *Sisters of Sword and Shadow***

'A gut punch of a debut, this book is both
vital reading and a call to arms'
Laura Wood, author of *A Sky Painted Gold*

'A powerful, ambitious, unforgettable read
about freedom, rebellion, love and hope'
Liz Hyder, author of *The Gifts*

'Compassionate, brave, authentic, educational.
Everyone should read it'
Abiola Bello, author of *Love in Winter Wonderland*

HOW
FAR
WE'VE
COME

JOYCE EFIA HARMER

SIMON & SCHUSTER

First published in Great Britain in 2023 by Simon & Schuster UK Ltd

This paperback edition first published in 2024

Text copyright © 2023 Joyce Efia Harmer

This book is copyright under the Berne Convention.
No reproduction without permission.
All rights reserved.

The right of Joyce Efia Harmer to be identified as the author of this
work has been asserted by her in accordance with sections 77 and 78
of the Copyright, Designs and Patents Act, 1988.

1 3 5 7 9 10 8 6 4 2

Simon & Schuster UK Ltd
1st Floor, 222 Gray's Inn Road
London
WC1X 8HB

Simon & Schuster: Celebrating 100 Years of Publishing in 2024

www.simonandschuster.co.uk
www.simonandschuster.com.au
www.simonandschuster.co.in

Simon & Schuster Australia, Sydney
Simon & Schuster India, New Delhi

A CIP catalogue record for this book is available from the British Library.

PB ISBN 978-1-3985-1102-6
eBook ISBN 978-1-3985-1101-9
eAudio ISBN 978-1-3985-1100-2

This book is a work of fiction. Names, characters, places and incidents are either
the product of the author's imagination or are used fictitiously. Any resemblance
to actual people living or dead, events or locales is entirely coincidental.

Typeset in the UK

Printed and bound in the UK using 100% renewable
electricity at CPI Group (UK) Ltd

To my mum,
my only wish is to make
you as proud of me
as I am of you.

I had reasoned this out in my mind, there was
one of two things I had a right to, liberty or death;
if I could not have one, I would have the other.

HARRIET TUBMAN

The world is but one country
and mankind its citizens.

BAHÁ'U'LLÁH

AUTHOR'S NOTE

Dear Reader,

I have always been curious about time travel. There's a radio show where the host asks famous guests where they would go if they could travel to any period in time. I marvelled when the guest would say 'Ooh, the Victorian era, to see Britain beginning to industrialize!' or gush over the 'Georgian era costumes – I'd just love to be able to dress for dinner every night!' I thought about how they had the luxury of being able to consider any period of time in history accessible. For me, the answer would never, ever, be back in time. I could only ever contemplate going forward, into the future, where, with hope, the lives of Black people have improved. There is also a side to British history that isn't told. I wondered about the silent Black voices of that history, and I could start to hear the echo of their cries in my head.

When I first heard the voice of Obah, a slave girl in the early 19th century, I immediately wanted to propel her forward, to shift her out of the abyss into a time of change and equality. The more I thought about it, the more I realized that time was not quite here yet. I wanted to place her into our 21st century world and have her intoxicated by the freedoms and inventions she found, but, also, to understand ultimately that the world we are in today is still very much wanting in terms of equal opportunity and status for all.

I was born in London to displaced Ghanaian parents, and my character is born to a displaced Ghanaian too. She is the 'me' I would be were I to go back in time. The 'me' of my nightmares. Had I been born in Ghana, I wouldn't stand out in the office as the only non-white face, I wouldn't hear taunts behind my back as I pass in relation to the colour of my skin. I understand displacement, to not quite belong in the world into which one is born, and I also understand that I had been taught from an early age to accept this as normal, that as a Black woman my status was inferior, and this was unchallengeable and unchangeable. Through my love for reading, I discovered that words had the power to transform, and I could travel to different worlds. Obah has been conditioned to accept her lot in life. In this story, she gets to do the unimaginable: challenge and change her position in life, and she discovers the liberating freedom that comes from the power of words.

I want people to read this story and be inspired to challenge themselves to do something extraordinary. They can see that anything is possible, despite seemingly impenetrable odds. They can journey with Obah, walk in her shoes and empathize with her plight. They can challenge themselves and others to face the British history they haven't been taught in school. They can resist stereotyping others and fight together for social justice. To move forward in the creation of a world where there is unity of vision, and anything is possible, we need to understand our history first.

I am an optimist, and should I ever get the chance to propel myself two hundred years forward like Obah, I hope to be pleasantly astonished at what I find, and much more satisfied with humanity's progress. There will be stumbling blocks along the way, but I invite you to travel with me. Let's walk arm in arm and hand in hand.

Joyce Efia Harmer

PART ONE

UNITY PLANTATION, BARBADOS, 1834

CHAPTER I

When I's running, me feel free.

I don't feel the rough scratch of grasses snapping on me heels, I don't feel the lash upon my back.

I'm in the time before here time. Me see the world so soft again, and the warm and the wet. Me remember.

I be running and colours blur. Gold-greens and blacks spin and melt into themselves as I pass, the chipping sparrow songs my ear with the breeze, and I knows the way. I feel the way. Like I be a' arrow shooting through the sky. My course be set. Wish I could run and be free for ever. Wish there was somewhere to run to.

I can run faster than any of them other slave on the plantation. Including the men, even big and strong as them is, they is no match for me in running. That's why the mistress always send for me whenever she got a message for the field from the Big House. I be pleased to serve Mistress Frida. She kind. Only ever hit me once with the back of her hairbrush, and I know that be my own fool fault. I know I do fine when I deliver her letters. Even him, that nasty Overseer Leary, seem happy when he see me come.

'Girl, anyone seen you come up this way?' he ask, placing his night-time pot at my feet. I don't pay a mind to it, but that don't mean I don't have to clean it for him. His eyes is looking over my head into the thick cane as he pocket the letter. His can of liquor swill some and he wipe his mouth with the back of him hand. Always, he ask me the same question.

'No, sir, me run real quick, and I go round, past the outhouse, just like always. Just like Miss Frida say.'

Overseer Leary's top lip curl a little, his whipping arm rest light at his hip, his forefinger caress that cowskin hilt, it tap once . . . twice. Me breathing stops. Then him look upon me with them pretend kind eyes that be smooth and flat as stones. Him smile. But I is wise to his ways and now me not stupid enough to smile back.

Fingers press a way through him damp hair and he seem ready to turn on his heel but sway a little and step short, as if he remembering something.

'How old you is now, Orrinda? 'Bout twelve? Thirteen?'

Me look down upon the dust. Ants is crawling on me toes. Him call me Orrinda, but this is not my true name. I is named Obah, as me mother name me herself.

'If it please, sir. I don't rightly know my age.'

I is near seventeen, but that be *my* secret. Aunty Nita tole me how I is born same day as the masser and Miss Frida's own daughter, Miss Lynette! She always say, 'On that indigo night, two sets of wailing did pierce the sky at the self-same hour. Me no work out which babe was which from the bawling alone!'

4

Nita rub at her sore eye, but it weep on, still. 'Only ting you two got in common was them falling tears, you know for why? Me go tell you. It because, lickle babes know what's coming, that's why them crying. *Hmhmm*. Tears of pain, Obah, that's what fly out from you like a new-sprung well. But that Missis Frida? Ha! Her babe's tears is purest joy.' She nod her head, hard and heavy. 'Babes born white cry drops of silver, but the babe born black like we? Him cry salt tears.' She laugh then, big and earthy and show me the pink drop at the back of her mouth, her own salt-tears wets her apron and she wipe them away, wincing as she bring on pain from the tender eye.

I know Miss Lynette and me, we cries different tears, but in secret, I is thinking this being born together be an omen. A good one. Maybe life got more in store for me than work, beatings and death.

Leary wipe his hands upon his thigh.

'Master Cooke is planning on taking some of the negroes to auction next week. Reckons *you* will fetch him a handsome price. You will be a good breeder when the time comes. A healthy chattel bitch is gold in this pigsty of a country.'

'Please, masser, don't sell Orrinda away. Me want stay, me tend to Miss Frida real good. Me a hard worker, masser, everyone know.' The words trip out of me mouth. Even though me know me shouldn't, me beg same way. Me palms slip upon themselves with sweat. Please, Lord, how me don't want to be sold.

Him fingering his whip again. His fingers is all-the-time restless and me keep me eye upon his hand because I know it can move fast. Me can feel him daring me to lift up me head, but me tell meself, don't look at his black eye. Me don't forget the hurt that caused me the last time. From his night-time pot, a rotten taste settle at the back of my throat, but still, me no stoop or cower, me pray him take a little pity on me for once.

The thin breeze caresses me as it pass and as it lift up the low branches of the pine behind Leary, me eyes find something be moving there, it is white with eyes, and a face. Me cannot stop myself from jumping up with fright.

He is waiting on me lifting up me head; it be a sure sign of my insolence. Him don't need an excuse to hurt me, but him like to have one same way, so him give me a blow to the crown with the butt of his drinking can. Me feel meself fold, knees touching earth, knocking the piss pot over. His mess slides through the wet dust to kiss my legs and the stench stings, but me stays still. I ready for the something worse, waiting for the lash to fall.

Turning him head he spit. 'Come on, we're friends, I'm only playing. We won't sell you, Orrinda. I know how much Miss Frida loves you as her plaything.' Me look up at him, watching the spittle dance a little from his bottom lip, then it breaks its chain and flies off to freedom. Him stroke my arm, gently, top to bottom, with the tails of his whip. Teeth stained brown with tobacco give me his crocodile smile again. But he no see. Him no feel the eyes from the trees staring upon me now. Satisfied, for now, him take another swig from the can.

'Clean up that mess and be back in the usual time.'

He is already turning from me, making him way back to him

lodge. Him always read Miss Frida's letter there as if to hide the secrets that she telling him. Them is secrets from the masser too – that much I know.

Me take in new air, breathing heavy, but all me smell is Leary on me, even as he walk away. Me bow me head and thank God for his mercy, but the Lord is too far away, high in the sky and can never hear my mutters.

Me look again at the tree for the pale face. It be gone, but in the breezeless heat, the tree still sways.

CHAPTER 2

As me step away from Leary me see how the sun have place my shadow long and high in front of me. The black shape on the ground is tall and thin, but the top rounds where the knotted scarf sit at my head. The threads that fall from my dress hem shake like spider's legs and me pause for a moment to watch them shiver and press upon the air.

I pick up my pace. Making my way away from Leary's cabin and past the bearded fig tree to where the tamarinds begin their standing tall. The first quarters me pass be the men's. In this quarter there sit six wooden cabins, facing each other with a piece of empty red dirt dividing them like a dried-up river. Nothing grows here, as if the ground itself shuns life. The warped wooden fencing ring around them cabins keeps me from seeing more than the gap will show but I press my eye against the hole by the front post and look in. I know that here is where Uncle Hector and the other mens stay living, or at least, where they sit and ponder in the small hours that them have to themselves.

A cough ring out from within the nearest cabin and me

jump a little as if me has been caught standing here staring. The cough come again, heavy this time and when it die down the cursing that follow it make me cover me ears for shame. The coughing one must be Apollo. He have a pipe that he love to fill with dried-up leaves and puff at – fashioned it himself from whittling bark. Aunty Nita say that if you ever try to keep smoke inside, it will do all its best to get out; just how it climb out of a chimney, it'll climb outta your chest, and that is why Apollo sound how he do. I just glad it ain't the cough from no ailment. Them coughs is the ones we all fear. The ones that put us into the ground when no doctor come.

Seeing how it is Sunday, me know the men will not need to make a way towards the fields for the cane harvesting. Masser Cooke be a tyrant, but he also a true servant of the Lord and his hand will never raise against us on a sabbath. The morning is full upon us, but these men refuse to rise, enjoying the sojourn of the Lord's day.

The dirt is warming up nice under foot and I bend to scratch away a ladybug that be inching up my leg, but when I see her, I let her stay upon my finger instead, counting up her spots, one, two, three . . . and then she open up her back and fly away. I watch until she just a speck of dust, wondering where she flying to and if I can follow.

A warning sound come from the tawny owl who live in the sassafrass tree, as though him have open one eye from him slumber to warn me off. So I pull my prying eye away from the plank and I walk along some more. I tap the letter in my pocket but dare not take it out to examine the lines written. Even though me cannot read much, sometimes me love to cast my eye over the lines Leary and Miss Frida make with their feathers. Wondering what the river curls of twisting ink be saying to each other. Running my thumb upon the sharp sweet edge of the parchment. I stare and I stare but it never make no sense. Me can't take it out now, though, I need to be careful. One thing me know for sure is how these words cannot be seen by Masser Cooke – Miss Frida most particular on that score.

Me is approaching the women's cabins upon the other side of the path, up aways from the men's, after the storehouse and the well. The women ain't like the mens, them up and about working already. Don't seem like they have the same respite, even though it's the Sabbath and all. Them women have eyes that will see what I hold. What I hide. Masser Cooke will be delivering his sermon and that is when I can lay the letter from bad Leary at Miss Frida's door. That be the time when she prefer.

The first cabin in the women's quarters belong to the weavers, Rosemary and Anna. Both of them is ancient ladies with hair that sit upon their heads as though a cloud come down out of the sky to rest a while and forget to leave. I see them now, grass broom in hand, each one bent over and brushing away at the never-ending rusty dirt as it fan about them. Them sure is proud to keep their quarters neat and straight. Next cabin along belong to Bertha. Bertha used to work in the field but now she taken over with the soap making after Eunice passed away. She sit looking out upon the courtyard, hand playing with the soft hair beneath her scarf. Her hair is long and silky black, falling upon her back, not like the rest of us. She laughs at how we other women has hair that seems to stand upon its hind legs. At her feet is her younguns, two little heads that look like hers sit upon their necks with hair as curly and fair as hers is dark and straight. One of her babbies, Bella, be chewing on a husk of Guinea corn and the other, Hanna, hold a slither of dried fish in her bunched fist and my stomach growl with jealousy at the sight. These are the end of the crop times, when the weather is dry and the sugar plenty, but we still feel as though we hunger all the time.

Next to, in the cabin with the broken door that wheeze when the wind blow, is where Mad Lizzy reside. She ain't nowhere to be seen. But it is day-time and we know she hate the sun for fear it brown her beige skin. More women pass me, entering into the quarters now with wet rags that they has beat against the rocks to clean. I curtsy to them and turn away, the weight of the letter heavy against my leg as I work towards our cabin, the one I share with Aunty Nita and Murreat, it sit at the far end of the quarters, under a little pip apple tree.

Further along, beyond our fence and pass the fields, is where Mimbah's cabin be. Not by the nearing thickets, where the trees are bigger and the baobab we call Martha have grown old. Not in the men's quarters nor the women's. Not by the sugar mill or by Savio the blacksmith. Mimbah stay alone. I send a longing look towards the weeds that lead to where she stay, thinking of her, my dear and truest friend, in her solitude. I will visit her soon, but now, I has to remember my duty.

CHAPTER 3

Me have a little time before Leary will be ready with him reply so me pick up him pot, gather up what slip out with a twig of cane, and walk down towards the spring in the valley to clean it. I trying not to dwell on the bump forming on my temple. The spring water's song groans, tender and pitying, she call me on as I step closer and closer. She love me for true, me can hear it in her voice. Me toe curl over roots, grasses straighten their backs from under my trekking heels, I be making my way. I stroke the tree barks as I pass, me fingers trace all them hollows and grooves, their history, their strength that's bound up in years and in that moment, me feel safe.

Maybe I did dream up that small white face by the tree just now. Maybe I did dream up them eyes, me sure they was blue, that did look upon me like them was sad.

Sometime, me love to dream. Me love to dream that me is a person, a proper one, like them white folks is. In me dream, I be eating meat with a spoon, and me hair kiss up me cheek because the wind is blowing gentle. Aunty Nita say, she worried me dreaming is going to put me into a whole heapa trouble one day. But I know that dreams are not the same as truth. I is not a proper human. Masser himself confirm that at every Sunday sermon. I is nothing close. I is just like a dog or a chicken excepting one difference, I dream.

The cold from the spring climbs into me as I bend, bidding me welcome and I cup both hands to sip the cool water. I study my hand in the stream, looking at how black it be all over, me turn it to and fro, seeing it grow darker and darker still. Then me hand gone – disappear! I lift up me eye, searching for the light, but the pot-belly sun is gone. All is dark where the sun did glow and silence come with it. There's only nightfall all around and even the rowdy blue birds stop their chatter to bear witness to the sudden dark sky. I blink in the blackness for a moment more, listening to the silence, even the spring has stopped her mouth. The darkness rests on me as if she be weary, waiting for a time to rest her aching bones. What has happened to the day? How can it disappear in but a moment? I never saw the like of this before.

I turn about, alone in the day-dark, my eyes searching for light. And then, slowly a golden scythe appears in the sky, growing bigger and brighter till I have to turn my head away. And with my blinking the night-time fades, like when one of my dreams is dying. I rub a little on my temple, staring at the strange sun. That brutish and wicked Mister Leary did hit me harder this time for true.

Shaking my aching head, I sup some more from the spring, but me thirst don't quench easy because that growing, silent midday sun is beating down hard again. Me know me got time enough to sing me lickle song three times over before Leary be ready with his letter. I sip more water, clean and bubbly cold and sit down at the old baobab tree, thick with ash-white bark. Me run me fingers upon her thick veins. I know this tree, I feel the familiarity of it and hug its life to me for protection. This be the tree I call Martha, living and breathing, a bit like me. Me press me back to her and open me mouth to sing. This day, somehow, new words flow out of me, a new song, a new gift. The melody pour forth as though it a song of past times, as though it from an ancient memory.

'Oh, lickle lamb, why you tremble so?
me not gone
me not gone
Oh, lickle lamb, take me hand so.
me not gone
Yet.'

Me get to sing it just once before me see him, a stranger from behind the pines, coming for me.

Stepping out, me see him. He be looking on me and like he calming a babe, him have arms outstretched low. It be a white, a white around my age, but me no recognize him from here, him not from Unity. Me feet is itching to run because them know something about this don't look right, but they stuck fast, me can't get 'em to move. 'Stead of running, me fix to gaze upon him. Him

14

so strange looking that me eye want to take in all his looks before my feet will move. He be tall, higher than Master Cooke, with a slender limb and hair darker than charred tin. Him features be even and regular, skin smooth and pale as the cameo Miss Frida like to rest at her throat. Just a freckle or two on his left cheek, sky-blue eyes is large, sitting under the longest dark lashes me ever see. Him strange garments be so clean they almost gleaming like him no have a speck o' nothing living on him.

This white boy, this stranger in the brush, he breathing, but nothing else. Me stare still and him stare back at me, the both of us quiet. Seem him eyes is as round and scared as mine, his head twist and turn about as if confusion sit upon his shoulder as he stare at me hard, his eye taking in my stained and ragged garments, my unshod feet, my rag-tied hair as if him have never seen a slave before. Them be the same pained eyes on me as before, in that tree behind Leary. Why him follow me here? A cold wetness sit on the back of my neck as I watch him, waiting for his next move.

His pitying eye open larger and his mouth open too, new sounds start to come, such as me no hear before. What is him saying? His voice mellow in colour, soft, it wash me up, wrap me into it even though me cannot understand him words. Sweet and kind, him voice is not gruff and angered. Me have lean me head close to him, as if to hear him well. Me have never heard a white speak like this. Him voice make me lose myself a moment, me enjoying it, him word sounds prickle my skin, prickle my blood.

15

Suddenly, him stop his words and his eye meet mine. I stare into the warm blueness and him stare back at me. We blink, together, and somehow, I is certain me is looking into the eye of friendship. But then, I straight myself up. Me wake up from me stupor. Me look to see where he carry him whip but he don't seem to keep it in him belt. Like a negro, him don't have any belt! Me can't feel any comfort when me can't see a white man's whip, can only mean he hiding worse things for me to worry about.

'Please, Master, me not fixing to run, me just do a little errand is all.' Me voice break up as me plead with him, this stranger. Me not supposed to be seen in these parts, not in the noon time. Miss Frida say to make sure of it and me don't want to get in no trouble. Where Miss Frida concerned, me must be straight and true, me no want her to become vexed with me. Him keep him eye on me and keep mouthing words me cannot understand. Me cannot understand him body neither, twisting and turning about his head from tree to sky to me and back again, looking all about him as though him is lost.

Maybe this young one here be a new overseer. Maybe he been sent out by Master Cooke himself. Have him come out to check upon we, and have follow me up from the Big House? Master Cooke do like to keep we upon we toes, like to make sure we not lazing. Him known to lash us himself; him not just leave it to nasty Leary. This boy do seem young but that don't account for nothing, everyone must work if them not own land. If them is able and have a limb that can swing in the sun, them work. Me know that well enough.

16

Me have bad feeling in me belly 'bout this. Me mind run quick and me trying to work out how me can get out of this situation whole.

Slowly, him advance, stepping his foot towards me like him gliding. Me blink. Me want to scream, but it seem like dirt sit in my throat. As him slip up to me closer, on silent feet, me do what any sober slave do if she see a white man pressing upon her person, me turn on me heel and run. Heart jumping in me chest, like it want get out, me breathe shallow.

Once me reach the other side of the stream, me catch a breath. Set down behind the hanging tamarind, me find a tallish thicket to hide by. Crouching low, but me can still hear him voice coming at me from all around, like it know where me hide. Me think this time me understand him.

'It's okay. Look, it's okay.' *What do 'okay' mean?* 'What is this place?' me hear him say. *What? Him don't know where him be?* Me cover me mouth with both hands. *What him be?*

A five-finger of sunlight slide through the cracks in the branches to warm me in my hiding place, but me feel only cold. Him going to find me and what then?

Mimbah did give me the warning before about this little wood, she tell me how there be persons living here *that is not from Unity's parts.* Them talk different. Them have moved from the earth and gone to the other side. When me tell her about how me must carry message for Miss Frida, she tell me, 'Obah, mind yourself out there, hear me now? Me warning you for true. After you pass by mill is when you soon start to see duppy roaming, duppies is them peoples that be dead but come back, thinking them still living! Did me never tell you how me see one there before? Them harvest the tamarind there. Him use him teeth to bite straight off the tree while me watch.' She open her mouth wide and bite an empty bite at me.

Mimbah, she have the sight, so she know all the ways and habits of the dead. She know how when them restless, them seek to feast on we that's living, but me never believe her, till today.

Him voice come nearer again, like him playing some kind of seeky-seeky game on me. Me must get back to the lodge but that mean running back into the clearing, no trees to hide me. Overseer Leary expecting me to return for his letter. If me not there . . . me fingers graze upon me elbow and me shiver, rubbing at my scar from before.

Me feel a hard fear. This white duppy must be here for my blood. Me scream out. Me can't keep it in no more, it fling out into the trees, up to the sky. Slow, me head stretch out from the bush and the sun bite as me come out. Me nail stinging from when me press hard at the white bark, but me all right. Him gone. The way is empty. Me start to laugh at me foolishness. This have to be a dream of mine, Mimbah must have put a little fear in me is all. There is no ghost upon me.

'Please, don't run again. I'm not going to hurt you. I . . . I need your help. Where am I? What is this place?' Him back and he be speaking to me in him strange tongue full of fear. How him right beside me? Me never see him walk, me never hear him footstep. Me swallow.

18

'Please, masser, what me can do for you?' Me voice be weak with fear. Slow and strange, I watch how him turn his body all around, him arms stretch out and touch the tree but shrink back, as if it have burn him. His eyes widen and his head look up at the trees and all about, as if he a stranger in this place. Maybe duppies have no memories of how the world be?

'Masser? What do you mean? What's a masser?' Him breath stings the cut on my cheek. Him voice have a soft lilt. Me never hear a white man speak soft so. We stare upon each other in the quiet like neither one of us breathing.

'Is you living or dead?' I says. Me say it real soft, soft like him speak to me. Me scared to death, but me use all me courage, me must try to save meself from this elsewhere visitor.

'Dead?' Him clear eye be as curious as him voice.

'Yes, sir, is you living and breathing?' me says. 'Kind sir, I beg you tell me now, if you is a duppy? When we all fall dead, is it a white skin we must wear?'

Him laugh, throw back him head and open his mouth so I can see how him still have all him teeth. Him laugh make me ponder if him have a duck living in him belly, but me don't know what is the joke. Only thing this can mean is, maybe him not a duppy at all, maybe him just white, and that is worse. Me no laugh with him, me keep me face stern so me can be ready for him when him turn. For when that laughter stop and the joke be over and the whipping start and the pain and screaming with it. But he don't switch. Him hug up him sides, body bending like cane pushed back this way and that. Me lick at the cold wetness

19

sitting above my lip. Me waiting. And suddenly him stop. Him face turn dark and me feel him chill.

'Look, you know what? I have no clue what you're saying or why you're speaking like that? All this sir and masser stuff? What is this place? Who are you?'

Feathery tamarind leaves hanging low from the branches brush me shoulder, them smell sweet and clean. Funny, me never did notice that smell when I been here before, never notice how them pods be dripping with scent. Me head say, 'Run, Obah – you know you can move fast, you can get away from him.' But, from above me, the swaying brown pods send out another word, soft, soft, them tell me 'stay'. Like me have nothing to fear. Me take in him dark head of curls and the bright clear eye and the clean teeth, the strange words and me wonder how come all these dead things put together, don't make me feel terrible afraid.

CHAPTER 4

Overseer Leary don't seem to pay no mind to my absence. Me must have gone for a high time, but it seem him only just be coming out the lodge as me now return. Most days, him not take much time at all on him writings, but today him letter be long and thick. I glad for it. One beating from him be enough for one day. Them black eyes scowl and him inky black nails leave prints like raccoon tracks on the letter he press on me, weighty in my palms.

'Hand that straight to your mistress. Don't tamper with it, or tarry. I will know if you do. The good Lord gave us whites special eyes in the back of our heads to hunt down the idle.'

'Yes, masser.' I bob my head. Me can well believe him. Me hate God just a little more for that.

Clutching his hot letter in me hand, me run back to where the strange white boy be waiting. Lord, me can't believe him stupid enough to want to follow me, like a puppy, and the whole time me have to explain to him that he need to stay out of sight. Only thing me can tell for sure is that him talk like we is friends and that mean he don't have no sense. Me wonder if he gon' be there still and me surprised that he is. Shoulder against the tree, him finger stroke on something in him hand, a ball of shining silver it look to me. Him slip it into his shirt pocket when him see me coming. I look on his strange clothes, the colours sing bright, his shirt be blue as his eye but him breeches be dark night and a heavy material. The shoes on him feet be strange too, white as a china plate! Never see a shoe shine in the sun like them, even though them standing in all the black of the earth. Me wonder where him have left his hat.

Living or dead? Me not sure, but me can't seem to mind. Him eye be kind, with a small speck of damp.

Me wonder for a moment if him know me is black. Slick black as a wet creek, me face is shinier than oil. No high red or pale tones in my skin, no way me can pass for white, not like baby Emmie and Mad Lizzy. Me is just black. Maybe a duppy can't see colour?

'What's that?' him ask, pointing to the letter in my hand. I tuck it inside me apron pocket, but my hand stay firm on it so it don't slip out of the hole that's there. Miss Frida say these letters be our special secret. Me must keep my mistress's counsel.

Him don't press my silence, instead he nod and accept my secrecy. 'So, what's your name?'

'Me name? Them call me Obah . . . pardon me, sir, Orrinda.'

'Obah or Orrinda, which one is it?'

'Pardon, masser, them call me Orrinda, negroes call me Obah.'

'Er, sorry, what?'

'Begging pardon?'

22

'I can't believe you said that!'

'Sir? Me sorry if me spoke bad, me did mean to say niggers.' Him take a step back as if me have slap him and his pale face get more white, shaking him head from one side to the next as though him having a bad dream that him cannot wake from. There is a silence between us before him speak again but the colour stays drained from his face. His voice is soft when him finally open him mouth.

'I like Obah. Does it mean anything?'

Me eye move down to him hands, me must be sure him hands and my free tongue match up. Him fingers be playing soft with a branch, picking at the leaves, but me know that sassafras tree limb not strong enough to make a good whip. Me eye stay upon him white fingers, marvelling at them clean nails, everything about him seem shiny and unsullied, my opposite. A rustle behind him drag me eye away to the tamarind branch where a hummingbird sit, watching us converse, green neck cocked curious at this exchange.

Me know who named me, and me know what it mean too. But can me trust this stranger? Can me tell him my truth? Me can hear Nita's voice telling me to hush me mouth, but me no listen.

'I be given that name from my own mother, before she leave,' me say, pride walking in my voice. 'But Miss Frida, she give me Orrinda.'

'Your own mother?' him say, questioning if he hear me right.

'Yes, sir.' Me courage is all at the front of me chest as me speak

23

what is true. 'Me mother, she come from Africa, the Guinea coast. Me don't remember her face good, but Nita say me face be hers anyway. She have one pickney before me but him die before him can take a breath and Nita say, when she pull me out and me mother see me breathing, she give me my name. It mean, "she have come".'

'She have come.' Him pause, thinking on something in him mind. 'I'm Jacob. That's my name.'

Me hear the kick in his voice, and me look hard on him, my new half-white, half-duppy shadow. In that moment, the voice, the clothes, the softness of him; me legs feel like them be sinking down into earth and darkness. Like him burying me dead with him.

Me must get back to the Big House. Miss Frida will be wanting this letter and me have chores calling for me too, there be yams to peel, the yard to sweep, and me must tend to the pickney hunger. Aunty Nita gon' bite my ear when she see me come. But, somehow, even though trouble be waiting, there be a pull keeping me here that's just as strong. This half-dead Jacob may be bearing a peril I can't see, but me think, if him feeling to beat me, him would have done it already. White men can't resist a whipping, them not like dogs who can bury a bone and keep it for later, them bite when them hungry.

'You no come from Barbados, sir?'

Him eyes widen. 'Barbados? Is that, this? Wow . . .'

'And, you not gon' hurt me?'

'Why would I want to hurt you?'

'Why?' I ask him back and we stand staring at each other. Me is blinking at his question and him stand blinking back. Me have me confirmation. Him is most suredly a duppy from the dead.

'The thing is – I'm not really from around here.'

'Sir, me know it.' I curtsy to him low, keeping my head down as I speak more. 'Me happy not to be beaten, but still, I is sorry you dead. You seem young to die. Was it a fever that did take you?' My tremble has lessen, now that I have say out loud what I know, I feel the release of all my fear. Me do not fear this ghost. Me will go ahead and tell him about me mother. Duppies only stay for three days before them have to leave earth, me know that from Mimbah. Maybe that's why me tongue go so loose with him.

Jacob blink at me and leave a silence in the air. So I tell him what happen. 'Them say she run off. Them say she did make it to Haiti, where the negro can live free. Either way, she be gone ten year now and them never find her.'

'Your mother?'

Me nod me head. 'Me think she get away. Me think, she push herself into a ship, in a hogshead bound for Haiti, Nita did tell me how she clever.'

His eyes is lowered, but me know them seeing me, them following my words. So me go on.

'Me never been beyond Unity. Me cannot picture what this Haiti do look like, but me know you must cross a big body of water to reach it. Apollo talk of freedom soon come for us negro, just as in Haiti. I was a small pickney when him did tell we what him overheard from Masser's own mouth, how in England, them have stopped the slaving. Meaning them cannot bring more of we from Africa, massers must be making do with we on the plantation. When the time come, when freedom come, Mother will return and bring me to her home, because all should be free as she!'

Gasping, me finish. Me have never said this aloud before. And now him know me secret, I will know if him living or dead. Me lift up me head and look into him eye which brim with strange tears.

'Listen. Did I hear you right? Are you some kind of *slave*? Trapped here?'

'What else me could be? Me speak free with you on account of how you is a duppy-man.'

'What . . . what year is it?' Him hand have climb up to rub at him throat, once, twice.

'Year?'

Him exhale a breath hard and long. 'This is . . . wow . . . Okay, listen. Obah. You need to understand something, I don't know why I'm *here*. I'm not like the others you know, who live here with you on this . . . plantation. I'm from the future.'

The eye is earnest, the blue of it seem burning black at me with its sincerity.

'Me have never heard of any "future" – it near to Haiti?'

Jacob open him mouth, but before him speak, we both of us hear it. The angry rumble of the sky above us. Him tilt him face up at the sky and me can see it too, a tight fist in the air, rolling towards us like Mother Nature been beating at her rug. A storm soon come.

Him turn to me, pick up me hand and shake it, like one white gentleman to another. Him hand feel soft like the cloud above.

'This is so messed up. But I'm gonna fix this, okay? I need to go and get help.'

And as me blink, him gone. Him leave me standing, looking at me hand, wondering why me still can feel the warmth of him.

CHAPTER 5

Miss Frida snoring gently when me tap against her door. It resemble the soft thunder that continue all about the house outside. Me press it open and see her lying in repose against her chaise. Me hold me breathing in as me watch her, me feet silent as they cross upon the rugs that line her chamber floor. Her bosom rise and fall with every breath, as if she carry a heavy burden upon her. A small fire have been lit in her grate and the room is warm with the smell of charred rosewood. There is warmth from the cool of the storm outside, the sound of rain pitter patters on the panes. Me tiptoe in and pull the paper from my pocket, gently placing it upon her vanity. Me turn to walk out when she stir.

'Orrinda? Is that you, my dear?' Her voice is thick with slumber.

'Yes, miss. Is you needing me before you dine?' Me curtsy, pulling out me apron a little at the hem.

'You have my correspondence?'

'Upon the vanity, miss.'

'Good. You've seen Master Cooke on your way?'

'No, miss.'

'Good. Good.' She settle back upon her chaise and the emerald blue velvet dip as her head twist to one side and she close her eyes again, unable to fight against the want to sleep, her voice is slow and thick. 'The world is changing, Orrinda, but not for us. We won't let it change our ways. My husband doesn't understand what needs to be done. How important it is to maintain what's ours, even against the threat of . . . modernity. Do you understand?'

Me not sure what she want me to say but me take her heavy and slow speech for a signal. These is the times, when the room is warm and the sun lie low, when Miss Frida have taken a drop of wine and her heart beat soft for me. Me can ask her a question and maybe she will answer true. The duppy. Him say him coming from a place far from here, maybe Miss Frida will know where it stand from Unity.

'Miss,' me whisper. Miss Frida's eyes open a little, making two dark lines in her white skin.

'Leary. He understands. He understands me. We will save Unity. And Master Cooke. He doesn't know it yet, but this is the best way.' Her words is mumbles now.

'Miss,' me say again. 'Where be "the future"? It far from here?'

'The future? What do you mean?' She strain as if to sit up but me sidle up to her and press me palm gentle against her crown, as she like, to settle her still. This half-repose bring less scrutiny for me questions.

'Is the future a place that stay far from us? Far from Unity?'

'You want to know where the future is? Why, we just turn a corner, and it's there,' she say, before closing her eyes and drifting away into a soft dream.

As me close the door behind me gentle, leaving my mistress in her repose, me feel a hand squeeze hard against me shoulder, holding me captive. When me look up, me meet Master Cooke's eye.

'Miss Frida rests?' him ask me, as if him do not know her ways and customs.

'Yes, masser.' Me tip me head downwards to look at the black knots and turns in the mahogany boards, me don't like to look at him eye, him eyes is not as Jacob's, the blue may be just as bright, but the malice shine there plain to see.

'Good. Good. She has had a pressing time of late. Her sister's death still unsettles her. The months may have passed but her feelings still run somewhat raw. Attend her well, Orrinda. On no account must you let your mistress down.'

CHAPTER 6

As me approach the Big House today me break off running early. The red sun hangs hot and low above me head and so me measure me walk back. The Big House look handsome in the half-light dancing with the shadows and the bearded fig trees wave their falling roots at me, beckoning me home. Today's letter sits stiff in my pocket.

These last two days, Miss Lynette have celebrate her own birthday, she did open presents of silk gloves and bonnets, skipping about with delight at all the activities. Guests come and go in them fine garb and I tell meself a new dream, these is my merriments, these is my gifts, that me be seventeen too. How me feel every one of them years; me is so tired of living this life. Me think of the duppy boy – me never did know him age and now him gone, to him final resting place, as me have not seen him since.

'Obah, what tune you hum?' Uncle Hector have finish him Big House weeding and is heading past me, back to the second gang. 'Do not give Miss Frida cause to push you from the Big House and back into the third gang. Keep the African song in your chest.' Him pat my shoulder, him wrinkled fingers kind and warm.

'Begging pardon, Uncle Hector.' I curtsy to him.

Him nod and shuffle off, him bad leg dragging him back with each step. Me watch how the dust swims about him, as he scorpion-walk away and a memory stings. Something Nita say yesterday make me pick up my heels and chase after him. Him turn then, just as me reach him shoulder, like him know me is upon him. A deep noise press out of him throat to let me know me have him ear.

'Uncle Hector,' I whisper. 'You did know me mother good? You did know the story about where she run to?' Slowly, him blink at the dirt, then him check over him shoulder for Masser Leary before lifting him eye to meet mine.

'Your mother?' His head is not far above my own, on account of being low standing, but him lean in towards me to make sure no one else can hear. As him bend, him hair – crisp like black maize – scratch me forehead. Slowly, the three teeth him have left appear, candles in the dark as he part him lips. 'Truth be, your mother a strong, fine woman. Mighty brave. Mighty powerful. She living still, me sure of it. Me have no doubt she living, and free.' I open my mouth to gasp. Him have never tell me this before, why now?

'Me want to follow her.' The words is out of me before me think them and make me stumble with surprise. 'Me want to leave this place, Hector, for all of we to find freedom, just as she did. Freedom is not just for the birds.' The words hit heavy in my soul. Me have never voice these thoughts before, and I feel something waking up in me.

'Birds?' Him look about him at the sky and turning back, him eyes burn with amber as if a fire have kindled there. Just as quick, blackness return. 'You growing up, Obah. You have the same fire in your belly as she. But listen, child, freedom is lost. When your mother did find it, she close the door behind her.'

'Why? Why it be just she who can live free?' Me lift me chin and hold his stare in mine. 'Possible for all if it possible for one.' Hector's chest rise and fall slow.

'Child, you think such things. But none can help with freedom. None here. Listen, there be some things you old enough to know about your mother, but not here – it not safe.' Before me can press for more, him turn to limp away. A red-feather hen, busy with pecking, complain with fear and weave out of his way. Me want to follow after, grab and shake him and make him tell me what him know, but the sound of a window closing and blond ringlets bouncing by the top left window catch my eye. Miss Frida is looking for my approach.

The corner of the envelope I carry from Overseer Leary caress me thumb as me start to resume me steps to the Big House, pondering again on the duppy. Me singing this song of mine all the time since me met him, making circles of sweetness and sadness in me head, like a trapped honeybee, as if to conjure him back. Him not here to ghost me, but him haunt me still. Me pick up my heels now, running a pace to close the last distance to the house. If me don't get this envelope to

Miss Frida soon, me gon' be the next duppy.

Miss Frida be admiring herself in her dressing mirror when I enter the room. She drop the brush and put a smile on her face like me have brought her a tray of sea grapes when me hand her the note from Overseer Leary. Her fingers snatch the envelope like them is hungry to eat it. As her eyes be on my delivery, me take this moment to push back the tufts of hair that be poking out of me head scarf, neaten up a little, so Miss Frida can't complain me is haggard. Then me study my mistress' profile. One time, me did hear Leary praise Masser Cooke on him wife being great beauty, but even though her skin be fair as breadfruit, and her hair yellow as ackee, there be something no right about the set of her face. How she chin curl up and she teeth peek out even when the mouth close, so me wonder if this be an honest truth.

Without knocking, Miss Lynette open the door to the apartment and march towards her mother who slip the correspondence into a drawer at her vanity. For a moment, their voices become a quiet hum in me ear, I turn them voice into mosquitos, let them buzz about me, as me look around this room. The moss-green velvet curtains be hanging heavy, the fabric coiled up on the floor like a green dog resting from supper, its softness bathes my eyes. On the dresser, beneath the mirror shining golden bright, be a portrait of the family. Me marvel at what the painter have done. Like him did use some kind of mischief to make them small and trap the family in him paper.

There's Masser Cooke standing proud, shiny black hat pushing skywards, body turned to the side and one leg bent a little at the knee, his arm hold a walking cane pointing to the ground. Him body is still but something about them eyes staring out on me be making me feel a little unease like him can jump right out. Seated to his side be the mistresses dressed up in rosy pink skirts and jewels aplenty. Every finger be ringed, them white necks trimmed with stones, Miss Frida have her favourite pomander on her lap, even from here me smell how it filled with scent, how it sparkle on her lap. Me have never known a day when she have not worn it close to her person.

'Mother, I simply cannot decide. Must I wear the rose feathered bonnet or the indigo with the French gown?' Miss Lynette breaks my dreaming, her plain face sullen. She sigh, 'Can you fathom it? Seventeen and still no official engagement to speak of. Shall I die on this island an old maid?'

Miss Frida gathers her skirt together and head for Miss Lynette at once, kissing her on the crown and taking both hands in hers.

'Lynette, my dear, indigo has never been a friend to your complexion. It shall be the rose of course. And, my darling, whilst seventeen is a most accomplished age, there is yet time enough for courtships and engagements. There, there, dry your eyes, dearest, Cousin Thomas will soon come to see sense, Papa will talk to him and rectify his lack of conviction.'

'But, Mama, he should have been here to celebrate with me. What if he should shun me anew?'

'It is the passing of my dear sister that causes his despondency.

35

He must understand it was her most ardent wish that you two should form an attachment. If he is still indifferent in the coming months, we shall arrange for you to come out in London! A debutante amongst discerning men of distinction. Have no fear, my dearest, there we will find you a match most worthy.'

'Not England! I beg you, Mama, to reconsider! The pirate-ridden ships and fog-laden streets described by Defoe quite complete my grief at returning. How shall I know a scoundrel in that country? I shall not survive it. No, I shall die here, a creole maid.' At that, Miss Lynette swoon and sit herself down as if to catch her faint. Me cover me hand to me mouth to hide my laughter at her antics.

'Lizzy!! Lizzy!! Oh, where is she?' Me jolt at the mention of Lizzy's name. Miss Lynette's maid be no friend of mine.

'You are hysterical, my dear. Do *not* speak of that book. I remain most injured that your own cousin would have counselled you to read such an immoral work. Now run along, I must attend to matters of business.'

The door have open and Mad Lizzy stand there, her eye cutting mine with loathing. Even with her hostile stance she look a beauty and me heart pang with pity that me cannot ever look like her, so fair and light-skinned. As they leave, me ponder would me life be easier or more troubled if me were a slave as white as she?

Miss Frida smile a little longer on the empty doorway, then like the air being slowly sucked out of her, her smile turn in on itself and she open the drawer, pulling out the letter within.

I watch her fingertips trace the letter, stroking it and a little sigh come out that sound like it been trapped in her all day. Then, with a real test of her patience, she set it down on her bureau, her fingers resting at the paper's edge like she don't want to let it go; like how me do when I must place down a plate full of food on her table. Her body stays facing the letter on her dresser, but her head twist and turn to me.

'Who was that negro I saw you talking with, Orrinda?'

'Begging pardon, Miss Frida?' Me trying to understand who she mean.

'Earlier, just beside the young screwpines. I believe the poor wretch had a limp of sorts from what I could ascertain; dragging a foot behind him.' She make a laugh like a small bell ringing and her hand cover up her mouth daintily. 'How remiss of me! That description won't help much, your sort do tend to carry ailments! Come, Orrinda, do not tease me. Doubtless, I should of course know his name, but sometimes it is hard to remember who is who.' Recovering her composure, she dab away a tear of mirth with her kerchief. Her eyes widen. 'But the black scoundrel came quite upon you, Orrinda, almost as though he was desiring a private conference. What on earth could a buck of that age want to discuss with you my dear?'

'Miss, I – I—'

Miss Frida sigh, tapping the letter against the dresser. 'What matter passed between you? Your conversation? For goodness' sake girl, keep up!'

'Please, miss, him never say nothing 'bout nothing. We's just passing small talk.'

'Orrinda, come, with me you must never be coy. You are duty bound to confess it. I simply *must* know. Was it something indelicate, my dear? I shall have him whipped if he spoke to you with any profanity.' Miss Frida's rose-pink tongue pokes gentle from between her lips.

'Oh no! Miss, him say nothing not delicate! Me swear it true!' Me heart beat heavy. She stand up and draw herself close, three of her fingers be pressing them coldness on me arm with a heaviness, scented powder tickle me nose and me feel drowsy with it. Her cold breath moisten me cheek.

'You must know I do try to always act in your best interests, Orrinda. You are so very dear to me and I am very protective of you!' Her hazelnut eyes are so round and sincere looking, me think she really meaning her words.

'But you must be on your guard. I cannot protect you all the time and the slaves have eyes. They can see how you are fast coming up to the age of nubility and it simply isn't fitting for you, a lady's maid, of sorts, to be fraternizing with any old field trash. Why, I thought it might be a personal experiment of mine to arrange a union for you myself, when the time comes. Be assured, I will choose the right buck for that very important job.' Giggling, her voice comes to whisper, even though is just she and me in the room. 'Let me tell you a little secret, just between us ladies. There's word of a shipment coming through any day, so long as we can elude those officious devils of the West

38

Africa Squadron, and this,' she tap the letter hard against her bureau, 'this will be the confirmation we have waited for! We'll have a thoroughbred squire for you, my Orrinda, to make such delightful pickaninnies.'

Me no have no word to speak. Me standing as still and as dark as all the other piece of furniture in the room. She want arrange me for breeding?

'Now, of course, favours beget favours. Stay true to me, Orrinda, and no ill shall ever overcome you.' She push me to arm's length eyeing me all over, them eyeballs sweeping up from my dusty toes until they're crawling through me hair. She lace her fingers together, letting her hands fall on her lap, her face is calm.

'We understand each other, then. No more consorting with . . . ?'

'Miss, him be Uncle Hector.'

'Indeed. Then, it's settled.'

She turn away with a smile, but it gone from the looking-glass when she sits back down at her dresser. She breathe a little, steadying herself, then slow and delicate, she open the letter seal with her ivory knife, her hand shaking a little. She unfold the paper and start reading, forgetting me now, like the paper got a magic and be pulling her down, drawing her in. Her back face me but me see her clear enough in the mirror glass, mumbling something quiet to herself.

Me reckon she no need me no more so me curtsy, turn and take me leave, me heels pat away from her softly and me turn the handle at the door.

'Wait, Orrinda. I still have need of you. I feel one of my neuralgias coming on and should like to repose a while.' She place the letter under her vanity with the others and beckon me back to her with a wave of jewelled ivory fingers. Her voice lowers as she whispers intently. 'Oh! It is wonderful news, Orrinda. You are sworn to secrecy, of course, but heed! The shipment is not far off. There is not long to wait, my dear.' She stroke my cheek with such love and tenderness then and her eye seem full of a watery happiness for me. Me glance again at the curl of parchment upon her bureau, wondering how it be this sheet can bring such news about my future. Does it speak also of the end of me that surely must come after?

Miss Frida take a lying place on her chaise. Me pick up her hairbrush and settle to me knees beside her. Gently, me brush her soft ackee hair into silken waves and as me do, me song come out, breezing over Missy Frida and sending my mistress into a quiet slumber.

CHAPTER 7

Jay-kobb, not *sir*, not *masser*. Me play over the words in me mind, as I pour the molasses into the hot pan. Even him name be as strange and foreign as him comportment. Me can see him formed clear in me head, this spirit that come to me from by the valley spring, somehow, him face calm and true even though it white. More strange even than him apparel, is how gentle he touch me hand. My choring hand have never been touched kindly by any man, living or dead, black or white. Him gone now, me sure, but him haunt me still.

Aunty Nita's creased-up face peers over me kettle as she pour in the meal and ginger spice.

'Quick now, pass me the butter stick,' she say, squinting into the mixture. As she stirring up, the smell of the biscuits climb up me back, and make me belly moan because me can't eat even a one for meself. Miss Frida love up the biscuits and she know the yield from the kitchen just as sure as Moses know him commandments. Nita stir quiet today, she not complain yet about Apollo's late-night carousing, or Mad Lizzy's tardiness with the breakfast tray this morning, so me guessing she be in a good mood.

'Aunty Nita,' I say. Me have me back to her and me reaching up on the cool shelf for the butter, but me turn me head and look into her eyes now. 'You did ever see them that's passed over? You did ever see a lost duppy with your own eye?' Me finger prick a splint of sharpness on that shelf and me press it to me lip to suck up the little blood. Nita tut, and shake her head for answer. She take the stick from me and place it into the kettle. Me mouth water as it hiss.

'Is *me* have to kill and pluck up that chicken or you gon' grab him?'

'Aunty, me will catch him, no worry.' The chicken must have hear her, for she start running, but me chase her to the door and break her neck quick-quick. Flinging her down, me reach for me stool and get to work. Her look up at me from the floor with an angry eye and from her open beak, a little pink tongue taste the dirt.

Seem Aunty Nita not in a good mood today. As me pluck out the chicken feather, me no like how her dead eye watch me still, so me reach for the chopper and cut off her head.

'What you know of duppy?' I ask again. Nita lift the kettle off the heat and drop the spoon to rest against the wood pile. She prise her finger under her hair kerchief, just above her hairline, start to scratching deep at her scalp. Me know she got her own scars under that bit of rag-cloth, hidden under her matted hair and how it itch her in the night-time. She do scratch at it in her sleep aplenty, but me never see her working it before sundown

42

come. One night beside me, she scratch up so hard and did pull off her rag, that in her sleep it slipped away and me did see what was there beneath. Instead of hair, she have skin like dead snails sitting coiled and naked, where her skin have raised up angry from beatings and cuts.

Nita harden her eyes and turn to me. Me can feel her wrath coming on.

'If you did beg to know what *I* think, me would have to say yes, me do believe in spirit persons and duppies. And me believe too in voodoo and Anansi and that witch Obeah who puts wicked thoughts inside we weak negro minds.'

Her voice is darkening and she train her eye on me now, losing patience, she point her finger outside. 'When me did hear that sooty owl hoot-hoot in the night, and me see him big claws and big eyes watching me from him tree, me knew the devil have come up, out of him hiding place to make mischief.' Nita bring up from her pocket the little *Book of Common Prayer* she keep there, she find the picture of Jesus with him sore heart on the first page and she press it to her lip. 'Obah, love Jesus, we the negro have to stop up that juju nonsense. We have to know our place on this earth be for toil. We will get our reward in heaven. No matter how big a piece of gold rise up and shine each day, me and you will be here still, slaving for Master Cooke and him kin. Better we put our trust in Him and no bother with no duppy.' Nita press the little book of salvation back into her apron. She proud to be the only negro who have words in her pocket, even if she can't read what them say.

43

'One time,' me have to tread soft with what me say, 'one time, Aunty, me sure me did see a person that seem like him dead. Me can't be sure, but him so strange with me, me can't explain it.'

'This be the devil working you.' Aunty Nita be shaking her head for me to break off my address and sighing she reach for the pan again. Me carry on plucking the bird.

'But why the devil send me a *white* duppy, Aunty? Dressed up strange and talking like we be friends!' Me see her eye open wider, she turn her head sly.

'What the duppy say?'

'Him young, but him not like the other buckra be, him show a kindness.'

Me have her attention now, her lip twitch like she want to chastise, but she want to hear the story too.

'And him shake me upon the hand too, right here.' Me hold up me empty palm, as if evidence of him white touch still on me as testament to what passed.

'Child, does me look like me have time for story-making?'

'Aunty, me telling the whole truth!'

'Jesus will come when the time is ready. When we have finish with the work that him have set. He will take we by the hand and lead we through the jasmine grove on the winding path to God's heavenly door. Till such time as that, we must abide by him law or choose hellfire and burning!'

'Aunty, but what about a duppy? Can him take time to roam a little for mischief, before him make him way to God? Him no have to rush like we?'

'Once we pass over, we got no reason to be roaming here chit-chatting and making friends. Orrinda, stop now.'

And me do, me stop me word and quiet down. Aunty Nita only call me by me white man name when me have tired her out. She turn round to the biscuit kettle, putting it back onto the fire and she pick up the spoon from the wood pile. Me watch her stooped shoulders raising and falling as if she being pulled up and dropped down by a mighty wind. Turning back to me, her voice be a little softer.

'The Lord will give and the Lord will take away. Only him know the wisdom in him ways, amen.'

'But Mimbah say—'

'Mimbah? Did me no tell you to stop consorting with that witch?' Her finger set to scratching under her rag again and me see a trickle of blood run down her finger, to match mine. She take the hand from her head and place it over her chest, staining her bib with a line of red.

'So, Mimbah have frighten you with her fool-fool talk. Keep your distance from her, before her blindness come upon you.' Nita's eyes blaze heavy.

'Aunty?' Nita wipe rough at her face and sit over the tray with the sweet cassava roots. Me reach out to pull on her apron hem but she pull away and start for peeling.

'Too much dreaming, Obah. You have the same trouble in you as your mother, Occo. Lord, me remember how she would carry you with her to the field, pressing you deep into the pit of her back with that little cloth you sleep under now. She did fix

45

you so tight to her, me could see she was trying to sew you in and make the both of you become one. When she left and gone, me did think she took all of that Guinea devil jabber with her, but me wrong, seem from all her wrapping, she did press a piece of Africa into your head for true.' Nita chest thrust forward.

'Me mother be a strong woman, most fine. Uncle Hector did tell me so. And him say him have more to tell. Him a good man.' Me raise me chin but the look upon Nita's face cause me to lower it fast.

'Hector a good man. And him speak true. But she is gone. She gone and we still here. And we need to survive our truth. Now take the mush out to the pickneys before them tear down me kitchen.'

She point at the boiled corn meal in the kettle drum with a jerk of her head. I know the conversation be over so me walk out with it, hot and heavy in my arms. The hot earth burns at my toes and as me reach the trough stand, the barefooted, naked pickney slaves is already rushing up, yanking on me skirt, screaming out their hunger. Me shoo away Remy the mangy dog with a light kick and place the mush into the trough. Them rush in, jostling and filling up them belly as fast as they can in the race for food.

As usual, Benjen be the last to arrive, crawling since him can't walk right, and me scrape up the last spoonful of mush into him outstretched hand. I know him grateful, though hunger stop his mouth from doing anything but swallowing the tasteless mix. Me give him a half of the biscuit me did steal from when Nita's back is turned. She know I always take it but so long as she don't see, she don't mind me, and Miss Frida don't miss what she don't know about. Him swallow it whole with a big toothless smile filling him infant face and me try not to grieve too hard over me loss. Aunty Nita's eyes is shiny from the butter as them meet mine from where she stand at the kitchen door. Me know how much she hate to watch feeding time.

CHAPTER 8

Nita snoring peaceful, her low noise make a steady rhythm that settle in me ear and me realize me will not sleep more tonight. Me tired outta me skin from labouring and though me love me sleep, tonight, when me close me eyes, the only thing I see is that spirit boy. Me draw me knees to me chest for warmth because Aunty have pull up most of the rag cloth upon her side of the mat, as usual. The night be cool so me rub me feet together, trying to keep them from touching the damp ground and turning to stone and I kick at the mouse that tickles me foot as him pass. The grey moon is fat and round, and as me feel him looking on me through the opening, him one-eyed stare is harsh, making me shiver more as him study me.

Me mind twist like the cerasee leaf in the sunlight as me thoughts remember the white dead duppy and him strange ways and words. The way him seem to breathe out a warm type of air, even though his pallor, speech and curious look mean him cannot be one that's living. Whether it be the thoughts in me head or the moon's hard stare, something make the breath in me stop and me sit up, chest aching. Me need air.

Gently, me slip out from between the warmth of Nita and Murreat and me move to leave the hut. The wood door strain and creak as me push it wide and step out. Me arch me back and twist about, arms raised skyward, to unlock the aching that stay there at the end of a long day. The night is noisy. Crickets chirrup, mosquitos buzz and the grass creak with the sound of creatures swimming in the stalks. Lowering me arm, me stroke the back of me hand, gentle, the way him did to mine, to make that feeling of clouds return. Instead, the rough callus on me forefinger catch against me skin.

'Obah?'

Me jump, as if me thoughts did conjure him.

Him clothes is changed, them is grey now but somehow, not from aged wear! How can grey shine so?

'Duppy-man, you come back?'

'Duppy-? Ah . . . Maybe I shouldn't be disturbing you so late. You look tired.'

Me take a step back from him, this wandering ghost with nothing better to do than follow close to watch the toil of one like me. Feeling a confidence rise, before me can stop it, me mouth open.

'Let me tell you how tired feel. Me been choring hard for the mistress all the day long, me run here, me run there and then me must help Nita in the kitchen.' Me surprise meself at how free me feel speaking with him. Him demise have give me courage. 'Why does the white folk love to press down on we so heavy, sir, work us, grind us down, till we can barely stand on us bleeding feet? We cannot all take our tranquillity in death. We cannot all lighten the load we must bear!' Something about him allow me tongue a freedom never known. Jacob close him eyes for a moment and him throat stone move up and down. Him reach for me hand again and me watch in stupor as him stroke it with him thumb, gentle across me cracked knuckles, them tingle at him touch.

'I didn't mean to upset you. Where I'm from, kids like us, regular kids, we're in school, not out doing field work! Not being servants! It's not right. Everything about this place is so . . . wrong, you know. Everything. But I'm here to help. I think I can get you out of here. Will you come?'

Him bite him lip now and the blood move away from him tooth mark, leaving a pale line, me watch the pinkness seep back into him slow and him understand he must explain more.

'Earlier, I watched you feed the kids, right, but you didn't eat anything, did you? In my world, the adults look after all kids, not just the little ones. We might be young, but we have rights. We have our own voices. We have options.' Me watch him mouth open and close and try to follow the quick, quick words, but understanding him be hard on me. Him notice me confusion so him stop, run a hand through him black hair, shake him head a few times and smile all at once before him place both hands in the air, showing all of him fingers. 'Okay, so, me for instance, I want to be a lawyer. I want to fight for justice. I want to make a difference. So, I'm going to study law, got an unconditional offer for uni.' Me do not understand all

50

him words, but one of them ring in me ear.

'Sir, if you must *fight* for justice, does that mean there be none where you is from? How is that so different to what we living here? Why must me come with you to a place where justice stay missing?' Me blink at him.

'There will always be injustice, humans . . .' Jacob make a quiet smile. 'We'll always need to fight against it. Difference is, where I'm from, it's not always acceptable. You can take a stand.' Him voice be sounding as though it scold me, and something warm tickle my lip.

'Hey, don't cry! Please!' And he is next to me, his finger dipping the tear that have slip from my eye and me skin heat at him touch. Him voice is deep when him speak next.

'Come back with me. You wouldn't have to put up with this torture! Come. See how life can be, Obah, how we're trying to build a society that is better!'

Me step away from him, shamed by my hot tears. What this crazed duppy-boy talking about? What him mean 'a society'? Him make no sense. Me remember how nothing him say make any sense.

'Me did ask Miss Frida about the place where you from. "The Future" – she have tell me it just around the corner! How it can be different to here if it be so close?'

Jacob laugh then and his voice is like the sound of gentle brooks, trickling waters that soften and cool. And I don't want him laughing to ever stop. In the bright moon, me watch all the movements of his face, the freckles dancing with delight, the

51

blue eyes watering, as him enjoy a joke that I cannot understand.

'The future. It isn't a country. It's . . . a time. A new time. Right now,' him point around at the huts behind, 'I think we're in the old times, in "history", but things can change, Obah. There's a new time. Why stay here when you could come with me? Let me take you.' Me see him hand reaching out towards me.

'Why should me put me trust in you? Why should me believe what you say? How can me be sure you not steal Obah away? Even your voice sound strange and fanciful.'

'But that's your evidence right there, isn't it? My voice *is* different. I *am* from another place. It's not perfect, my world, maybe it never will be, but one thing is sure. Slavery is illegal. People can't own each other.' His eye don't blink, as if him believing all him strange words for true. 'Obah. Come, come with me.'

I close my eyes and try to see it in my mind's eye. There is nothing but blackness.

CHAPTER 9

Lying back onto the pallet, Murreat stir, moaning for the little warmth that Nita took from we both. She be sleeping with a heavy tiredness that come on when a child do a full day of toil. Me glad to have her near me. Nita tell how Murreat be my true kin. Her mother and mine is same-same sisters, stolen and travelled together across the big water to here. Occo and Jimba, sisters from the motherland. Oftentimes, me wonder why them never run off hand in hand, how me mother can leave her behind, but then me remember, she did leave me too.

What me remember about Murreat's mother, before she fall dead? She did talk in a strange language of whispers. Nita tell how them sisters speak an African tongue whenever them be alone. But them never speak them language when a buckra man near. Me have a memory of her and Jimba, walking graceful side by side, them head laden with the green plantain provisions as them step light to balance them load. Nita did tell me what happen when the master find out me mother gone, him take a hot poker and swearing blasphemy, him brand Jimba upon the face to remember which one she be. Jimba stop her speech after

53

that, she no talk again. Even when she did birth Murreat, Jimba never cry out one time with the pain. That be why Murreat come to be born a mute.

Murreat must be four years younger than me, but we have the same rough life. Her tongue don't speak, but if she do something wrong she smell the rubber lash upon her skin just the same as any. I look at her sleepy black lips pressed into a rod of iron; her lips never open except for food. She must feel me breath on her because her eyes open and meet mine. We have the same eyes and like sisters, blink at each other, black with understanding in the darkness. Even though me can't sleep, me have to rest, me no want no night-time talk with her. Me turn me face straight up, away from the slumbering bodies on either side, me eye probe the cabin's rafters for a flaw, a crack, a way out.

Me thoughts slip towards my mother, is she there, in that lonesome valley, dead with *him*? I push it away. Strange how him smell sweet like flower, not dead, like his nearness bring honey and warmth. Nita say me must have dream him up, but how can me dream up what me have never seen before? Him garments, boots and bare head be like nothing me know.

This Jacob's voice be different to the whites' here in Unity Plantation, him speak English like Leary and Masser Cooke but it sound like him must have travel from a different part of them homeland. Him speak like him have learned from books. Me remember back to the dry season, when Masser Thomas Abel did come and visit from Jamaica. Miss Frida did curse how him no bring no rum, no relish, not even a little guava jam from him

54

plantation. All him bring is him mother, 'Miss Jane', fresh from England and him reading books.

Miss Frida open the silver pomander that hang from the chain at her waist, pinch at the powdery content and inhale. She blink from the smelling salts and as if them boost her spirit, she start her complaining again, no wine or jellies, and how him can come with no lady's maid for him own mother too? 'My poor sister! Orrinda, you shall tend to Miss Jane.'

Miss Jane be Miss Frida's older sister and the two of them did huddle up with each other like a pair of doves in the nest, no air could come between them. But Masser Thomas, him huddle instead with him book and it prop up his arm the whole two month he stay. Him speak seldom, but me can still hear the sound of him voice, like him have some hot soup upon him tongue.

Young Miss Lynette be fifteen then, and starting to become a fine beauty, them say. Miss Jane give her a hand fan made of 'ivory and a rare silk straight off the merchant ship from China! How now! Quite the fashion in England!' Miss Lynette, she start to walk herself back and forth, up and down the length of the drawing room, twirling the new silk against her pale cheek and all the time her brow furrow up as her eyes did perceive that her cousin did not study her like we. Even though her hair have an emerald ribbon, him never look up from him book. As if magic be there. What them words and writings did tell him?

The day them part, me carry Miss Jane's bag to the gig only to find Masser Thomas already seated inside, him rump spread full upon the bench and him eye happy in the book.

'Jane, Henry and I are very disappointed you could not stay longer.' Miss Frida did sigh as she kiss her sister's cheek farewell and Master Cooke tip him hat, rocking back and forth on him heels.

'Dearest Frida, dry your tears. Thomas must attend to business. Every English morning, one reads some account of how the negroes succumb to slovenliness when masters quit for too long. Without due care, one's prosperity can be quickly undercut.'

'Indeed, madam, most sobering.' Master Cooke nods, his cheeks red. 'I am glad to hear your account. Of late, the newspapers are filled with fashion for the negroes' claims to freedom! One would think the men writing such nonsense had no stake in the business themselves!'

Miss Jane, bored of politics, turn back to her sister. 'And besides, when will you return to us in Bath? Father is becoming quite frail and would be restored, were he to hear about your jungle adventures in person.' Both sisters tinkle with laughter at the thought of them father. 'My dear, farewell! I will leave my Thomas in Kingston, quite content with his library for company. Fear not, however, I am most determined to remind him of his obligations. The engagement will be secure, sister, and the affection will develop with time, you have my word.'

Miss Frida kiss her sister's finger to her lips.

Cooke tip him hat to them again.

We watch the coach ride off, swimming red in the sunlight, a hogshead of Unity Plantation rum teetering from side to side on its backside as the melody of Miss Frida mutter bitter and low against the breeze, 'Security is everything, sister.'

CHAPTER 10

She know me before me speak, lifting up her needle to pause her crafting. The bowing ferns ornament Mimbah's face with green ribbons, framing her like she sit in a painting in the Big House, only there be no darkies framed upon the walls there. Disturbed by my steps, the white ash from where she burned her fire flutters from the ground like moths.

'Me hear you humming from afar.' She smile. 'Don't stop, Obah, sing it again.' Mimbah's needle is raised in the air as she sits rigid for the sound of my voice. Its bone tip flash gently in the sun like some far-off star.

'Again.' Her voice is stern.

Me be humming the lamb song over. Me can't sing nothing else. Since me have met the duppy, them words and then him appearance is linked. First Uncle Hector and now Mimbah get to hear it too. The melody slip out of me, sprinkling the both of us in sorrow. 'Obah, them words you hum come from another time, another place,' she say. 'What them mean?' I shrug. Even though she can't see me shoulder lift, Mimbah nods her understanding and I know the sadness of it cut her deep. Me

57

wish me knew why me sing it still.

Mimbah stand up and gesture to the stump with a dip of her head, and I take her cue to start our customs. She take the kerchief from off her hair and use it to beat off the dust, flies and ants for me. That's how Mimbah stay, she love to make you feel comfortable. She point at the cleaned-up worn-out stump with orange palms and a smile.

'If it please, sit down, my dear Orrinda, have you come to pay old Mimbah a visit?' This be Mimbah's favourite game, when we meet, we act like we be white ladies calling on each other for a society visit. We like to sit off the floor and converse for a time in pleasantries about the weather and us temperaments. Me make me voice sound as white as me can.

'Good day to you, miss! I have wake up this morning, thinking, what a fine and glorious day! I will not sit idle, no, I will pay me dear friend Mimbah a society call.' The both of we giggle.

'Why, you must be parched! My dear, will you be pleased to partake of a refreshing lemonade-and-ginger punch? I have prepared it myself this morning!' Mimbah beam.

'Why, don't mind if me do!' I say. Mimbah reach into her pail and scoop out a little rainwater into her empty gourd.

Mimbah not an old woman, she can't have more than two or three year over me, but her skin be tinged with a heavy grey. Her unseeing eyes smile like them know all me secrets. Aunty Nita say Mimbah be a witch and practise Obeah, but me think the blind eyes taint her. Me pick up the needlework she have put down by her and me mouth dry up at how beautiful she have lace the collar. She have a gift for sure. Me eye the work up close, since she lose her sight three years ago, her needlework have become sharper and more fine than before. Me even hear Mad Lizzy say that Mimbah must be a false blind, *'How she can do so fine when her eye empty?'* But all can see she imitate nothing. Her eyes pale all over, like the white have kill off the black.

Since the reckoning, the day that Mimbah go blind, Miss Frida have say Mimbah must have her own private cabin, that way she can know where everything be when she working at the loom. Ask any negro and they will tell how she give her a hut of her own to appease her guilty conscience, but me think Mimbah did ask for this herself, so she don't have to feel all the black eyes staring on her white ones.

Mimbah sit down opposite me, folding up her knees high as her fingers be feeling to place between us the little wooden log-table she use for her embroideries.

'How you do today, Mimbah? Me hope you bearing up in this heat. I bring some more cuffs need mending for Miss Frida.' Me place the little bundle into her hand and she slip it into her pouch.

'Me see to it later. Watch this now.' She beaming. Her mind is not on stitching. 'Me have a new game for you. Bertha did give them me, she say the father of her babe bring them off the ship!' She reach into her apron pocket and pull out a deck of crumpled cards with dark patterned backs. With long delicate fingers she stretch out her arm, offering the cards to me and say,

'Cut, Obah.' Me feel a shiver run through me, even though the sun biting harsh at my rag-top head.

'Cut? Mimbah, what is this?' Me have never seen so much paper held in a black hand. The misses play at cards, us negroes do not.

'Them be messages, Obah. Them be communications about life. Me will tell you what the message say for you. Is you bear one babe or two? Me tell you. Will them get sold? Me tell you.' She hiccup a giggle and her hand wave the cards in a circle. 'Me can tell you what will pass. Pick the card now.'

'Mimbah, Nita say to stop the witch talk.'

Her hand hover under my chin and me feel the scratch of the cards as her skinny fingers float on the heated air. Me stare a moment too long at her missing finger and me feel guilty.

'Pick three.'

Carefully, me lift the cards and then Mimbah grab them from me. Briefly she close her eye, then with care, she lay the cards out, face down.

'Past, present and what will come – which one you yearning for, Obah?' Her foot be tapping quickly at the heel, sending fresh puffs of dust to rest up on the old on her skirt.

She tapping on the third card now. Her soursop eyes is full of mischief.

'How you can tell me my fortune, Mimbah? You must have sight of the cards to do that!'

'Turn it over,' she says and her body is still, rigid as she waits for me to move.

60

'This give me doubt, Mimbah.'

'Do it same way.'

Me reach over and my small finger gently strokes the card's back, feeling it massage my callus with its worn-away smooth. Mimbah's breath have stopped, her back is straight as I turn the third card.

'What you see?'

The image is faded and worn and me wonder how many hands it have passed through. Slow, as though an image through water, me start to see the shapes appear.

'Mimbah, me see a fire burning, bright and hard upon a high tower. Two persons be falling, them arms pressing the air, mouths open with crying as them falling down.' As though it sting, me drop the card from me fingers, and jump up from me stump, knocking the other cards into the dirt. There is a quiet now, as though even the tree birds hold them breath for fear of what I have say. Mimbah do not lift her head and her eyes do not open to mine as she speak, her voice dry as husk.

'Obah, me see only death.'

CHAPTER II

Mimbah's word hover just above me head as me start running towards the spring. Me must take care that no one see me, especially not Leary as me have no letter for him today. The grass be soft under me running feet, caressing me, but it don't quell my troubled mind. As if me haven't got enough worry, with buck-breeding talk from Miss Frida, me must add another about them cards. Mimbah say my future be set with death, and me never even tell her nothing about the white duppy boy Is him the death she speaking of? How she did know?

It be counting day and we negroes must all gather ourselves up just before sundown for Masser Cooke to take a good survey of all him possessions. Him like to see us together and count we up from one to a hundred and twenty-seven, one by one. Me not sure if it take him a full hour to do because him can't count good, or if him just enjoy seeing how much wealth him have, spread out in one place. We have to wait in line, heat beating us, hunger paining we belly while him counting up.

The counting did start when Overseer Wilmett stole away a couple of slaves for himself to start him own plantation, them

62

say him gone to Trinidad. Masser Cooke never did notice him slaves gone for two month or so. Not until one of the pickney did tell him what Wilmett have done. By then, it was too late, him long gone from the island. Since that grievous day, Masser make it him business to count up we for himself, every Friday, so him not receive mischief again.

I need to see if him there. Hogs, mules and cows lift their lolling heads, staring coolly as me sprint past them. Me smell the tamarind and gentle, me press me ear against the tree to hear its heart beating. Me think me hear a rustle in the branch and me call out, 'Hello, sir, that you?'

'Orrinda? Is that you lurking? What business have you out here?'

Masser Cooke come into view, him slow his horse next to me, digging him boots into Bessie's flank. A coldness fill me brow and a weakness fill me legs.

'Masser?' I look around me, taking in the empty clearing. 'Masser, me . . . Aunty Nita did ask me to fetch some tamarind for her, sir, me be gathering.'

'Is that so?' Cooke look at the trees, turning his horse in circles about me, as if sensing something not right. 'Hurry along, girl, and back up to the plantation. The boundary here is off limits. It is the count this eve, and you miss it at your peril. Old Nita ought to know better than that,' him mutter and he flex his fingers for a moment on Bessie's bridle. Him give eye on me, it follow slow from me feet to me thighs to me chest . . . Me drop me gaze when it reach me face and me hold me breath.

'There's no way out, you do know that, don't you?'

'Masser?'

Him smile remind me of a cottonmouth snake, his voice is smooth and steady. 'It is 1834. These are fine and modern times we're living in. Your late mother may have *thought* she was finding liberty in her defiance, but how can one know where she ended up? The horrors she was subjected to? The price of that "freedom"?' Him pause, as if truly awaiting my reply, then him lift up him tin from the saddle and take a swig of water. Finally, in the pregnant silence, him turn Bessie about, click-click him tongue and ride off.

Me breath start again. Me mother! Him dare to speak of her? Cooke grow small as him dart away on Bessie and unable to stop myself, me find me closed fist raising above me head.

The tamarind feathers touch me cheek and me can see the white duppy boy is sitting solitary beneath the trees. Him black curls shine with pomade or sunlight, me not sure which, and it seem him have misplace his hat again. Though me still unsure if him dead or living, me watch him for a moment, taking in his slender limb, him skin pale as any English madam. Him have a softness about him, like him have never carry a hoe or pull a cart before.

Mimbah's dead card talk did give me a fright, but here and now me feel safe.

'Obah!' Him stand, kind eyes upon me. Him smile is warm. 'I have something for you.'

I watch from my place, trying to understand what him just say. Him have something for *me*? Me never get anything but tribulation from the buckra. Slow, me feet start to move towards him.

'Can you hold out your hands, like this?' He demonstrate, him arms outstretched, palms up. Me eye never leaving his, me do as him say. Him reach into him satchel and draw out a package, to place on my palms. A box, wrapped in brown paper, ribboned with a bow of red shining like the ruby ring on Miss Frida's finger.

'You want me deliver this to the Big House? For Miss Lynette or Miss Frida?'

'Erm . . . No, it's yours.'

'For me?' I whisper, keeping my eye on the prize him place in me hand. The box rest on me fingers heavy, me not know what to do with it. Hanging from it be a paper tag with a writing. Me feel him nodding, and me can't hide a smile. Him lean in close to me, pick up the label and say, 'Look, it has your name.' I stare at the writing on the label. Black lines scratch on white, but me can't see me name. 'Sir, me can't read.' Him trying to play me? Me foolish, but me not a fool.

'It's not "sir", remember? I'm just Jacob. Anyway, open it, come on!'

I kneel down on the ground, tuck me toes under me and flatten me skirt, brushing off as much dirt as I can, then me place the package on it, careful of the dust, me look upon it. I stroke the red ribbons, then me lift it to me nose and smell how it handsome. It mine for true? Me try hard to stop asking what him want in return.

'Sir? What I must do with this?'

'Jacob.' He eyes the packet, softly he says, 'You need to take the paper off.'

Hardly believing, my fingers pull on the softness of that ribbon, my heart beat fast and loud from me chest and then I is tearing at the paper quick before he can change him mind. Inside be a book, old, creased, bound in tanned leather. I run me fingers over its ridges and turns, I open it up taking in its pages and pages of writing.

'But me no have no lettering knowledge,' I say, sure that this is what him want to hear.

There was once a time, when Miss Lynette and me were no higher than the spring corn, that she did show to me the words in books. Me did learn the 'alphabet', she call it. Me did learn to spell out the name them give me, 'O-r-r-i-n-d-a'.

'Miss Lynette, me have done something! You will be pleased with me when you hear of it!' Me jut out my chin, pride pressing as timber girders from my chest.

'What is it?' she say, not looking up from her doll whose auburn ringlets she tend.

' "O-b-a", Miss Lynette, this is how me spell out me true name! Me have used the letters from the alphabet, me think this must be Obah? Is I true?' Miss Lynette must not have hear me right because me see a cloud come upon her eye and she pick up her doll, press it to her chest and say, 'Orrinda, you are not to read with me again. Not ever. And I don't want to play with you today.' She turn her back on me and I stand confuse for a while before walking away. That be the last time we play together.

Me have many question for the duppy. Why he give me this? What me supposed to do with it? What him want in satisfaction?

'Listen, let me read a passage to you, follow my finger.' Me bend to settle beside Jacob, a warmth come off of him as me breathe in him fresh scent. How him smell so wholesome?

Him begin, speaking in a melodious voice about some strange place named Narnia where there be snow and a young girl named Lucy. Him touching each scrawl as he speak it, me see how there be an empty space before each word.

'That be what it say?' He nod, repeating his words and actions and me watch him finger touch the black shapes again.

'The other light?' I say. I turn to look over my shoulder and am satisfied there be no one nearby, 'What else it tell?' Me don't want the words to finish, even though there be a biting in my rib that this be dangerous.

'It's a story about travelling.' He points at the words again. 'See how the winter never ends? It's one of my favourites.'

Me stare at the words and as me reach out to touch them, me feel like little stars be blinking in me fingers. The black lines and turns on white paper, how he make them sound so beautiful? But me shake me head.

'Me? Learn lettering? Nita will surely kill me dead first, if Miss Frida haven't finished me already! Me can't take this book.

67

Anyone see me with it and me will be whipped for thieving.'

Him close and open one eye quick, like a flying beetle have touched it. 'Then we won't tell them! I'll keep the book for you, I'll look after it. We can meet here every day, for as long as you can spare, and we'll read, okay?'

Him like that parlance, *'okay'*. Him say it a lot. As him continue with him talk, me turn and examine him profile in secret. Me can understand everything now – what Mimbah's card mean and why God have sent him back from the dead. I smile wide. This boy spirit have come to teach me how to read! I sit at him side, weaving the red ribbon through me fingers, as me listen. Me hear the spring bubble up alongside him voice, making a tuneful harmony. The tamarinds watch we too, them branches swaying along to the words like them already know the story. Me close me eye, forgetting where I is, who I is. Me can't understand all the words him say but there be music in the melody of him voice so me follow that, following the girl called Lucy on her journey.

When him finish, I open me eye and see how him seem sad. But I feel happy. Even though me never understand half the words he say, the sound them make be like my voice, them sing. Me never know them little black words can bring a happiness like that, how they did take me to a place far and distant from here! I want to say all this to him, me open me mouth ready to speak, but the tamarind shadow has climbed upon my foot, telling me dusk have passed. Masser Cooke's big counting have finish, and me weren't present. Me smiling stop. This reading of books have make me forget myself, and now me see the danger.

The sound of gunfire in the distance disturbs a pair of doves in the tree above, them flutter them wings away in quick agitation and a white feather softly floats between us. There be a price to pay for this gift after all. Jacob see my face fall and his brow knit together, concerned.

But me don't have time to explain. Me jump to me heel and run.

CHAPTER 12

The yard be quiet when me reach back. Quiet not like we have by the brook, where water tinkle, tinkle, this silence be laden with the promise of a reckoning. Might be my own. Dogs barking in the distance sound out them baleful hunger to the wind. Them hounds only be set loose like that when them chasing for negro. Dear Lord, if him think me have run off, what the masser will do when him find me?

As me near in the kitchen, there be Nita sitting by the fire, wringing her napkin to and fro and her body rock forwards and back like the broken weather vane on the chicken coop. When she see me she open her mouth so wide me reckon me can climb in, but all that come out of her for sound be a little 'Oh!'

Murreat run up to my waist and press her head deep upon me chest, her bony arms fold and sharp elbows dig into the small of my back. I stroke her head gentle and she look up at me, shiny lashes, shiny eyes. She open her mouth as if to speak, but as usual her eyes do the talking. *Where you be?* them ask. I look away, turning me guilty face towards Nita, me don't expect no sound from Murreat, but Nita's quiet scare me.

'Me sorry me have miss the count, Aunty. Me did lose notice of how the time pass.' My voice is thick as monkey hair, me can't hardly hear meself, my words swallowed up by the pounding of my heart. I know she hear me, but still she stare. Her eyes be screaming at me, but no words pass her lips.

'That no excuse,' say Bertha who have come to counsel Nita as she give milk to Bella.

'Aunty, me truly sorry.' Me breathing is heavy and the words be rushing so fast out me mouth, them tumble over. I be sure the masser will murder me this night if she don't help and me can't understand why she silent. Me pull me hand away from where me stroking the ribbon resting in my pocket and me bite me knuckle.

'Me begging, Aunty. Me can hear the dog, them barking loose. You gon' let Masser kill me?'

There be a sting in the side of my head and me blinking hard as me see Nita's hand moving back to her side.

'You! Like your African mother, you bring me nothing but trouble. First she and she sister with them voodoo, juju talk and now you starting up nonsense with witches and whites. You can't be satisfied with that? You have to send poor Hector to him grave too?'

'Aunty? What? What me do to Uncle Hector?'

'You no hear me good? Hector running, it him them dogs be chasing.'

'Why? Me can't understand.'

'No. Is yourself alone you care for, don't it? You no stop to think about any other. You have kill Hector today, Orrinda, just

71

as if you did pick and tie the noose around him neck.'

Hot tears be falling from me eyes as all of Aunty Nita's words slap me one by one. Me can barely see her shape, but her angry form be clear, even with all the wet in me eyes. She grips me shoulders and start shaking me hard. Me think of Hector's mashed-up leg – him must know him can't get far? That hound will scent him out before him can reach any ship. And why him running because of me?

'Where you been at? Where you been at?' Each word she say she couple with her shake of me shoulders, and me bones twist inside me. She tap at me temple with a hard finger. 'Me not know what Mimbah have put into that head, but you must find a way to set it out now, you hear me? Your game playing be dangerous. A man's life. A life, Obah. You never, never miss the Masser count. You want what happen to Mimbah, happen to you next? So you can sit useless and blind, sore in the sun feeling sorry for yourself?' As Nita rage, me feel the warmth of Murreat's hand slide into mine, her fingers curling through my fingers, knitting we together. She stand by me side, her face guarding me from Nita's anger.

I sniff, but tears slipping out me nose, like them cross too and want to witness my reckoning. Nita raise her hands above her head, they pause mid-air as if to praise the Lord, before me realize them ready to fall on me for me beating. But she let her hand drop onto her kerchief, her fingers reach under for her hair and she start her scratching for comfort instead.

'Lord, what me can do with you? Hector must have gone to search for you when him don't see you ready in the line-up like the rest of we and now . . . well, him must pay the price.' Her sore eye weep and she wipe away the water. 'Me never see you yet, but still, me know you must be coming up. Late, but coming. Masser point him finger at Judah and start him counting, me watch him mouth twist and move as him do the tally.

'All the while, we praying for you to come soon. Me praying, please, Lord, make this child stop her waywardness, make she turn up soon. But then, jumping from the line and running to the masser me did see that pickaninny Tom. Him butt naked, but still him reach up on the tips of him toes to Masser Cooke's ear and whisper with him. As me watch Masser's white face pale, me worry start. Then him cry out, 'Fetch the hounds!' And me heart stop. Everybody a-mutter, and what the pickaninny have whisper start to weave through the line.

' "Hector have run off," Apollo tell me. Lord forgive me, me did thank sweet Jesus that it's Hector, not you the masser chasing.'

'Mother Nita? Is that the blackie? She have come back?'

Nita's chastisements stop sudden, as Mad Lizzy appear. She peek into the kitchen but, as usual, she don't come in. She use her forefinger on the left hand only, to pry back the door and look in upon we. Her green eyes and brown curls peek at us from under her grimy-rimmed bonnet. Her other hand be holding up the kerchief to her nose where she dab it to and fro to protect herself from the smell of we, like she smell sweeter. She so pretty, me think. But something rotten sit just beneath her beautiful countenance, a shadow that repulse me.

'What you need in here, Lizzy? Me can fetch something for

you?' Nita wipe the sweat upon her lip and quick step in front of me, shoving me roughly behind her back so I be her shadow. Murreat move along with me, to thicken it. My view short now, so me press me head round to see. Mad Lizzy no come down to the kitchen much. She prefer to take her meals alone, outside in the courtyard on the cold bottom step of the Big House, her raggedy skirts spread out like them be the finest silks. She will put her own plate on her lap, spread out she breadfruit neat and delicate. She always use a fork with her meal, she did tell me Miss Lynette give she it, but Murreat did see her fashion it herself from a tree branch. When you see she eating, her tiny finger stick out, like it separate from the others, different.

'Heh! Nita, me can see what game you playing.' Her cheeks blush rosy and her finger look for me at Nita's back. Lizzy's voice be dark, like she growl with each breath she take. 'Me can see that the pup have come back from she wandering travels, you can't hide her. Where she been?' She tip her head and a vein throb here with a face intending spite. 'Come out now, girl, me just want to pet you a little bit, me no bite!' Me feel Nita press her finger on me and me stay put. Lizzy growl some more, 'Me scare you? Why? Me no kick, me no harm you.' We three stay quiet. Waiting for her to give up. Mad Lizzy let out her long sigh, she finally tired of we.

'Suit yourself. We play the game again tomorrow, if please you better!' She giggle. 'But come now, come see the thrashing Hector having in the yard. The dogs have him.' Me can't tell if the news of the thrashing or the light of the fire cause she to glow, but she looking so radiant, like a true flower in bloom.

'Masser Cooke have tell Leary that him want do it himself, now in the firelight. Say him can't wait till morning as him have business, come now, the whipping starting.'

Again, she jerk her head in my direction. 'Me know Obah behind you never show for the counting, but Masser? Him no know, do he?'

The pink-lipped smile broaden as she shake her head. '*Me* did see she was missing – soon as we line up – but why Hector set off to save her?' Lizzy find my eye. 'Little pup, know I will find out the truth, even if you no tell me youself.' Lizzy step back and stretch her spine up straight, her voice bold and bright. 'Anyhow, a good whipping only improve the darky condition, come see old Hector catching stripes!' And with a light laugh and a swing of skirt, she slip away.

'That poor child. See how she think she white?' Nita be shaking her head in pity as Lizzy leave us. Me look at Nita and her red eyes look back on me. If she have pity for me before, it gone now.

'Where did you go, Obah?' she whisper again through gritted teeth. Me look down at the floor, ashamed. This be my offence, Hector cannot take my guilt, me have to stop it. Nita silent, waiting on my answer. Me can't tell her me been learning reading with a white duppy or surely she will put the dogs on me herself! Murreat taps me foot gentle with hers, me turn to her and she place the red ribbon me did not know me have dropped, back in me hand. She curl me fingers up and over it, then kiss one finger to her lip.

CHAPTER 13

Outside, the darkness has come on thick and black. No moon be in the sky, no clouds neither like none of them can bear witness to what is about to take place. Above me head be the heat of the day, as if the sun have drop some of himself when him run off too. There be a fire burning bright, and though me can barely make out the negro faces around me, me can see them white eyes, scowling. Them know of my guilt. Me step forward, ready to stand by the post. To tell Masser the truth, that it was me who miss the count and must take the beating for Hector. Hector arrive, arms bound together as Leary lead him in, pushing me to one side. Slow, him unravel the rope and try to tie him hand but I shake my head, holding firm to the post. It must be me.

'No,' I say.

Leary eyes grow small and him push me away from the post again, firmer.

'Move along, child.' Hector speak. 'This here my place.' Him bloodshot and naked eyes bore into me and him shake him head. Me try speak back but me mouth no open and me eyes drop away like a coward swallowing my questions. Why him flee? Why him make Masser look for him and not for me? I open my mouth again but another voice speak before mine.

'What's this? Is there something you wish to say, Orrinda?'

Masser have come and him sleeve rolled up to him elbows, suspenders pulled off him shoulder and hanging against him thigh. Him eye meet mine, expectant and ready for my explanation.

'I . . . I . . .'

Murreat appear by my side. In this fire light, she look like sweet bread, pale and golden at the same time. Quick-quick, she tug my arm and pull me away. Full of shame, me let her lead me off until we reach the outside of the circle where all of us must stand.

Lowering me head, tears stinging and blurring, we continue, me pulling her as we push out of the ranks, too ashamed to be amongst my own, waiting on the very brink of the crowd. Finally out of the full gaze of all, the anger burns inside me and the tears of my cowardice begin to fall. Murreat's grip stay firm, standing small beside me, her pretty head wobble on top of her frame, too heavy for her bones. Murreat tap me choring hand three times, this be her signal that something urgent be 'bout to befall. 'Me know, Murreat,' me tell her. 'Poor Hector, this be a trouble I have heap upon him.' But Murreat shake her head weightily and turn to look over she shoulder, out into the misty fire shadow by the side of the house where me follow her eye, squinting at the figure me find there. Darkness shroud him, but me see it is Jacob! Instinctively, me drop Murreat's hand and turn to him but she tug at me skirt pocket to face the post. The beating about to begin.

Masser take off his hat and hand it over for Apollo to hold. Apollo exchange the hat for the cow-skin. This night heat do make Masser look shiny and slick with sweat before him even start, or else, the light of the fire be laughing on him. Pickaninny Tom throw more stick, more branches so the blaze crack and hiss with hot red and yellow flame so we can see what coming. But we no need eyes to know.

Him have send for the misses, they standing on the landing too; a whipping always draw out the whites to play. Miss Frida and Miss Lynette both, they fan themselves gentle in the night with no breeze. Miss Frida yawn. Miss Lynette be looking bored too, her creamy satin toe be tapping slow, anticipating the rhythm of the falling lash. Miss Frida lean and whisper something in Miss Lynette's ear. The shoulder shake and the auburn ringlet bounce with the amusement, even though she place her finger to her mouth to muffle the sound. Me eye turn again to the shadowed figure, me recognize him outline, it seem to be *him,* but me cannot know for true unless me take a chance and head across. Me can't move yet, too much silence. Too much quiet.

Master Cooke hold up the cow-skin, checking it over. Him call Lucifer and me hear him have a hilt made of crocodile teeth. Lucifer drips with the blood of a hundred slaves at least. The blood, meat and bone that Lucifer feast on, have mingle with him leather curls and the black hair have a russet sheen. Master's hand sways to and fro and Lucifer's legs dance gently in the dust, warming up, ready to drink more wine. Mimbah be here too, she

78

don't need to see the post to remember how it feel, her face look straight on, but she show her pain in those empty eyes. Behind her stands Overseer Leary, hands on him hips, thumbing his waistband, him mouth set in a cruel smile. This be me chance. With everyone eye on Lucifer, me drop Murreat hand and make me way quick-quick to the figure in the shadows.

'Lord, have mercy, it is you! Why you come here, duppy?'

'Obah, you're okay? You left in a hurry. I knew something bad was going to happen. I just had to make sure you were all right.' The darkness mean me can't see his eye clear, but me believe him is earnest. He point at them fire-bathed figures glowing before us. 'This isn't . . . he isn't going to : . . ?' There is tremble in him voice, as if him have never seen a man tie to a whipping post before. Me press me hand upon him lips then, 'shh,' me whisper as Masser's eye point in the broadness of our direction. We both hush up as Masser continue him address.

Master circle the crowd, Lucifer trailing by him foot. Him step slow with leisure.

'The negro condition is such that you require constant training and discipline. Here, at Unity, it is my duty to provide this correction. If the rules are broken there are consequences. There is pain. And this is how one learns and improves.' Lucifer follows him as him make him address, hopping in anticipation, bending and flexing for action.

For a moment it seem his eyes meets mine. 'Running away will not serve you. You will simply add a hundred lashes to your backs. Your black skin allows you refuge here, you will

79

not find another master so devoted to his flock. Elsewhere, there are masters much less cordial.' Him point Lucifer over his shoulder at Hector, but him body and face stay trained on us. 'This half-lame wretch believes he is above the rules of Unity.' Me cast me eyes down, but me can't escape his voice.

'Let this serve to remind you, then, of your duties to your master and to Unity.'

Master Cooke stop for a moment and we watch him in silence as he genuflect and roll him shoulder to warming up. He bend each of him ear to the shoulder, then turn his head a slow circle, like a terrible owl.

'Well, then, negroes, watch well and learn and should any of you turn your backs on my instructions, I will remove a toe from his foot.' And with that, Lucifer springs up. The lash fall and Hector cry out as him prickly pear back split; scarred and welted skin tear open again. Lucifer land again and again, feet dancing to a terrible rhythm and with each call he make, Hector respond, shrieking and writhing alongside the pain. Our chorus be the count. One, two, three, on and on our voices low, each time the lash falls. Masser pause at fifty lashes and for a moment me think him going to show mercy, that him stop there, that we have learned. But him just let Apollo mop him brow, then take a drink of water from his can. None of we move but a burning anger bright as the fire spring out from me. From the back of the crowd a baby be screaming hunger, but no one minds it. We count. We can't read nor write our numbers but we can say them just fine. We no cry, any tears from watching whippings have dry up long time.

In the shadow of the count me turn to the duppy beside me, him face as porcelain as Miss Frida best breakfast plate. 'Obah, you need to leave here. Right now! Come with me . . . this place . . . this place, I can't even.' Him gulp as if him breath have left him and I see fear. 'You don't need to put up with this! I can't help this man but I can help you. Please, I told you before about the future, it's a place far away from here. You'll be safe.'

Shaking me head at Jacob, me make me voice a low whisper. 'Wherever you is from, Jacob, you must see that me cannot go with you! Hector need me here now. Me must stay and tend him wounds. It is me that cause Hector such grief. Him is being whipped on account of me.' With his soft thumb, Jacob wipe away the tears that line me cheek and for a moment me feel that me have left this place, that me have travelled somewhere far from here, somewhere safe. Me reach up to touch his hand as it caress me face and look into his deep duppy eyes trying to understand what them saying.

'Orrinda, what you doing standing in the shadows?' Overseer Leary shove me forward back towards the rest of the crowd. I right my footing, terrified him have seen the duppy. But I look behind me, and Jacob have gone.

When Masser reach eighty-five him stop. Him tired. He steady himself and throw Lucifer down before him pull him suspenders back on him shoulders. The mistresses take this signal and stand, fanning arm in arm, them adjust them shawl and turn back into the house. Apollo take up Lucifer before Cooke can change him mind, knowing by rote what to do when

Masser tire. Him whisper something in Hector ear, patting him on the head with a loving touch, as if all be forgiven. The rest of we shuffle off, wearied, hungry, ready for our small slumber. From the Big House hallway, Miss Lynette float a giggle into the slave silence. Aunty Nita rummage her apron pocket and take out the can of aloe unguent she have brought with her. Masser must be tiring because him did forget to rub the vinegar and bonnet pepper on Hector's sore back.

'Go tend to Hector.' Nita press the can into my palm, before she mutter and turn herself to the Big House. She still have the beds to turn down and chores to finish up before she can rest. Me can feel the red ribbon in me pocket, still binding me fingers. If Nita or Mad Lizzy have pick up this ribbon when it fall from my pocket and not Murreat, me would have a back sore as Hector's.

Them cut him down now and start to take him to him cabin in the men's quarters, by the piglands, furthest from the kitchen where we rest up. I press on close behind him procession with small steps. When we reach, Apollo and Cato take him and rest him upon the ground, on top of him matting pallet, him lie face down. Rosemary and Anna, the weaver women, is ready for the bathing, both of these ancient ladies have seen this spectacle too many times. Silent and grey, one holding the pail of bloody water while the other dip the rag. The torn flesh on him back rise and fall with him breathing and me swallow back the sickness as me settle beside him.

We none of us have anything to say. Me reach into the rub

and spoon a little onto the wounds patting gently the trembling back with me finger. Hector not dead. Him eyes be closed tight, but him back convulse each time me put on the medicine. Him whispering now, calling for water so me push the can towards him, but him don't partake. Me stoop now and as me try to avoid him blood staining my bib, me can hear what him saying better.

'Me think,' him say, 'your mother, Madam Occo. She would be proud today.' Me wipe away me tears, full of shame and anger, shaking my head. Me have let Hector down, me have let me mother down. There be no pride in what me see. I press my lips against his ear and almost spit my words into him, me want him to feel me anger, me sorrow, me disgrace.

'Proud?'

'Of me. Me have take a stand, for you.'

'Uncle, me sore sorry. Me have shamed me mother today. This be my fault. Me will find some justice for you, somehow.'

Him speech slurred and slow, each word hanging with pain. 'Me not taking another beating. Not ever again. You want to give me justice, Obah? Then fight. Fight back. Do like your mother and find a way. A way out.'

'Lord know, we need a way out,' say Apollo, he and Cato looking upon Hector's back with a woebegone spirit. The weaver women nod them heads.

'It time for change,' say Rosemary. 'A change soon come,' echo Anna. Them dip the rag and tenderly, them place the wetness upon Hector, over and over again.

CHAPTER 14

The first toil bell tells me morning have broke, even though the sky be black as Masser Cooke's no-good heart. Me stretch out me arm and yawn mighty big like me want to fall back inside me dream again, but warmth from the night before is creeping up me legs and then a little sun bite through the holes between the branches. Me can tell another heated day approach.

Me start thinking on the happenings of the night before. Rosemary did tell how Masser have give Hector two days' rest before him expected back for lifting. Masser, him lenient of late, usually a whipping no give nobody excuse for leave.

Me still not clear why Hector do what him did. Why him left the count and make himself the missing negro. Him have never show me a kindness before, so why now? For a moment, me imagine the stroking heat of that little sun be me mother's proud hand like he say, and me heart surge with joy, until me remember that it is my fault and what is the pride in that?

Me must go to him. Maybe him like a little of Nita's molasses brew-wine? She always say how it see off the pain. Me have seen them, Monroe, James and Cornstalk, swigging it round the fire,

84

and it seem to put them in mind for smiling . . . or crying. Me have never see Hector touch a drop, though. Him never smile or cry neither.

Me porridge is lumpy and dark in me cup; and when me try to eat, I just see Hector's back running with blood and me can't swallow nothing down. Even Nita seem quieter and smaller today. She have no shout in her, but move about the kitchen, her weight soundless, on them broad bare feet.

Nita will never forgive me for what have happened unless me do something to make it up. Me can't call on her for favours today, so maybe me can make up a little brew for Hector myself? Or better still some snail soup, to fetch back him strength. Me must finish me errands quick, then me will find him some snails and herbs from Mimbah's patch.

'Aunty. Me go fetch Miss Frida her cuff.'

'Mmmhmm.' She shrug her response. She stay that way when me have upset her. All me see be her back, hunched up under her ragged shawl, all me hear be a muffle or a grunt. If she do look in me eye, she have a deep scowl, mouth set hard. Nita turn to Murreat. 'Go on now, Leary watching the third gang himself today, no let him whip you, run on with the gourd and work what him tell you to work, you hear?' Murreat scoot out, her shirt tails flapping. Once she gone, Nita turn to give a private conference.

'Me sorry,' she say.

'Beg pardon, Aunty?' Me look upon her with confusion. Nita have never before give me apology.

'Me no say it again. You hear me the first time.' Her eyes

85

squeeze shut. 'When me never see you come back, me did remember your mother, how it be when *she* disappear. Me have misgiving it happen again.'

'No, Aunty. I must show remorse, not you.'

'No, it is your blood. Your mother, she tell me how she have been born free in the negro land.' Nita look on me then for a moment as if she sorry for me, sorry to bring up the old story again. She set back her shoulder. 'And, when the buckra catch her in him net, she scream. She scream all the time she in the boat, though many days pass over water. When she and she sister arrive here with we, she did always remember the free feeling. She never forget how real living be. Your mother's eyes was always screaming for freedom.'

Me running. The dust swirl about me ankle, me riding along quick with the wind and none can stop me. Me right about the heat today, me run two hundred yards before sweat slide and settle down at the pit of me back.

When me reach Mimbah's cabin, by the end of the flat way, me call out.

'Mimbah, me here! Obah. Me have come for the cuffs and me is taking some of the herbs for Hector. Me gon' make him soup, me gon' take a little cerasee and one of them hard christophene you have here in the patch, Mimbah?' There be all kind of leaf growing in her patch, me don't know how she tell them apart with the blindness she have. I pause, then pick out the cerasee, which have a gold-green, tender stalk and the pointing leaf, me

86

take care to mind the nettles don't sting me skin.

From the corner of me eye me surprised to find Mimbah sitting still and quiet in the yard. She fronting like she no seen me here.

'Mimbah? Me just take small-small for Hector, a snail porridge for the pain.' Me walk to her and place me hand on her arm. She jump like me have throw cold water on her. Me take her hand, the one that have all its fingers, it ice cold.

'Mimbah, why them beat on him so? Cooke whip as casual is if him walking slow on a balmy day! It senseless, Mimbah, like the world upside down.'

Mimbah's white eyes glisten a little, but she don't move more when she speak. 'The world? What world you know outside of this here plantation? How you don't know that everything, world over is any different? That upside down is not right side up?'

'Mimbah.' Me pull up close and even though no eye be watching, me glance over me shoulder before I whisper in her ear. 'Me hate the white – me hate them all. One day, them gon' pay for what them have done. Me feel it. We will be free to live how we please, go where we go, earn we living. We will run free, just like me mother did do.' Me hissing, but even though me words fierce, me murmur low for Mimbah's ear only.

'Hush now, Obah,' she tell me. 'You can't talk so. No good can come from that.' She press her hand against my crown and rub it gentle as if that can wipe away my ill thoughts. 'Hate will never answer your question no matter how many times you ask it. Leave off of hating, it don't help we.'

'Mimbah! What we have if we can't hate? Them hate we, so we must hate back. That a logic. If we can't hate, what else we must feel for the white? Love?' The red ribbon strains at me knuckle in me pocket. Me voice rise, me can hear it buzzing round me head. Mimbah look on me, her face steady.

'Obah. We is broken. Them have mash us up, but still, we must love them up harder than them hate us up. Them have an eye, but it be closed up, like mine, blind to loving. We must open them eye for them to see.' She smile on me, weakly, and me do realize she really believing what she say. 'Them will follow you, you know? Hector, Apollo, Cato – see what Hector done for you yesterday? Them look to you.'

'Me? What can I do?' Me raise me shoulder but Mimbah don't see.

'And you have one good friend, Obah. Start with him. Not all of them white have a sickness inside.'

'What you mean, Mimbah?' But she don't answer. She close her eye then, humming a little and swaying to and fro.

Mimbah stiffen and turn herself, a yellow dust rise up from her feet and twist about her head, washing her eye, but that's not what make her flinch and her voice dry.

'Obah, me can still remember the day when me did come here from the block. Them pull me off me mother teat and me did hear the scream she make when she try to grab me back. Me hear her cry for me still, it have never stopped.' Mimbah hold out her hand, wave it at me and her blind eyes examine the space where fingers should suppose to be. 'Me remember the grunts of the men, them make a sound so satisfied as them kick and kick her, but still she don't stop wailing. Them did smell like dog ravaging bone. Only when them cut off this here finger.' She touch the nub of meat in the middle of her hand, rubbing the empty space. 'That's when it stop. When me mother did quiet.' She drop her voice to whispering, her head come close.

'Obah, if you bear a love for Mimbah, no wait for the house to burn down! Run away!'

'Mimbah?'

'Listen to the card, Obah. It say you have a friend. That the two of you must travel, must jump together. That fire it show you, it coming fast. Run, Obah! Find your friend and do like your mother, steal away!'

Me knock at the door and enter into Miss Frida's chamber with her breakfast tray. She already awake and awaiting as me enter and she jump up to press her letter into my pocket before me put a word out me mouth. Her skin be flushed and her eyes dancing, this be she in a lively mood. 'I will breakfast alone, Orrinda. You run along now,' she whispers. 'And do bring back those embroideries from Mimbah, goodness only knows what's taking her so long to finish them. Anyone would think she was blind!'

Me know she waiting on me to laugh at her clever joke. But all me say is, 'Me have them, miss.' Me pull the cuffs from my apron and lay them upon her chaise for inspection.

'If that be all, miss.' Me curtsy and turn to leave.

'Orrinda?'

'Yes, missis?'

'I hope you enjoyed yesterday's spectacle. You have me to thank for arranging that for you. Perhaps you'd like to take this opportunity to do so?'

'Missis?'

'What was his name? Ah, yes, Hector. I had made a special petition my dear, to your master, for him to be disciplined and although Cooke denied me at first . . .' She cross her arms over her chest and sigh, a dark line appear momently between her brows. 'Once the scoundrel had *proved* his disobedience by missing the count, he finally indulged my request. If only he would always listen to my counsel.' Me feel her eye against me and her head cock to one side as though she confused by my silence. Her delicate hands rub themselves against her dress.

'All is as it should be. You did the right thing to report his inappropriate behaviour towards you and he certainly shan't trouble you again. Now, what do you say, girl?'

She sit and turn to the looking-glass and start to lift and place the blond curls about her face so them framing it nice. She look like an angel, like the one in Nita prayer book, perfect ringlets shiny and gold. Her sapphire-blue dress reveal too much of her pale chest, but Nita say when the whites them do that, and the chest be shimmering, it not mean indecency. Her white day-gloves caress her white fingers. In the mirror, standing behind her, black all over like a thunderous shadow, be me. Me gulp, thinking of Mimbah's words, of love and not hate and me know that them is a wisdom. But the purest, reddest, ire raves within me and me don't think me can get reign over it.

'Well?'

'Mistress Frida . . . Me thanking you.' I fight to swallow back the bad spirit rising in me, my fists clenched.

She open her pomander ball and me watch how it spring out its silver legs like a spider in her lap. She sniff a little powder from it, close it up, then wipe away the invisible dust on her lap with both hands, eyes still on me in the mirror. Before she can place it back on her waist chain, the pomander fall to the floor and roll over, a spinning ball of light that finally stop at my feet. Me reach down to pick up the pomander from the floor. It sparkle and flash in me hand, I stroke the silver and a feeling of calm come upon me.

'Orrinda?'

'Yes, missis?' I feel her examine me face. Her countenance have little lines that tighten at the corner of her mouth. She unfold her arm and her outstretched fingers, like dry pale twigs, curl towards her body motioning for the return of the silver in my hand.

'Who gave you permission to manhandle my trinkets? That pomander is most precious to me, it belonged to my dear mother and to hers before that. Never, ever, touch it.' The gravel in her tone is hard. Me have never hear it sound so.

Me hand her back the fallen jewel. She examine it with care, looking for the flaw from me tawdry touch. The lines around her jaw release but a little, tightening again as she start to speak anew.

'Mark me most carefully: on no account may you approach my jewels. Tell me that you understand.'

Me can't understand why she so upset, all me do is pick up what have dropped upon the floor. I nod me acquiescence.

'Now then, girl, I must ask whether you have been granting time enough for your errands? The correspondence I have of late seems rushed at best.' She clench her fist in her lap, but her voice is sweetness, like the tinkle of the brook. 'These letters are incredibly important, they relate to business matters that I simply must be informed of. Of course, I wouldn't expect *you* to understand the . . . intricacies of these communications, but Overseer Leary simply must keep me informed.' Her hand whiten as it tighten over the pomander in her palm. 'Now, tell him, if you will, that the correspondence is not optional. Remind him that it would be most distasteful to involve Master Cooke in these matters. I'm sure he will understand.' She nods and smiles at her perfect reflection as if it's a part of the conversation and she twist her head to place a pearl-drop earing against her ear.

My finger pinch at my thigh through the pocket hole. Me curtsy and move to leave but Miss Frida be looking on me. She clenching her little ivory comb so hard it seem like a dagger in her hand.

'Orrinda, I have taken it upon myself to ensure conditions here are favourable for you and you must do the same for me.' She don't have to say no more, the teeth of the comb glint at me.

'Do not return to me empty-handed.' And she show me all her teeth in her face as me turn to leave the room. Me shake and tremble as me close the door upon her.

CHAPTER 15

The trees watch me as me pass. The branches sigh as me gather pace and fly along. Greens, blacks, browns, them all floating past me eye as me go on and on, to whatever destiny awaits. Me reach the overseer lodge and Leary come out cursing. Him have see me from him spy-hole. Me hope him can give me something heavy today, or else me will taste Miss Frida's sour wrath. Maybe, from him raised and shouting voice, negro troubles be bothering him.

'You hush now, before I have to hit you 'gain,' him say as him close him cabin door and a high giggle muffle itself. Is that Lizzy? As him walk towards me I look upon the letter in me hand from Miss Frida, so that him can't see me scowl biting him. Me scan the letters, trying to remember that alphabet learning from years before and that Jacob did teach anew, is that 'T'? 'O'? me sigh.

Him walk over slow, stretching him arm over him head and place him two suspenders back over his shoulder as him reach me, then him take the letter from my hand. Him don't ask if anyone have see me coming. Behind him the door creak open a little and Mad Lizzy's flushed face look out upon me, her anger clear to see, but not against Leary, she angered by me. She watch the exchange between us like a hawk watching prey. Leary take the letter from me, unfurl it with him stained nail and get to reading them black lines, his mouth shaping each word real slow as he take them in.

'How many days at sea?' He roll his eye then as if to heaven before crushing the letter like crackling between him palms.

'Run along, then, girl, I will settle this later,' him say with a wave of his hand and I is horrified to see how the parchment have gone from smooth to creased. Me eye stay low and as me look upon him middle, me could swear him have a new buckle on him belt, it dark as tar, as if it reflecting what lie inside. Him turning to walk away from me, but when him realize me still standing, him stop him retreat and step twice towards me once more.

'Well, now? What are you waiting for, girl? Run along and finish your chores. Or do you need me to find you an occupation?' The warmth of him breath chills me. Brown teeth peek out to match him tanned skin. I smell the liquor on him tongue. I cross me arms together, fingering my elbow scar, it smarting raw as the day him did give it to me.

'Please, sir, masser,' I say, a lowly whisper. 'The mistress, she tell I to wait. She say me must wait for you to finish your correspondence and then, me must take it to bring her straight back.'

'Is that right?' Him smile, stooping low to snap a stick of tall grass from the ground. Him place the yellow stick in him mouth and fix him chewing real slow, black eyes never leaving my face. Me feet beg me to move, but there be nowhere me can put them. Me brace down, breathing steady, readying meself for the blow when it come.

'Yessir, if you please. Mistress say she do need her correspondence,' I say, me toes curl into the ground. Him favour me with him hard stare.

'And what are you to give me in return, Orrinda? If I give you something, would it be only fair that you give me something back?' Him cock his head to the side, eyebrows raised. Thumbs slip under his waistband as him adjust his breeches. Him black eyes be full of scorn. 'Fair is fair, is it not?'

Me know that if me don't mind him words then me heading for market and me not coming back. Me would rather stay in the grinding-room, the boiling-room or the filling-room here, running the cattle round the mill, or ladling up the syrup in the copper pans, sweating the sugar out of me until me drop dead, like Phoebe, Sambo and Roderigo did this last season past. The sweet sugar them whites love to eat have a cost of black blood and bone. At least me would die here, for burial amongst me own and not in a strange land.

I rub my elbow again, mouth is closed. Him can't make me say it. I'd rather face Miss Frida anger than agree with him. Him step towards me.

'What's that? Speak up?' him growls, tapping hard on the wood at his hip with his whipping arm, he know me see it.

I try not to move. From me watering eye, me see the familiar brown hair and a pale hand holding open him cabin door, Mad Lizzy standing there still. Me have a mind to guess what she be doing here with him but me keep me head down as him wait on me to answer, the empty air between us be heavy. Me focus on the stinging me feel from the little grey rocks and stones that be sitting between my toes. The stones have cut up me little toe and a trickle of blood make the ground darker. Me don't feel the pain no more, just moist from where the blood running out.

Who is me trying to fool? Me have no choice. Me lips start moving, me open up me mouth, ready for him, to tell him 'yes, that be fair.' But now, me see the shadow of Lizzy approach, soft feet patter in the dust towards us. Leary don't feel a need to turn round but instead raise up him chin and him voice so Lizzy can hear him message. 'Get back to the cabin, Lizzy, you don't want me to show you how quickly my charitable nature can turn!'

'But, sir, me just missing you, is all – me get lonesome here, you can please come to me now?' Leary turn and though me can't see him face, me can tell from Mad Lizzy's pallor that the message him eye giving her be void of him special 'charity'. Lizzy hang her head, brown corkscrews bob and turn as she, obedient, step back towards the cabin. Panic rises now as I realize Leary have won, the escape she try for me have failed. I must do as him please. Him start to press fingers at him new buckle.

'Come now, Orrinda, you're a fine girl. You'll soon be busy making picaninnies when the new bucks come in, so how about a little practice? Settle down on the ground and this can be over nice and quick.'

I am screaming inside. Nita have warned me of the trial we all must face when we come of age, she did tell me that one day soon me must expect it, that Leary or Cooke or some other passing male would come to take my innocence. But not today, please, Lord, not today. I look around me, searching for a way out. I can run, but where to? I gulp at the fear of what is to come.

Shakily, I bend my legs one by one and slowly drop to the ground, just as him say. The heat of the earth flows through my limbs, binding me to it, holding me fast like a squirrel on a spit. I will think on my mother. 'Brave and proud' is what Hector called her and this is how I must be now. I will call on my African mother, feel her energy, feel her strength, that way he only can take me body and not me true self. Me have closed me eyes tight but me hear Leary grunt towards me and him liquor breath slide across my face. Me hands press into fists that have no fight.

'Masser? Oh, masser, me must speak with you, it about the mistress, sir, it a matter of urgent concern!' I open my eyes as Mad Lizzy's voice rings between us again, closer this time and as thorny as if she have thrown a porcupine between our chests. Me see her now, face close to his, her hand upon his person, pulling him away from me. Leary close him eyes with irritation. Him dark shadow over me moves to one side and me see the sun once again.

'Lizzy! I think I warned you enough times.' Him rise to standing and begin to turn and walk towards her retreating form, me see the belt slip out from his waist and him fingers begin to roll it in his hand.

I press meself up in confusion as Mad Lizzy slowly walking backwards. Purest joy be passing from her eyes to mine and me realize she mouthing a word for me alone, 'Run.' Me stumble to my feet but my body stand firm, squinting at the opening cabin door as she enter it and watching Leary follow. A shiver pass on me as the door close. This be a true confirmation of her madness; her footsteps towards me is gon' cost her Leary's wrath. But why? She have no love for me.

Me mouth open to suck in a heap of air as me realize me did stop from breathing. Me have never listen to counsel from Mad Lizzy before but today me take her at her word. Even though me hands is empty for Miss Frida, me pick up me heels and me run.

CHAPTER 16

Me have reach the Martha tree, but the sound of Mad Lizzy's cry reach me still. Me sit down by Martha's feet and press me back against her strength, feeling her heart's low beat, but it don't calm mine. Me hands is against me ears, wishing away the sound of Leary 'ministering pain. Me close me eye against it, as if shutting out light will stop me from what I witness. Everything have turn bad. Mad Lizzy taking a beating for me. Hector have too. Me have no paper to give Miss Frida! And what about Leary? The next time him see me, what him will do? Me need a place to run to. Unity be unsafe.

Me jump as something softly trace across my hand and place a warm heat. I follow the softness to find Jacob's fingers against my own. I look up at him and the word slip from me tongue before me can stop it.

'Leary.'

'What happened?'

Him must feel the shiver in me because there be no smile. Upon his face there be a darkness now to make him grey. Even though me cannot see him move, it seem like him whole body shudder as if him understand what did take place. Shame travels through me as Jacob lets go my hand and takes a footstep away from me. Him turn towards Leary's cabin, face hard.

'No, Jacob. No. Him dangerous.' Shaking my head I turn and pull him towards me and for a moment there is a heat between us, as if a spark have jump from him, a living fire, into me. For a moment, I wonder at the warmth of him, how him can be so heated for one that is dead?

'Jacob, sir, come with me, it not safe, for neither of we.' Me tell him with earnest.

Lizzy have given me pause, but that is all! Now, we both must go before Leary can do his harm. Jacob drop my arm and him walk, back straight and purposeful, away from me and along the path that lead up to the cabin door. Me find meself following him as if somehow, where he go me have to follow, me cannot hold back. When we reach it is quiet. The screaming from within it have stopped but me cannot tell if this is good or bad. He turn to look at me one last time as me stand away, still shaking my head and begging him to find wisdom. Me cannot stay here and watch what will happen. Me lean upon the bearded fig tree. Jacob face set in him determination. What him doing? Crazy, headstrong duppy! Him hand is raised to knock upon the door when it open and Leary step out.

'Overseer Leary, I assume?' him say. I cover my mouth with both my hands at the sight of this! Young Master Jacob, in front of me with him hands on him hips, looking down on Leary.

Leary's face be more coloured than usual, as if him have

finished a heavy chore, him eyes turn small. He look up at the duppy, taking in him peculiar dress and bare-head appearance and him take a step back, puzzled as if him can't work out where him have come from. Him examine him dark curly hair, shining in the sun and me know, as him scratch him head, he wondering where him have left his hat. Leary's face turn about as if trying to find the place where Jacob have left him nag or evidence of his travelling party. He catch sight of me now, holding fast to the tree, crouched low. Him beckon for me to rise and me bend up to me knees.

'Orrinda, you still here? Come now!' him say.

'This girl is needed. Now. Back at the house. Cooke himself sent me to fetch her.' I hear Jacob voice falter a little, or will that be him strange tongue again?

'On foot, sir? And unchaperoned in this heat?' Leary pause remembering him status. 'I don't think we've had the pleasure of an introduction,' Leary say, him tongue flick briefly to him lips. 'Leary, Unity overseer.' Him stick out his dirty hand towards Jacob, but Jacob let Leary hand be left solitary, in the air. After a pause, Leary drop it.

'No, you haven't, er . . .' Jacob tell him, with him special drawl. 'I'm visiting. I'm Cooke's solicitor, just looking in on things here, checking the books are in order.' Leary's black eye make small then and him mouth set in a thin, thin line, me think me hear him breath suck in.

'A' attorney at law? Well, well, indeed? and yet, so . . . juvenile? Forgive me, sir, but you hardly have whiskers to pare!' say Leary, him eyes widening as the colour change from dark black to dark leaf green. 'And from the old country? Well, welcome, brother. Naturally, you hear the Irish in me, from Killarney. But I cannot determine your region exactly?'

The duppy gulp then and square his shoulders, though I see his knees shake. 'Brothers, Leary? I think not,' him say. I see Leary bring his hand to rub upon his chin as Jacob continue. 'I have heard rumours of mistreatment of these enslaved people and for this I will be watching you most closely.' Mad Lizzy have stepped outside the cabin door. With red cheeks and eyes wide as mine own, she watch the spectacle. Jacob's voice breaks a little as he point over at Mad Lizzy before hissing into Leary's face. 'You have no rights to them, they're not *your* property.' Overseer Leary take a step back, almost tripping on the rock that's there, somehow him steady himself with his hands in the air.

'*Enslaved?* Mistreatment? Now, sir, I am quite sure that what has been communicated here is inaccurate. These are nothing but falsehoods levied against me.' Him throw me a dirty look. 'You must understand you can't trust what these negroes say! They're prone to mendacity and deceit! Perhaps it is your youth, sir, that allows your sentiments to side with the abolitionists, but I would in earnest advise you to consider the natural disposition of the slave. They are quite simply fashioned for work, a light touch is what spoils them! That, Mister . . . attorney, is the truth. Your name, sir?' Leary chin jut out, his finger pulls at him shoulder brace and him shift dust from one creased boot to the other, eyes never leaving Jacob.

'On that question, we must disagree. Slavery is a disgraceful occupation, but my "sentiments" are my own, I speak now in capacity of business, Cooke's business. I will leave you now, Leary. But remember, I am watching. I am staying . . . locally, and I have Mister Cooke's instructions to pop in and out as I require. Remember that.'

'*Pop . . . ?*' Leary screw up him face.

Jacob turn to me, him tamarind smell fill up my skin as the blue of his shirt fill me eye. 'Now then, Miss Orrinda, you come along, back to the house and you too, young, er, lady, return back to your duties.' Mad Lizzy look from Leary to Jacob before turning around and running on ahead of us into the brush.

Me gulp as Jacob's gentle touch steer me elbow and we walk off as if towards the house, before turning back towards the spring and to the clearing, through the tamarind trees and the ferns that gently breathe out as we approach. Me feel nasty Leary's eyes upon we backs, sending out him evil heat, but that is no longer my concern. Me understand it now. This duppy be alive and well! Him not me friend at all. Him the living proxy of Cooke.

CHAPTER 17

As we walk away, deeper and further into the trees, me trying hard to fight back tears. Jacob really be living and what's more, him be working for the masser! Him here for manage him property! Me have no right to feel confusion and betrayal, but me do. Him have trick me. *Obah, you is a fool.* Me feel a sickness rising from the pit of me stomach as me remember how me did tell him all about me mother, how she run off. Me can remember now, him did press me to answer where she be – him did know me from the start. And the reading! Him have test me. Fool-fool girl, me can't believe me did ask him if him living, no wonder him laugh at me. Him must have been laughing at me foolishness. What punishment him planning to deliver now?

Cooke's Jacob is walking straight, head held up high, him say nothing, staying quiet. Me think of how him did shake up me hand, me should have known then how him trouble. When I figure him as a ghost, me never been scared, but now me know him real and breathing, me terrified. Me want drop to me knee and beg him and God to have forgiveness. But me know God never listen, him white too.

Jacob stiffen and stop when we reach the tamarind grove. The branches and fruits cast a cool shadow on the both of we. Leary no see us now and him likely back in his lodge, nursing a soreness from Jacob. We a long way from the clearing too, so no one can see we from the Big House. We alone. Me stop beside him. It a little cooler here, the earth feel fresh against me feet, a relief from the hot grasses. Jacob turn to me with empty eyes. Me have never seen the blue so pale. Him put him palms over his eye and slowly pull him hands down until the fingers reach his chin, him fingers seem to shake a little with him victory.

'That was – intense. I think I'm gonna be sick.' Him turn and pressing him crown against the white bark, him breathe out a long string of air and the branches above us nod to register him labour. Jacob body bend and crumple as him place him two hand against his knee.

'God! Look at me! I'm in pieces here.' Him wipe at his eye and me swear there is water there, him smile is thin. Me stare at him strange antics but me don't smile back, not now me know him not dead. Him soft eyes that me did think was true stare at me now with his lies. Him no go trick me again. Nita say, you can only trick we negro one time.

'I can't believe I just did that! I mean . . . what if he had . . . what if . . .' Jacob turn and run behind the tree and me hear him heave. It seem as though a qualmish notion have come upon him after all. After a time, him emerge, face grey, the tears now moved from his eye, run down his brow. Him wipe his mouth with the back of his hand.

'We haven't got much time. He'll investigate or . . . he'll be looking for revenge. Either way, Obah, we need to go. You need to come home with me. Right now.' Him take out of him pocket a silver ball what sparkle and shine in the sun. Me squeal out loud when me see that him have Miss Frida's pomander.

'Sir, Miss Frida be very much attached to this here pomander, me must ask you to return it to her chamber before she can tell it gone or we negro will surely feel her wrath tonight!'

Jacob look down at the glowing ball in him palm and then at me. 'You know this? You've seen it before?'

'It belong to Miss Frida, me sure. That be her pomander, she keep the shine just as sweet. How you have come upon it? Dear Lord, she put the blame upon me!' Jacob blink a couple of times and shake him head quick as to banish a roach that did crawl inside. Me feel anger rising in me belly. This part of him trick? For me to fall into trouble with Miss Frida? Me fingers the ribbon in my pocket, throwing it upon the ground, where it writhe like a red serpent. 'This ribbon, this be yours. Me don't want it. Me don't want anything more from you. You here to cause me grief, me see it now.' I fall to my knee, hands together in prayer position, staring down at the ground. What me can do to find redemption from this deceiver?

'Masser. Those things me did say before, me never meant nothing by it. When me talk about me mother, me was only playing on negro talk. Me don't know nothing about where she did leave to.' I know him don't believe me, but these words is all me have to save meself. 'And the book reading? Me have never learn nothing, me never understand no writings, me swear.'

'Obah?' him say. 'What're you doing? Get up! Come on, stand up!' His hand's shadow reach out to touch me, as though to help me up, but me move away from him grasp.

'Why you did play me so, masser?' Me don't know where the unguarded words come from, flowing out of my mouth before me can choke them back. Me words no care about beatings and the consequences of insolence, them just want to be heard.

'You managing we negro as stock for Masser Cooke? And you must laugh at we too?' My voice croak as me meet him eye, him still missing a whip on his hip and I wonder what he will use to beat me with. Him feet, likely, them as strong as any branch. I can't look on him, afraid me will see eyes that turn black with rage.

'Obah, no . . . no you don't understand. Let me explain what I did, what happened.' Him voice catch in him throat. As if him triumph don't taste as sweet as before. Him bend his head coming closer to mine. He whispers, 'It's not what you think.' His breath is gentle, warm. Him full of contradictions.

'Me never done harm, sir, not to anyone. Me do all whatever Miss Frida say – ask Aunty Nita! If me did tender offence when me speak about me mother, please, masser, find a little clemency for Orrinda!' Wetness splash from me, small upon the ground. I wipe roughly at me eye, not wanting him to see the tears or the pain, to know how his gaming have caught me.

'Obah? What I said, just then, you know none of it was true, it was . . .' him say, his voice soft as the breeze against my back, him hand be on mine again, me feel him hand fingers linking into mine, joining me, as if him touch can speak the words him cannot.

'That psycho Leary, he was going to . . . for God's sake, what else was I supposed to say? Can't you see? I had to make him think I was on to him? I mean, I couldn't just let him get away with it . . . I had to *do something*, you get that, right?' Jacob's other hand is in mine now and me look down at both we hands entwined, like storm and day cloud fusing together. Me think me beginning to follow him, what him said was to warn Leary off . . . but does it make my path any safer to walk?

'Look, we really need to go, now! He's going to ask questions, and then he'll find out the truth about me, that I'm not a lawyer, and he'll be after you again too. Come with me. Let's go. This place . . . The injustice.' Again him bring out the pomander and me eye focus on its shine, me cannot look away. 'This. This is the key. This will take us. Will you come?'

Injustice. Me think on all that have pass. On Leary and him wicked proposal of what be fair. On Miss Frida and the glint of fire in her eye. On Lucifer at the end of Masser's hand, Hector's back dripping with blood. *Injustice.* Me think on the soon-come buck stepping off the boat, the husband me must mate with. On the babies me must bring into this world for toil, for anguish. *Injustice.* On Lizzy and her sacrifice for me. She tell me to run. Mimbah, she did say to run too. Must me run with Jacob?

Me stare at our hands, both tremble against each other, the

softness of him against the rough callus of me. Somehow, in this mix, me spy a kind of truth, a kind of hope. Me don't know where him will take me, but me cannot stay here. Anywhere but Unity. Me have not choice, just as me mother before me. My destiny is as hers.

'Me coming.'

PART TWO

SOMERSET, ENGLAND, PRESENT DAY

CHAPTER 18

Me not remember being born the first time, but it have to be hard. Me have heard the pain that come with it. Me mother, she must have cry as me leave her inner world for another. Me stepped out of the before, where there was warm and wet, and me did openly wail at what I find in this plantation home. Dust. Dust that did sting me two fresh eyes. Dust that did bite me new lungs as I draw air. I only a lickle babe, but me can taste the air and sense how this new place be no good. Me was better off, safer, staying inside me mother womb.

Today, this second time for being born must be worse. On this new and second birthing day, me see meself, stepping straight-legged out of one world into another. Into *here*. With each step me make, me recognize nothing here, not sound, animal or smell. Me is blind as Mimbah.

Me is fresh again, fresh and new. Biting at the new air, me is hearing all of them new sounds. Seeing all them new colours. I blink at the callous dark sky above me, looking even more fearsome as it throw water on me. Me head be paining, shoulders moving, teeth making a sound of them own. Jacob be

113

here, him pull my hand from off the pomander but me empty fingers stay clawed, desperate to hold on to the surety of silver.

The shadow of the tamarind trees and them scent is gone. We be under a tree that look as frail as I seem. A handsome bird with a red chest sit on a thin black twig, blinking at my strange form. Jacob, him mouth be moving and his eyes is a friendship, but his words can't break through to me for the humming in my ears, from this cold rain. Him pull up me arm, fingers rubbing life into me, bringing me back from the dead. Me stare at Jacob, my tongue heavy, leaden with iron. I remember Murreat and how her mouth is stopped closed and I force my tongue to move, to lick at the falling raindrops. Me want me voice.

'We gone. Me feel it. We did leave Unity.'

'We're home. At *my* home. You're safe now. That tiredness comes when you pass through, but you'll be okay.'

'Home?' Me don't know where me is, but there is a calm here. A peace. A sigh.

'Come on, let's get you inside and changed and then you can meet everyone.'

Him eyes ask if me feeling well enough to mosey and even though me head spinning, me check that me can move me feet, them press against the ground and stand me straight. Jacob's hand is firm at my elbow. I breathe in coldness, ragged and heavy, wet air fills me with the scent of cooling iron, like when Savio dip a hot horseshoe in water.

Me have a new feeling, one that me never felt in any of my years before; me far from home. We in Jacob's promised land now. This be the future. As we start to run, Jacob's voice whisper assurance in my ear. But me heart heavy with the sadness of that red-chest-bird without a song.

At the door that Jacob open, two hounds appear, and I bite back my scream.

Instead, I make myself stiff, holding onto Jacob's hand and closing me eye to them open mouths that drip water as they roar and reach up on their hind legs to grab me.

'Musket, Drummer, no! Get down! Shoo and leave our friend alone.' Jacob voice singing with joy as he speak to the hounds and I open one eye to see the darker one obediently lie down at the commandment, his eyes a woeful apology as he look up at me. The lighter hound gently press him nose to my curled-up toes and give them a little lick before him circle after him tail and make his retreat.

'See? They're harmless. Come on, inside.' Jacob pull me further into the hall. I see dark wooden beams above that remind me of the Big House but nothing else familiar. Dark doors are closed all around, a faint light come from the gap between the bottom of the door and the floor at the end of the hall and me think me see a person shadow there. Jacob push the one near to us open and we step into a white room. There be a painting hanging on the wall, got a trembling negro an' a white giant in it, but when I looks again, I sees it's the looking-glass, with me in it. Him reach into a clear closet and turn a metal lever. Water start to fall from the ceiling, heat and steam begin to rise about we two.

'You need to take that off, you'll freeze to death if you don't.

Mum won't mind if you wear this.' Him hand me a red garment large enough for two of we to fit inside, softer than any satin and fluffy as a green-face monkey. 'Okay, so shower gel is in that dispenser thingy, just press here. There's a basket there for your . . . your clothes. A hot shower makes just about anything feel better. Take your time and I'll meet you in the kitchen when you're done.'

Then Jacob is gone, the door close and I am alone with the sound of hot rainfall. I bend me head and watch for a minute or two, how the spray falls, how the steam swirls and wonder what it is him wanting me to do here, me slip me hand into the water and pull it out quick. This is like him have place me in a room that is a Barbados rainstorm. Then as one bewitched me understand. The door have been closed for me privacy. Me do how we youngsters do in heated rain. Me take off me shift and me head scarf, me step into it. The water rains down hot. Me open me mouth and drink, me eyes open too and falling stars sting as me blink up at them. I squeeze me eye trying to understand where the water coming from and when it will exhaust itself, but me cannot comprehend it all. Instead me enjoy the warmth of being born fresh and whole again.

'In here, Obah!' Me hear Jacob voice as me leave the room where heated water flows without end. The red garment him did give, me have wrapped tight about me, warm as in a blackbelly sheep embrace. Me feet pat against the floor that feels heated by the sun towards him voice. Him smile when he see me. 'I'll be two secs,' him say and him walk back into the water room. Me hear the sound of that water fade and stop. This is the place him call 'future'! Outside, beyond the doors of this house is cold, grey, wet, but everything here, inside him dwelling place warms me, the water, the floor, the clothing, wrapping me in a welcome, making me feel safe.

'Come and try this, Obah! Mum is the best cook ever.' Jacob point to the bread at the table where him sit with a woman and a youth. All them six eyes watch me approach. The room and table is smaller than in the Big House and me guess that where that table have space for twenty guests, this one have a space for only six. Me covert glance see how the table laden with provisions for a banquet and me wonder where the footman have stepped to and when the other guests will come. Plates of yellow, white, pink and brown dispatch their inviting scent to me and me belly growl me secret; me sore with hunger, but me more sore with fear of *them*. Me knees tremble. Me cannot eat at this table with them, me have never break bread with white folk before and me don't know where them want me to go so me stand stiff and still in the doorway, eyes nursing me reflection on the shiny flooring. Tears form even though me try to hold them back.

'Jacob, quick, you'll need to get her. Go on.' The woman start speaking. Her voice is soft and deep as if she have many years of sucking on tobacco and strangely, it give me the same feeling of warmth, like she place a blanket over my shoulder with her voice. Jacob's touch is gentle, as him arm guide me to the table and place me on a chair amongst them. Me breathe in hard, trying to remember how, here, everything be different, me must

117

try to settle me nerve. Here there be much to learn, but the blue eyes on me are kind, not harsh and them steady my racing heart.

Me hungry eye rest on the meat at the table but me make out them silhouette shape, the woman and the youth is both adorned in black. Me fathom then, that the blackness this mistress wearing all over must be for mourning, to mark she master's death in a proper, righteous fashion. What me cannot divine, though, is why she be sporting him breeches? Me mouth open and close with the question me cannot ask and the mistress take it for the hunger in me.

'Jacob!' Jacob stand to and begin to place fare upon a white plate, me lick me lips as me understand this be for me and when him place it at my chin, me wipe away the spittle that have come to sit at the corner of me mouth with the back of me hand.

'It must all be very strange here. What foods do you normally eat? Perhaps I can find you something familiar at the supermarket. Will this do for now?' The words from the madam fall on me but all me can do watch how them forks move. Me lift the one that must be my own, then me copy them movements, pushing the food around the plate, until me can resist no longer and pull up the fork to me mouth. Quickly, me lips open and close on the meat, swallowing fast before them notice and remember themselves and place me in another room where negroes must eat.

These provisions taste better than anything Nita have conjured, even at Christmas. Me drop me fork and return to the way me know in answer to the call of me howling gut, me fingers curl over the bread, the meat, the gravy and me scoop the flavoursome mess dropping it down me throat. The table silent, except for the grateful sound of me supping. Them eyes glance from one to another but them say nothing and me grateful for them indulgence at me poor mannerisms, feeling a comfort spreading out from them to me and not a judgement.

After a time, me place me licked-clean plate down and me eyes start to move around the room, there be no sign of where this mistress have place her bonnet and me see how in this place no head is covered. Silver, black and white gleam at me from all about, hurting me with confusion. Me shift me eye instead to roam over the woman again. Her lady maid have neglected her coiffure, no loops, curls or coils adorn her brow, instead black hair like Jacob's be veined with white and stand on end in strange spikes. She have on a black shirt with the collar open at the neck and open sleeves up to the shoulder, me gasp, me never seen so much lady skin exposed. Coolly, me cock me head to examine her feet under the table and discover her feet almost as naked as her frame, white toes wiggle in happy freedom like a slave's and she show no pain in her demeanour even though her toenails is dipped in red, as if her feet been pressed by something heavy.

The youth beside her have fair hair that stop at him ear and a soft face like Jacob that have never seen a whisker. Him pantaloons have been cut down with shears to mid-thigh and the tailor has not locked the edges! Him expose legs free from hair and me have the unsettling sense that, like the mistress, him is a wench beneath the breeches. She pick up her fork and chin in hand start to move her meat as if she seem to find sport

119

in the taking of nourishment. Jacob break the silence.

'There's plenty more, Obah. Actually, the food here is the best, you wait till I take you to McDonald's and you try the burgers!'

'Jacob, you certainly won't be taking her there. We'll feed her properly, it's the least we can do.'

'And, yeah . . . this is my mum, Dinah – same hair.' Him tap at him crown. 'This is my sister, Kitty. Don't mind her, she acts like a twelve-year-old but actually, believe it or not, she's fourteen. They weren't as sure as I was that you would come with me . . . Obah, we're all really glad you're here. I'm really glad you're here. Welcome home.' Jacob eyes deepen then and we blink at each other, me swept into that blue warm again. For a moment me forget our surroundings and it is as though me see only him, smelling the scented tamarind about us once more, me head dizzy with it.

'At least give her a drink, then,' say Kitty and tip towards me a goblet of clear water. Me thirst be raging so me nod thanks to her and raise the cup with both hands, pouring the liquid down my throat. It is clear and cold but oh, too-too sweet! Me cannot help but spit it out quick, spraying the table. As me coughing continue, me eyes open wide with confusion. What have me done? What punishment will befall me? Me cannot find words to explain me actions, even though me must apologize, me cannot form the sound. Me eye dart from one to the next, waiting for them next move.

'Kitty, that isn't funny! Don't worry, it's not your fault. It's just lemonade and it was an accident.' *Lemonade*, so that is how it taste? Miss Dinah turn to me and place a pale hand upon me red fur arm. 'It's our mistake, we should have known you wouldn't be used to it.' She take a type of parchment and gently dab at the wetness me have spray upon the table, me watch it soak up, as if drinking for me. Jacob's eye be crinkle with laughter and a sound come deep from him belly at the scene of me misdemeanour.

'That's one way to introduce yourself! Don't worry, you'll soon get used to fizzy drinks.'

'Jacob . . . please. I think we could all stand to be a bit more mindful of junk food. Let's stick to water from now on.'

'Wait, Mum – what?' say Kitty, concern in her voice. But Miss Dinah ignore her remonstrations, instead she turn to me then and there is a glint of honey shining in her eye. 'Obah? That's right, isn't it? You're so very welcome to our home. We hope you'll be happy here,' she say. She look worried. Kitty, the wench in pantaloons, nod along with her mother at these words, but when her gaze meet me, me see how she smile with her mouth but not her eyes as she play with a piece of smooth stone.

'Kitty, no phones,' say Miss Dinah and Kitty groan heavy like she have a delirium fever before tossing the 'phone' onto the table. The groaning stop and I look at this 'phone' wondering whether it have cause or given relief from her pain.

'You must be exhausted. Come on, let's get you off to bed.' Miss Dinah stands and I look up at her giant form, me have never known a woman could rise so tall! Smiling gently she take my red-clad arm in hers and me look at her unjewelled hand as it rest against me, stroking me tender as if me be a cat in her lap. Jacob

121

stand too and beside her me note her eyes are a softer blue, as if her advanced years have mellowed them. 'Perhaps you should sleep in the dressing gown? It must be so cold here compared to where you're from!' The grate in her voice is warm as a hearth, it soothe me, making me eyelids grow heavy. 'Don't worry, you're here now. Leave your worries at that awful plantation. It's sweet dreams from now on.' Me hear her, but her voice is behind water as the tiredness grab me and Jacob catch me as me fall.

Miss Dinah and Jacob bid me good night and leave me in a room where there sits a bureau, a bed and a small room beside. I venture in and recognize that this must be where I must sleep. I looks 'round me at the shimmering whiteness of the room, the likeness of me in everything with shine. I examine the spigot, tiles, an' other strange things besides I can't recognize. From above me stares silver circles of hot white that burns at my eyeballs. I kneel down and press my head at the white pan, feeling the cool porcelain respite 'gainst my brow. I reach in the pan an' splash the clear water on my face, then sups a little of it from my hand. It's cold, fresh and sweet, no bugs to chew on, nothing for me to spit out.

There ain't much left, though, I's guessing I will need to top it up soon enough. I yawns, big an' open. Miss Dinah be most generous to let me take a little rest before I tend to her needs. I settles myself on the floor, its cold grates against my back so me takes the first of them cloths and lays it out on the white tiles, it works just as good as any matting. *What a kindness*, I say. Well, then, just a little sleep.

CHAPTER 19

Me have spend ten days here now.

For three days me did stay in my room. Fear did come upon me of all that is new beyond the door and them did set food upon a tray for my sustenance. Jacob read to me through the wood panels. Him tongue familiar to me now, it comfort me. Him telling of Lucy as she enter the world where it winter always, but never Christmas. Me feel for Lucy, it seem her journey home will be long indeed.

'Obah, you haven't been downstairs for a couple of days now. You know you can come down whenever you want, right?' say Jacob every time he leave. When me hear his footsteps quieten, me did open and shut the door quick, taking the food inside.

By the sixth day, me have discover the room with the bed is where I must sleep! Jacob have explain how the smaller room be a 'bathroom' where water, clear as glass, be running free and cool. When I twist at the silver tap, the water start to flow and, Lord, how it trickle and stream clear and fast like me have a river flowing out in front of me! I cannot stop playing with this instrument, me checking and looking at it all the time to understand how it work.

I am leaving my room more now and I see there is something foreign dwelling in this house with us, a secret potency that hide from sight; a kind of duppy. Jacob say she name is Lectric. She stay in the walls and control all the wonders that me see, the way water is hot and how lights have no flame. The Mimbah me carry in my mind smile, her white eyes round with marvelling. She would commune with that Miss Lectric, were she here with me.

How me pang for her now, my Mimbah. Me miss me friend. Me never say goodbye to them, not her not Nita nor Murreat . . . me heart hurt to think of how me leave without a word. Me need to go back to them, to tell them all that is here, to bring them back with me! Me will ask to arrange it.

The Lectric brings a sweet music in my room, music of many sweet voices and instruments that me cannot divine. Every day it wake me in the morning and it begin again at night as if to announce the time for repose. Miss Dinah knocks gentle at my door and me remember now to say, 'come in'. She have bring me new towels and fresh clothing.

'Do you like this kind of music? Or should I put on something more . . . upbeat?' Miss Dinah ask as she place the towels upon the bed.

And me answer her, 'Oh, yes, madam, the fruitsome melodies be very fine indeed.' And this make her smile broaden.

*

'There's a funny smell in here, though. What is that exactly?' Miss Dinah sniff the air and walk towards the bureau and me clench me fingers together, afraid at what she will say when she find my secret. Opening the top drawer she pull out a black-skin banana, three biscuits and a slice of gammon ham that is glazed with grey. She sigh and for a terrible moment, me think me see Miss Frida in her same countenance.

'Obah, you don't need to hoard food. I know it's not easy to remember, but, please, the last thing we want is mice.'

Miss Dinah not angered? She don't scream? She don't threaten? Instead, she have a face like a bowl of ripe peaches, and the scent from her is a nosegay. Softness and pink shine from her and me love her already. Me nod me head, shamed that me cannot stop me old ways.

'It's all new, I know. For us too – we have a lot to learn about you, about . . . about our past. Let's just take it day by day.'

Miss Dinah have gifted me several garments, so many choices of dress and breech and undergarment; the breeches is worn here by our female sex to fortify against the coldness in the air. Why, if Nita were to see me with this wardrobe of finery, kissing on her Bible cannot counter the attack of fainting that must come on.

Me have a pair of shoe now too. Me love me shoe, them feel like cushions upon me feet and not hard or sore. I take them with me into the field behind the house. *I run* and I see Murreat run beside me, begging her little feet to keep up, her face as happy as an apple. *I run* and I hear Nita's voice cursing my missing whereabouts low, as she chopping on beets and shelling beans. *I run* and I hear that red crest cock-eyed cock 'adoodle, strutting that song loud and mighty. *I run* and I hear the turn of wagon wheels, whistling that cranky complaint as they's pulled along towards the picking field; beside, them is accompanied by some old negro hand with skin that hang as if it means to walk off his face. His laboured tap-tap breathing be soft, but his cuss claps loud through the trees when thirsty mules be arguing each other for the little water left in the trough. *I run* and hear Mimbah's voice 'the fire coming, Obah, run!' *I run* and hear babes' cries cut up the branches with confusion, like they can't understand their mamas got to leave 'em for the field. I hears it all, here in this quiet place, I's the overseer of it, but I can't make it stop, their cries is louder with my every step.

My world before today was dark. Always. Hogs' snouts black with the same mud crusting round my toes, tree bark against me lips, skin, hair – all manner of shades of darkness. Even me foolish dreams kept no colour. Now, here, in this place them call High Ostium House in Greatest England, everything be bright. Above me stares silver circles of hot white that burn me eyeball. Colours swirl and shine about me here like me living in a painting. Even Miss Frida's finest silks, them don't compare a whit to the colours here.

This place Jacob did bring me to be the same England where Miss Frida's sister Jane did come from to visit we in Unity. But

126

him say this is 'modern times' now, and here them have finish with slaving.

'No slavery? Is that why me have not bear witness to negroes such as I at work on the land? But then, how can any master get the labour done?' me ask him. For once, Jacob don't look at me. His voice be low.

'Slavery was always wrong. There could never, ever be an excuse for it. I don't care what anyone says, I don't care who got involved. Even, even if they were related to me, it wouldn't matter. It's toxic. You can tell when something's rotten. We all can. You know, in your gut?' Jacob point at my belly, fuller and rounder than yesterday. 'Right here and now, you're finally alive, not just existing. You like it here, right? You can live the way you want. We can go to the pool, the cinema, I'm gonna teach you how to game . . . you're gonna love it.'

'Game? Who have a time for game? When there be jobs that needs doing? We got to have all hands working, each to him place or else there is surely chaos, Master Cooke him very self have say that.' Me stick out me chin, me understand the way the world work and me have misdoubts about this lack of arrangement of labour.

Jacob pause his step, close his eyes a moment. 'It's a lot to take in. But I'm here. I'll always be here. Just . . . trust me.' Him brush his hand over my own and me could swear this Lectric him talk about living under his skin. Him feel it too and jump, turning him rosy cheeks away to look at the wall for a moment and him cough. Him voice strain when him speak next.

'At school, right, they're all so behind. One day, this teacher, Mr Finch, he was talking like, the world, this world, is backwards, like we need to return to this so-called "golden age", to learn how to be better. As if! You've seen what it's like there! We both have! How can that make any sense?' Him scoff him distaste at this sentiment. 'What would Mr Finch say now, huh? If he could see you here, with me and know where you're from? Someone living and breathing from the actual real past could tell him where to stick it!' Him shake him head many a time. 'This weird thing that's happened to us, the pomander bringing you here, it's got to be for a reason, right? It's got to be to show you how we've moved on? How far we've come? All of us, Mum and Kitty too, we see this as a chance to put those past wrongs right. Helping you kind of helps all of us to heal.'

'That pomander belong to the mistress, why you take it from her? She must fret over it so!' Me voice stern at Jacob as me worry for Miss Frida momentarily, me can see her eye welling water with the loss of her favourite trinket. At me words, Jacob turn towards a silver glimmer at the shelf.

'I know it has its . . . history, but this is what brought us here, Obah. There's something about this ball, this "pomander" as you call it, that connects the two worlds, the past and the present, do you see? Somehow, it kind of creates an energy that flows between us. How can I explain? Niagara Falls! We went there once. It's like that. There's an energy there. It flows between two countries, Canada and America, almost like two worlds, connecting them, and nothing can split them. Not now, not ever.'

Slowly, me walk to the shelf and me fingers reach upon the pomander. A feeling come over me then and me can't tell if it be the 'Niagara' energy him speaking of, or the thought of Miss Frida's face at the spectacle of me, stroking this precious ball of silver in my palm. 'Hey, just, take care, okay? We don't want it to send you back, do we?' Jacob gently remove the pomander from me palm, but them tingle with a need to hold the ball again.

CHAPTER 20

The third week me here, Miss Dinah did send for the doctor as she say me was sick and in true, me did feel a strangeness for a time, the world feel to be spinning fast so me must lie down and close me eye plenty.

The doctor him have a kindly face the colour of golden sunripe mango, brownish warm, not white like how a doctor should be. Him did warn me that a sharpness would be felt, and me did take my red ribbon then and held it tight. When me question what me did wrong, him say this not as a punishment as me have done nothing wrong but then he did give me arm a thin scratch. Him say it make me strong and when him finish, him place a pale piece of parchment over me that stay on me for two days. The doctor, him did see the tear on my cheek and him call me brave. Then him tell me to swallow some small stones in a jar each day, him call them vitamin, as them will help me too. I don't like them taste, but these are the rules me must conform to for to be living here as a new person and that is fine with me.

*

We have finish *The Lion, the Witch and the Wardrobe* and Jacob say me a quick learner. Me love book learning. Me happy that the brothers and sisters reunite together at the end, me did not like it when them parted and me did not like the White Witch's evil ways. This evening as me ready myself for dining I press my hand to cool my hot head, the braids is still hurting. Miss Dinah, she have find a woman who did come and wash me hair good, with hot water and plenty soap and then use a hot air to blow and tease it so that it fluff up nice like a black dandelion. She did place a ribbon in my hair, between the braids, me sure neither Murreat or Nita would know me now. Me desire that them will see this place with them own eyes so that them can be as confounded as I. But each time me ask Jacob should we send for them, him just shake his head and say it dangerous, that the 'slip of time' from here to there cannot be guaranteed. But dangerous for who? Him or me? I must find a way to gain him permission to use the pomander, then me can go back to fetch them on my own.

Me look upon the shoes. Them sturdy black would fit Nita good and me see her shoulders release as she place them on; the sky-blue would do for Mimbah, me watch her spin and pivot round and round, as for Murreat, well, she would love them pink ones that have a shine, me watch how she stroking them, her smile wide. Why must only me have new living and them don't? There be plenty here for all, me trying to understand why them cannot come here too. As me walking down the stairs to dinner me pause as me hear reference to me name from beyond

131

the heavy walnut door at the end of the hall.

'For God's sake, Mum, can you stop shouting? She'll hear you!' The voices lower and me walk slow upon the door.

'Listen to me, Jacob, you've proved your point, okay? I can't even blame you, as I gave you this ridiculous stubborn streak, but what now? What you've done is time travel for goodness' sake! Believe me, if it had been anyone else but *her*, everything would be different. You cannot, ever, do this again. People are going to start asking questions! Everyone has a history, Jacob. People don't just suddenly appear out of nothing, from nowhere! Des is a friend but even he was suspicious when he gave her those vaccines. What if she has to go to hospital for something? What then? I'm not going to prison for her, Jacob, I won't do it.'

'Prison? Seriously, Mum? You're exaggerating! What's your problem? It's not like she costs us anything!'

'Cost? Cost! Don't you dare mention costs to me. Of course it's not about the money, there's a much higher cost to this. Don't you think I don't feel that pain? The shame you keep pointing out to me? What's done, well, it can't be undone. But you, you just can't play with time, it's a dangerous game. You have no idea what you've got us into.'

'Mum, she's safe, okay? Doesn't that count for anything? Can we not just be proud about that one small thing? Or do we have to feel shitty for ever?'

'Forever's not long enough.'

'It's rude to listen in on private conversations you know.' Kitty approach me now from the staircase, her gaze fixed and solemn.

'Please, Miss Kitty, me never. Me just . . .' Me shake me head from side to side, full of fear.

'Your face! Oh, my days. You're easier to wind up than Jacob, you know that?' Kitty shake her head and pull out her phone, walking away from me.

There be a handle turning and the door open, Miss Dinah's eye cannot meet mine when she see me standing there. Her face is flushed, but then she remember her smile. 'Obah, you look lovely. Come on, let's have some dinner, you must be starving!'

Just as we finish our fine banquet of pies and cakes, there come a chime on the door. Miss Dinah face observe the screen where the image of the visitors shine up like a looking-glass. She look from Kitty to Jacob before she finally frown on me and her hand begin to play with the chain of pearls at her neck. Her voice is a deep sigh, 'Caroline has a file to drop off, but I didn't realize Beth was coming with her. Let me do the talking, okay? I'll try to keep her at the door but, you know what she's like, Jacob.'

'No, Mum, you're gonna have to get used to it. I'm not hiding Obah. Deal with it, okay?' Jacob's chin jut out and Miss Dinah sigh and go the door. She whisper for a moment with her visitors before two gentle ladies cross the threshold. These madams have a skin that the sun have kissed but seem them shameless enough to show everyone that them have change from blossom to bronze!

'Just a small one for me, my lovely!' Miss Dinah's friend have join us at the table and she take a sip of yellow wine. From her ears hang small silver knives, they shake a gentle melody when she tip her head to one side and one long ridge of black hair walks across her face. The woman following her nod her head in agreement but then she see me and she stop in her tracks, her eyes widen. 'Oh, I *love* your hair! It's ever so intricate – must have taken ages!' She come close to me, to lift and examine one of the plaits between her fingers, bending it to and fro. I allow her inspection.

'Don't do that!' Kitty shout loud, just as Miss Dinah hand the woman a cup of wine. She look shocked and take a too-large gulp of her beverage, a little spill over her fingers.

'Me thanking Miss Dinah, for all of she kindness to me,' me tell her.

'But of course you do, my dear. Well done, well done,' she say, nodding into her drink.

'Me will work hard and do all my duty to pay her back,' me continue.

'Obah, you know that's really not necessary!' Miss Dinah complain, a pinkness filling her cheek as she touch my arm.

'Natasha *is* looking for a cleaner, though. She'd be perfect! It's so hard to get reliable people these days . . .' The dark-haired woman have spread her arms out wide as if in discovery of some new treasure.

'No!' say Miss Dinah, her voice cold. 'Obah's not available.'

'But, miss? Me can clean good,' me say. Smiling me agreement.

'I think she's tired, Mum,' say Jacob, a piece of grit be in his throat.

Miss Dinah have a shine in her eye as she stand. She push

134

the bottom of my back and I stand, understanding I has her permission to leave the assembled party. I curtsy low to the ladies and beg take my leave. As me walk away, I hear the one of them say clear.

'Well, what impeccable manners! She's out of this world isn't she?'

'Quite,' say Miss Dinah.

As we take leave from them, me whole body sore tired. Me unburden the shoes from me feet and the soft tapestry flooring give relief to me toes as I step up towards me room. Jacob quiet beside me as we walk. My mouth water as me hand feel the food that I did hide in my pocket for me bedtime snack, me must eat all before Miss Dinah find trace of the smell in the morning. As me reach the door, Jacob give up him silence.

'Hey, Obah! Wait a sec.' As him gaze at me it seem him have a touch of melancholy, him hair flicker with an invisible breeze like a candle about to expire. I slip the meat back into my pocket and curl my toes under myself, me hoping Jacob doesn't fret that me have remove me shoe before me reach me room, but he look past me as him speak, as if him talking to himself.

'It's hard for you, being here, meeting new people. I get that. Ignore Mum's friends, what they said . . . They're hateful and they don't get it – I'm not sure they ever will. But life can be good here and I want to try and take care of you.' Him smile and then him eyes stay on me until me feel some unease from him gaze that will not avert from mine. Me drop a curtsy then, low and gentle before me speak. 'Jacob, me hope me never cause any disgrace to you or Miss Dinah. She a kind and loving madam and I do thank her for her attentions to one lowly as me.'

Jacob look at me then, as if him finally see *me*, him raise himself up and squeeze my shoulder. As he step away to let me pass into my room, he turn his face in parting, it seem grey in his shadow. 'It's us who should be grateful, Obah. It's us who should be lowly.'

I enter into my room now, grateful for the sanctuary of the day. Me press me back against the closed door and close my eyes, my head is hurting from all the newness here. All the learning me have to do to understand. When I open my eyes me see the strangest thing. The looking-glass that don't show me is showing a scene from another place. Inside this glass got a young girl, surely she no bigger than my finger, and yet, this here girl be walking. She move all about that box in her pinny, even got a little mutt at her heel, but no matter how far she walk, seem she can't make her way out of it, can't find her way free.

Kitty is in my room, sitting upon my bed, her face looking up at the image, the light have put a gleam into her eye. 'I turned off that lame music . . . Mum and her crappy lullabies! Instead, I thought I'd show you how the TV works. Jacob said to wait, but you're ready, aren't you?' She lift up a black stick and point it at the girl and me see now that she is gone. Me jump! Now there is another place with small animals running. Me cannot speak for watching with wonder at this movement. Is Kitty a witch like Mimbah?

'Can I ask you something?' Kitty's low voice pull me eyes away from the screen. 'I've been wondering . . .' Gentle, she turn and press Musket off the bed and then slide upon my sheet, she prop herself on her front, cupping her jaw in cradled fingers. Her tan legs stir the air in my room forward and back. Her straw hair is grown some, it sit upon her shoulder now and make her look less like she here to be my overseer. 'What was it like?'

'Miss Kitty?'

'The plantation? What you went through . . . At our age, kids shouldn't have to deal with . . . I just don't think I could ever survive something like that. You're so brave.'

Me hear Kitty's words but me have no answer to give. Me eyes move back to the return of the small girl in the box, me cannot look away. Now she happen upon more; more of them same little people be moving 'bout with her, them got little houses, little skies, little trees – like they's in they own little world, and all the world be in that box; them moving and moving but they can't break free, like blue flies catched up in a spider's net.

'Obah? I'm sorry, are you okay? I don't want to make you relive it . . . Maybe Jacob was right.'

'What it is?' me ask soft, feeling more hurting in my head. My heart beating fast but me know me should not feel fear.

'This?' say Kitty and her voice perk some. 'Well, TV is like . . . it's like stories we read. If you close your eyes when you read, you see the characters, don't you? It's like that, it's the picture in your head. The TV brings the book to life, get it?'

Me still looking at the image. She singing now, singing and

137

dancing, seem she happy being in that box, her eyes is bright and hopeful. Me turn away from her singing voice then, pressing my hand to the ache that have started in my heart. Me not sure why, but I is suddenly full sad for her, sad on account of how she don't know she trapped.

CHAPTER 21

'Okay, let's check out what's happening in the big bad world.' My eye widen at his words, but Jacob have a smile upon his face. Him reach into the carriage beside me and as he lift up him arm, his breath against me forehead is warm as soft embers dying. I eye the few whiskers he have grown in the night. Them is auburn red, not like the black him have on his head; they scratch gentle on me. Me have a strange desire to touch them, to reach up and stroke them tiny stiff flecks of red with a gentleness. Me hand start to move up but just before me reach, he pull back him face, his arm have got a belt with him now, thick and black, he pull it over me and me hear a click as it tighten on my chest and pin me to the chair. Me body stiffen.

'That's a seatbelt, to keep you safe. I passed my test recently, so it might be a bit bumpy.' Him voice have lower to a whisper and him eye laughing already. 'But it's a new day, and you're here.'

As is customary now, I don't know what he mean, but me know me must trust him; even though the tight feeling of this belt as it cut across me chest and neck reminds me of being tied to the whipping post. I tries to hide my shiver with a nod, like me understand what's happening. Jacob retreat from the carriage and go round, climbing into him own seat. He is beside me now but for a small gap where him assign the cupped draught of morning tea from him breakfast. Him pull the door closed.

We be going on a 'scursion, me think that what him say. But this not like any buggy me have seen before. Everywhere me turn there be glass, and we be closed inside, how can we breathe the air we need in here? Me have never stepped inside a buggy before, that's true, but me have seen the one used by Cooke and him visitors and me know for true that them never have a buggy full of lights and buttons and levers like this.

Jacob's hands fasten on a black turning circle and though we have no horse at the wheel, with a soft jolt we heading off and how me belly jump into me chest! I press the yellow flat of me hand against the cool of the glass, this a cold barrier, me can see out but me cannot touch all I see. The breeze blow but me don't understand how it reach me from beyond the glass. Me eyes widen as me press me head against the glass and wonder if small horses somehow be under us and me never see them when me enter? No, me believe this buggy be moving, from that same Lectric as them have in the Big House that make things work. Somehow, we is moving. With a soft sound, the buggy take us quick-quick straight out of the safe harness that is High Ostium House and into the surrounds of this future world for me to see.

There is no dust in the road as we move, it stretch before us, black as tar and empty. At first there are only trees, birds and sky but then there come others, more buggies like this, different colours, different sizes moving ordered and straight, making the breath catch in my mouth. None of them have a horse neither, the buggies move by themself, with people controlling their travel. The trees are becoming less and then more houses be appearing, people walking along the side of our black road on flat stones that glint with dew.

We slow down and I press me head against the window, gulping at the air to stop the sickness forming. Jacob seem to understand me because him command the glass slide away from me and the air outside be mine to breathe in. 'It's okay, just breathe. It's travel sickness. These help.' Him give me a white morsel, so me place it in me mouth and chew and the whiteness become as bunched mint leaves in my mouth! Me wince and close me eye for a time, as if me body know it be too much to feel, see, smell and hear all at the same time. 'Okay, you don't look so good. Hey, let's pull over for a moment, yeah? Give the sweets a minute to work.' The buggy stop and Jacob come to the door, him open mine and pull me out lowering me to the floor, head between me knees as me gasp for air. Me feel Jacob hand on me back, rubbing warm circles against me as me sway, and him hand be on me hip, a hoist to me falling form. We sit upon the bank then and me lie back upon the cool of the grass, not minding the wetness that gather against me skin as me look up at the sky. The sky be the same here as back home. Sure, it more thick with cloud, but where it should be, high, high above.

'Hey, Obah, are you okay? We can't really wait here much longer, that traffic warden's sniffing at the windscreen and

Mum'll freak if I get a ticket.' Jacob pull me up and much as me want to stay against the solidness of grass and ground, him attend me to the buggy once more. The sheriff standing there shake him head, with displeasure, him mutter at Jacob a word me cannot comprehend and move on. As me take me seat again, me head sit cold by the carriage door and as we move off, gentle and slow, a soft music begin to play and me feel safe again, as if me back in time, alone with tamarind leaves and a disappearing sun and a white ghost. Me turn to Jacob.

'This is my favourite Beatles song. Something about the broken wings, it always gets me.' Him carry on with his driving. Me don't understand how beetles are singing, but this song help me feel calmer. Me can see that bird, trying hard to fly, with its broken wings. I press the red ribbon – never far from me hand – against my fingers, soft and familiar. Me observe from the window now as the music play gently, there is more folk starting to move about; me watch as them go by. Mens, womens, babes, all of them countenances inscrutable, passing on the small patch of grey land. Like leaves that fall from the breadfruit tree, they float soft and slip pass each other, careful not to touch.

We be in a *car park*, say Jacob. Lots of empty buggies is lined up here, in rows, neat as a harvest of cane. Him help me out of the vehicle and Jacob's eye twinkle as him pat the top of the buggy like she a fine nag. I jump at the noises about me, grunts and groans gnash against me ears from the other buggies that swim about us and I press myself close against Jacob, clutching his shirt and inhaling him scent of mango and lemon like Miss Frida sniff salt from her pomander when she feel faint. Me settle into the warmth of him. Him stiffen at my touch for a moment and me hear him sigh low. Then him hand rub across my shoulder, him always make me feel safe again.

'We made it,' him say. 'It'll be worth it when you see the menu. McDonald's has nothing on this place!'

Me ponder not on Jacob jargon, all will ever be revealed. Instead, as we enter the street, me rub me eyes from what I see and look up. These domiciles here, they're not made of tree wood but something hard and grey, they climb tall, heads aching for the sun as them block out the trees and sit on the grasses. The buildings have writing all over. Me never know words could be all out in the open like that, not secret, but big as you like for all to see. 'Are you hungry?'

Me no answer. I understand him japes now; this not a serious question to ask such a one as me.

Mistress Frida have talked aplenty of partaking in 'afternoon tea' when she live in England and me and Mimbah did love to play this game together, practising the lifting and lowering of our conjured china cups. Now, I is here, in the England she did talk of, walking into a such a place as she describe to enjoy eating tea. In this parlour, there be tables all around the room set for service, although the cloths be missing, the cutlery is laid and little chairs be tucked beneath.

A quantity of tables have occupants, them forks be glinting silver as them carry fare to them mouths. Me stumble as we walk towards the table destined for we two, but even as I look around me, afraid me presence may offend, them eat their provisions undeterred. Jacob pull out a chair and sit down, I stay standing, looking side to side, can't see no Blacks like me sitting in here and me not sure if I should seat myself on the floor beside him or stay standing. There be a grating sound as the chair slide out.

'Miss?' A young white youth put him gaze at me, his hand gesture to the seat and as me reckon him telling me to sit, I do so, obedient. Me hands start to swell up with sweat and I look down away from him, breathing hard. Me look down at how the table is made of looking-glass, it shining so high my face shadow be staring up as affrighted as me. Quickly, me lift me fingers off the table, not wanting to smear it with my touch.

'This is where we used to come for birthdays. It's pretty full-on, but for every now and then it's, you know, a bit of a treat. I haven't been back here for a couple of years, though, not since I was about fourteen. I can't remember why, exactly.' Jacob look away from me then, and a darkness appear like cloud across him brow. It is as though him have remember the reason, but him have no disposition to announce it to me. Him shoulders bunch and him pick up a tall book, and scratch at him brow. Him seem intent on his reading now and quiet, so I look about me while him busy himself. The cover of him book look to be the same as the book that sit in front of me; every table have the same book placed on it. I want pick it up and look through it, but me not sure whether me can do that in the open with so many white folk about. The man who did pull out my chair still hover by us.

144

'Coffee?' he ask. A piece of metal shine and flash in him mouth when him talk, like him have kindle a small fire there, upon him tongue. I look from him to Jacob, him still have his head in his book but it is him who must answer the youth, not I. Me put my gaze down on me fingers.

'Yeah, two lattes, please. And we'll have one of those and one of those,' Jacob say tapping at the picture in the book. 'Oh, and tap water, please.'

The youth scrawl upon him parchment then head off and Jacob take back to him reading, I wonder if the words he reading is as rousing as when Aslan fight the White Witch. The back cover of his book got a set of pictures, look like fruit, custard and heavy cream in wine goblets, only someone dressed them as ladies heading out for dancing. Them have coloured beads, ribbons and pearls all over, like each one trying to be prettier than the rest. I smack my lips together, I reckon there is candied mango and fried apple in them puddings for sure. Me never knowed food can dress to look so beautiful.

Our table sit beside a whole wall made of sheet glass. I fix to gaze to the outside of where we be. Buggies of black and blue grunt and growl as they pass on the black strip. People be walking, their eyes not seeing others as they step. I spy one who prefer not to walk today, she using that Lectric to seat herself in a chair that can do the walking for her. Them all stay mighty careful not to look upon each other. I thinking this must be because their heads is bare. Can't tip your hat and say 'Good day, sir' if you forget to wear one.

'The last time I came here was with my dad.' Jacob voice soft, but him eyes still face him book and his head stay bent. 'It was just us two – Mum and Dad had already split. Supposed to be a birthday treat, but yeah, we kind of had an argument. Funny thing is, I can't remember what it was about exactly. Probably me not studying hard enough or something like that and the trouble is, I haven't seen him since. He moved away . . . to the States. He said it was for work, but who knows right? Maybe he'd just had enough of me.' Him eyes glisten as him talking. And me think, poor Jacob, a parent have forsaken him too, like me.

'I miss him,' he say. We look at each other and me heart skip at him pain.

'Him still love you,' I say. 'Just as my mother still love me.' Me touch his hand and we stay just so for a while.

'Look, Obah,' he say, after a pause. 'I've been wanting to talk to you about Mum's friends who came round the other day. Kitty was worried about you – they shouldn't have treated you like that and . . . we should have challenged it more. Mum . . . she tries, but it's not enough. Some people think they're not racist by having black friends or colleagues, a cleaner or whatever, but they don't understand that showing racism can be more subtle than that.'

'Racist? What you mean, racist?'

'Racist? Wow! I guess, you wouldn't even have heard that word before, right?' Me blink at him.

'It means when you judge someone based on their skin colour. You think of them in a certain way, a negative way.'

146

Me think hard for a moment.

'You mean how me living at Unity? Where black is called ni—?'

'Shhhh . . . You cannot say that word here!' Jacob look over him shoulder to check if anyone have hear my language. 'Yeah, it's words like that for sure, but it's more than words too.'

'Yes. Me understand. It how we treat others. How in Unity, we black is treat like objects, not as persons. Me understand racism.'

'Yeah . . . you do, you really do . . . I could never. Even though I try to, I guess I could never understand it, not the way you do.' Jacob put him gaze on me now, as if searching to find something, some writing to read on me that can give him the answer.

Me look away out at the glass where the people roam, but me don't see them. Me see the racism me left behind. Me see Masser counting people as if them is cattle, me see Hector at the whipping post, me see Mimbah's white eyes, blinded by Cooke, me see Leary stroke him belt buckle and lick him lips, me hear Miss Frida's talk of bucks for me . . . But Jacob have say the racism be here too! I look about me and all is quiet, all is calm. Where be this racism? Where it hiding? Where will me find it?

The white waiting youth return, and me drop me gaze. Me cannot look upon him, this be a white gentleman, carrying fare on a laden tray! And him conducting service to me! If only Aunty Nita could bear witness! In front of me him place the belle of the pudding family with pink pearls all over her thick cream. Jacob laugh, 'These sundaes are bigger than you are!

147

Don't tell Mum you got the knickerbocker glory, I told her I'd just let you try one scoop.'

Me not sure what to do with this, must me eat her, in all her glory, right here and now? Or beg them let me take her home, so me can gaze in wonderment at her each day? Nita in my mind roll her eye at me and point at the spoon with a huff of hot air. Mimbah in my mind spoon a little and place it in her mouth then giggle. Me will show my courage, for them sake. This first bite of it pains with cold. Next comes soft, cool, hot and a sweetness so strong that it twist inside me. The white youth have moved away, but him and Jacob have both them eyes fixed on me, watching and waiting for me response.

But me remember Mimbah, me imagine she here with me. Me manners be sweet. Me spoon go back for more and more. Me take a mouthful for Nita, one for Murreat, one for Mimbah. Don't take me much time to finish up the whole of the glass. Me look up at them two white faces and smile as sweet as the pudding me did eat.

But the sweetness is a mask, hiding an untruth. After the sweetness comes a wretched pain in my stomach. This sickness bite me so hard me think I must be dying. All of the lies comes out then and me see clear, all of the wickedness that was masked in sweet glory.

In the evening, me still feel only half recovered. Me have a blanket on my lap in the study and when me not nursing peppermint tea, me doze soft. Low voices float across my path in a blur from beyond the wall but me cannot hold them still.

'I've put it away. Somewhere safe. It's better this way, Jacob. Look at the mess you made today!'

'Mum, you can't! I need it – what if we need to go back? What if we could help others? That's what she wants.'

'Like I said, it's not happening, Jacob. Put that out of your mind entirely.' A door slam hard and me jolt, sitting up. Me yawn, but stretching out my arms make the tear in my belly hurt and me fold again, groaning as me reach for the cold tea to sip.

Jacob press the door gentle and come into the room, but when him see that me eyes is open him look sheepish.

'Did you hear any of that?' him ask.

'Hear? What me should hear, Jacob?' me ask, soft.

'Nothing,' him say quickly and him pick up a book but don't look at its cover. Sitting beside me, him start with reading upside down and there be a restlessness within him.

'How are you feeling?' Him voice softer now as if he remember himself, and him eyes is grey with concern. 'I'm really sorry about today. Let me get you another tea.'

'Please, and thank you,' me say weakly.

Murreat, Nita and Mimbah sit beside me, just as them did at the parlour, unseen and unheard. But me know what them want. Jacob stand and return to the door.

'Jacob? We bring Murreat, Nita and Mimbah here? Please?' Me voice be weak but me know him hear me, even though him eyes don't meet mine. 'We can bring them here. I know them will work hard for you and the mistresses. This house so big,

Miss must need help with choring.'

'I'd love to bring them all, you know that, don't you?' I sense him waiting so I nod my head in the silence and him continue. 'When I think of them there, I hate it. But you know how my mum is, she'd never allow it.'

'But . . . why we cannot even try?'

'There's no way. I can't even bring it up with her without her flying off the handle. She thinks it's too dangerous. But maybe she's right? I mean, the fact that you're here is miracle enough. It's incredible.'

'Jacob, maybe it will work again if we both of us go? Both take the pomander in our hand again?'

'But what if it doesn't? What if you get stuck there and can't come back again? What if I can only travel with one person? I can't risk that. After everything that's happened to get you here, I won't take any chances with you. You know that, please don't ask me to.'

'But why only me, Jacob? I am only one. So many others is still suffering. Please, can you try?' I brush the back of my hand against my eyes to mop the moisture that gather there.

'You're the one I care about.'

'Begging pardon?'

'I mean . . . it's . . . it's complicated. But it's you, Obah. It's you . . . you're important to us.'

'Nita, Murreat, Mimbah – them is important too, important to me.'

Jacob have come by my side now, and him forehead press

against mine as me sob gentle. The tears come and me do not try to stop them. So much have happened. Me cannot think. Me need me friends, me family. Jacob, Kitty and Miss Dinah, them is not enough.

Jacob pull away and wipe a tear from my cheek. 'Obah, I'd do anything for you, but, going *back*? Right now? It's out of my hands.'

'The pomander?'

'Mum took it, okay? After what happened today. We were exposed and I . . . I put you in danger. I don't have it any more.'

'The pomander, it gone?' Me fight back the tears that want to form again.

Jacob stand up and me watch him walk towards the dark shadow of the door. As him reach the exit, him turn him body back to me and stare for a moment as if arguing with himself on if he should speak. Musket the dog tickle me toes and I rub his golden muzzle with my chin.

'It's strange. Bringing you back was actually her idea, in a way.' Him whispering, but I think that what him saying.

'Her?' I move to stand up from the carpet, but Jacob wave him hand, bid me stay put.

'Mum. She's the one who left it in my room. *"This was your great-great-grandmother's."* That's all she said and just kind of left it on my shelf. When I told her I'd been to Unity, through the pomander, she didn't laugh or question, like you'd imagine someone would, right? It's almost like she wanted to go herself but didn't have the guts.'

Him laugh to himself. 'I guess she didn't think I'd actually do it. Maybe she was just testing me all along.'

And him leave then. Leave me in the room alone. Why? Why is it that I must be the only one? Why is he the one who always get to choose my way? Jacob say that there is injustice at Unity. But me see it here now too.

That night in bed I tuck my knees up to my chest and bury my face into them. Me have learned how to weep in silence from a young age. Nobody wants to hear their property cry; cows and chickens know it and a slave learns this quick enough to stay out of trouble. We cry without sound. But today, I howl, my fingers dig into my pillows as I press my face head down into it and I scream over and over and over.

CHAPTER 22

This night me cannot sleep. Me have a curious notion that this bed desire me for her supper. Blankets, sharp like teeth, gird me and chew upon me body until me feel as if me being swallowed, pulled down and cannot catch me breath. I open my eyes and am sure that it is Miss Dinah bent over me, there is no smile, her eyes reflect the cold moon, I close mine again, open and she is gone. Me move off from the mattress to take my nightly repose upon the floor, soft still with carpet. The bed's two pillow-eyes watch me, angry that I have escaped them grasp, me comprehend that the bed cannot eat me if me don't give her permission.

Early morn me feet say, 'Run, Obah.' So me come to the door at the back of the house to go outside and move me limbs. Everybody but the dogs be sleeping and them kiss me feet when them see me. Them big-big, but kind. I try the glass door but it is locked hard. Some keys sit beside the wall and I try a few to open, but the door stays shut against me. A knot in me twists at my trap. Musket has put a ball in his mouth and waits at a door I take for a cupboard, looking at me with expectation. Me turn to him and examine the draw bolt at the top and bottom, I use the chair to pull myself up and pull it back at the top, it stiff but it budge eventually, the bottom one is out easily and then the door is open. The dogs run out and I follow. Looking up, the sky is still a weakened ash, never that rich blue I know from Unity.

This house be set on a plantation just like in Barbados only them have no crops and them have no labourers to drive up the soil. Instead, the land is rolling verdant green, soft, lazy and untilled. Around be trees that stand like brooms, them frame the perimeter of the land in a arc so me know me have plenty space to run, even though it look like the bars of a gaol. The door shuts hard behind me and me hope me have not disturbed the slumber of me new family. Biting my tongue, I shiver raw in my new pyjamas as I face on the cold dawn and look out at the new world. My feet slip across the wet terrace boards in the too-big, too-soft slippers Miss Dinah has give me. As soon as I take them off my toes strain, waking up to catch the droplets of rain. I turn, no curtains is twitching. No one is watching me. Me step off from the veranda stair and into the soft rain.

My feet press down over moss and grass, damp and dewy with night-time, and then the coolness seeps into me. I take one step, then one more. My body be righting itself, adjusting to the tree roots running at my feet. I turn my face up to the sky water, it pitter-patters on my head and down my nose, my mouth yawns wide and hard drops bang against my teeth. Then I am off, running ahead across the ground, taking the dogs with me. It is half dark, but the scattering moondust weave through the trees making way for the early sunlight. There be something warm about the connection to the earth that come when me leave off them shoes and run barefoot. Me fly and the dogs them chase to catch me, happy and barking. My hands sparkle and slide with wet and I breathe in the damp. I want to laugh at the trees I pass, if only they could run like me, then they would not have to stand there, roots stuck in a past time, their bodies shivering in the here, in the now.

As me passing these oaks and ashes, seems I see Nita's face in one of them, and Murreat smile in another, the bark shift and change in texture for the eyes of Mimbah to appear before me. Me family, all watching upon me and me feel like me not alone. When me think of them toiling hard and me living free here, the anger rise in me and me want to run to Unity and drag them away. Where am I? If me is not with me family is me truly living or not? Is me ever really home? Miss Dinah is a kind woman, she smiling at me all the day, she hug me, feed me and give me clothing and me feel a comfort that she want me to be happy. But when me think on Murreat and Mimbah and Nita, even all of her kindness don't have a start on the way me feel sadness from the lack of them. Me will ask kind Miss Dinah herself, she will understand what Jacob do not, she will hear my petition to bring them all here and agree to me request. Me sure of it.

Just as me slow me running and stop to breathe the cool wet air, me hear a roaring coming from above the trees and me look up expecting to see a small animal remotely in the tree, growling in complaint that him cannot get down. But what I see there is more than beast, it is monster. I squint my eyes into the early

155

sun, gentle and cool against my face. This creature is flying in the sky, higher than the top of the tallest tree. Black wings spread like an eagle, but bigger than any bird, his beak is pointed and mad, cawing his anger at me. This animal be making some heavy grunting but not like the way Overseer Leary do when he beating up one of us, this be darker and louder. What it is?

Copying my screams, Musket and Drummer bark at the thing in the sky. We turn and set off back to the house. Trees tremble, them leaves jigging from the breathing creature following on, them as afraid of this beast as I! My feet is fast, but I know the creature be faster, the back of my neck got hairs there stirring up from its breath. My tongue stuck hard between my teeth. I trip and fall, I close my eyes.

'Hey, whoa!' say Jacob. He got me by my shoulders, blocking my run and I buries my head in him chest, shaking as I point fingers up at the sky. It's so close, close enough to pluck us both up and swoop us off. Jacob laugh soft, and be rubbing on my back. 'What? The drone? It's just kids probably, they like to practise around here. Did it scare you?'

I hold on to his shirt, balling up my fists, my nails pressing sharp on his cotton. I nod into his chest. 'It's like a really small plane, that's all. Everything's different here, but it's all good, always remember you're safe.' I look up at him, and he nod, blinking back. Gently, he turn me round to face the beast soaring away in the sky, sounds softening as it take its leave from us. Getting smaller by the second. 'Look, it's gone now. See that bigger one, higher up in the sky? That's a plane.'

'There be . . . inside that . . . a man sitting there and riding the sky?'

'Yeah, that's it, exactly that.' His face is straight as a hoe, this is not one of him japes. 'And beyond the planes and the drones, higher than the moon even, there are other planets amongst the stars, other worlds! Mankind has started exploring them too . . .' I squint up at the sky. The drone and plane have disappear now and the sky quiet. Other worlds? Like mine. Like his. I check his profile. This have given me clear vision. Me know what me must do.

'If all such things is possible, if a man can ride his wagon into the clouds, if me too can pass across the lines of time to follow you, then why cannot Mimbah, Murreat and Nita come to here? Me going to ask Miss Dinah for the pomander, and if she will not grant me request, me will find the pomander myself.' Me straight me back and open me eye against the falling drops.

'Obah, what I love about you . . . I mean – like, is your strength. You don't *ever* listen.' Him eyes crease and him sigh. 'We'll need to distract Mum so that I can find it and then . . . Then, we'll go back and we'll bring them here.'

'You will help me?'

'Let me find the right time, okay? Right now, she's on her guard, there's no way I'll be able to get at it.' Jacob press him hand against him brow.

'Jacob, Murreat she just a child, me cannot think of her under Leary grasp, what him will do to her. Nita, she old, health failing every day, here we have a medicine that can make her strong. And Mimbah, what of her finger and eyes, we can make her

157

well again if we bring them here.' Me press me hand against him face with my words.

'You're right.' Jacob eye grow large. '*If* we can get the pomander. I can't guarantee it'll work as smoothly as it did before. It's going to be a risk, you know Leary's already on to me . . . God . . . these people . . . they're pure evil! You remember what they did to Hector? That could happen to us, Obah! Nothing's guaranteed. Are you still sure?'

'Jacob, we must help them.'

After our dining today, Miss Dinah say she have something to show.

'It'll cheer you up,' she say. She lead me gentle down the staircase and her shoe click and clack like goat hoof against each step. We walk to the end of the corridor to a room below the kitchen, she push the door to and inside is windowless and dark. 'Once upon a time, before my knees gave out, I bought this.' Miss Dinah press the button and light fill the space. 'Cost quite something at the time. An investment, the salesman said. Anyway, no one else is interested in running, but Jacob says you are. You ventured out yesterday, didn't you, and got a bit of a scare, right? There's no pressure, but if you want to give this a go, I'm pretty sure it still works. Let's see.' She press a button and red numbers light up an' flash. 'Look at that? Okay. So, you just have to run, like you would ordinarily, only you don't have to be all out in the open, in the awful English cold and rain!' She laugh at her joke but arrests her noise when she perceive my eyes be scanning the floor.

'It's not as scary as it looks! Technology, don't you love it?' Dust swirl and swim in the yellow light of the one hanging bulb, as she start to instructing me on how it work. I steps on it and sure enough, this machinery be moving himself to let me run, complaining as it do. My feets move one on one and she watch and nod her head. 'Yes, yes, that's right, like that. Push that if you want to stop!'

Miss Dinah, me loves her mightily, me do, but she don't understand. How does I tell her? The running ain't just motion, ain't me legs moving. The running is the being, it is the mercy. The running be the dust my toes stirs as I pass, the smell of raccoons hiding in the wet thicket, the early sun-thrown light on fallen cypress logs. Running be like what I seen happening in the sky with them drones, with the planes – it be flight, out of myself and into creation. Running be my eye catching fresh green berries on the dog-wood tree, showing the coming of Maytime. The touch of freedom. How does I say all this?

Miss Dinah pilot the control and the floor slow a little so now I is walking, not running. The machine wheeze to a stop and Miss Dinah look at me with eyes patient.

'Thank you.' That seem all me can say.

'Pleasure. Now, stay down here as long as you like and make your own way up once you're done.' She kiss me on my cheek, a peck that's so light I don't feel it, then she take her leave, waving as she go. I steal a breath of unstirred air, it fills me up and I press the green button again. As I move my legs, I begins to see the trees walking in my head.

159

CHAPTER 23

Today be me first day at school, this be where all the young go to get education and me tummy jig with fear. The school house is far from High Ostium. Me draw apart the curtains but little light fills the room and me squint me eyes trying to imagine me can see it from here, but there is only trees. Miss Dinah will drive me there in her own buggy, this be me opportunity to speak with her in private and state a clear case for me brethren.

'Hey! First day at school, huh? Don't be nervous, it's gonna be fine.' Kitty enter and sit herself down upon my bed and draw her knees up to her chest.

I walk across the room to seat myself at my bureau swallowing my sigh so she cannot hear. Me need to make some distance. Me cannot establish what Kitty want. Me feel a tightness growing against me chest.

'Look, Obah. You might learn things at school that we haven't talked about yet . . . Our family . . . well, we have a history that I'm not proud of. In fact, I'm ashamed of it. And . . . I'm sorry. Sorry that it happened.' Kitty's eyes is earnest. She lower both her legs to the ground and stand, her mouth opening to speak again.

'We all are.' Miss Dinah be at the door now and Kitty, sheepish, lower her head. 'Everyone should be sorry about the past. We should never have treated people so unfairly. But some of us are doing our best, these days, to put things right. Now, Obah, are you ready? Come on,' say Miss Dinah looking at Kitty and not me, 'we don't want to be late on the first day!'

We is in the car. Last night under me covers, me did try to form the words I want to say in my mind so I will impress her with me argument. I want to ask Miss Dinah about Mimbah and Nita and Murreat, just them three. Jacob say not to bother with requesting, that him will find the pomander himself, but I have developed a confidence that she will not deny me anything, me have seen how much she love me. As we travel, me mind turn again to marvel at how this buggy without horses can move so fast. We ride along on a wide, dustless road and the buggy's movements roll inside me and under me. I press my brow to the glass, looking out at the shadow-filled sky and the emerald and jade greens of the round tree leaves, as soft music play about us heads. At Unity, me did have a notion that me can outrun a buggy, if the nag be tiring, but I could never outrun this car Miss Dinah driving now.

More people appearing now on the street as we passing. Them still have nothing to cover them heads and this me have finally understand, it be because the sun is weak and cannot burn as in Barbados. But what confuse me still is how them wear clothes that hardly cover themselves too. A young fella with as much black skin as me be running through the street, his skin shine, gleaming and glassy with him effort. Me see the sweat beads sitting on his head like bitty jewels and me marvel in the knowledge that him have no requirement to look behind him for the hounds, or the Master, or the chase party. Small white stones block him ears like the ones Kitty like to press into hers so I understand that him listening to a melody as him go.

I want to ask him who he be, how him did come here, is it from the pomander same as me? But we pass by him too fast and me know me cannot get answers. We stop at a red circle of light and my stomach roll again as the buggy settle down. Next to us an aged woman, her face lined as crumpled linen is sitting at the turning circle of her carriage without a companion. Her vehicle have no top cover to keep out the little sun there is and her head is bare without her bonnet. The gust make her white hairs blow about her head like plucked feathers, but it be her plump pink lips as thick as my own that seem strange on her. A pair of black eye-glasses sit on her nose and I frown confusion at how she can steer her passage but she ride off confident and strong as if she see her destination. As her car move away I see something from the corner of my eye that send me straight back to Unity. A man, face lined and ancient, eyes hollow and empty, sit on the ground alone. Him skin is dark, but not through race, it is dark from the dust that pass about him. How long he been sitting there me don't know, but him don't make any sign to stand.

'You have Jacob to thank for this, you know. I didn't think

it was a good idea to have you out in the real world, too much of a shock to the system.' Miss Dinah still face the road but rub hard at the ring on her finger with her thumb, the jewel flash and sparkle its blue light in response. 'I've arranged everything with Sarah and we go back many years so you'll be in very safe hands. I've told her you're here on an exchange. It's a tiny class and just for a couple of weeks, okay? There'll be kids there who have English as an additional language, but my tip to you? Try not to say too much.' Miss Dinah lean over and rub my arm but keep her eye on the road. Despite her warm words, her touch is icy cold. I straighten me back to speak, me moment is now.

'Madam?'

'You know you can call me Dinah by now!'

'Miss Dinah,' I say, placing my hand in my pocket rubbing the red ribbon there. 'Please excuse me impertinence but me have a petition to make. Me have family behind me that still suffer a heap of troubles at Unity. Me have left them home alone. Them be hardworking and can earn them keep. Madam, me see them with me every day, even though them not here-here, me feel them breath on me, them warmth. Me see them eye and the hurting of each passing day that them must rest there. Me begging, miss, madam, to let them come to stay here with us.' Me shoulders square proud and me breathe deep, me have made me petition well with all the right words.

Miss Dinah open her mouth as if to speak and then shut it again. The sound of fiddle music against the buggy's roar, fill up the cabin about us. She bite her lip but no words come from

163

her mouth. I blink at her and wait, did she not hear my plea? Must I petition again?

'Miss Dinah?'

'We're here, just let me park up.' Her lip is a thin line as she bring the buggy to a stop. Her hands stay tight on the turning circle and her strained knuckles shine. Her head turn to mine as she speak and her diction seem slower than before.

'Look, Obah, I know it's hard to understand, but there's just no way this is happening, okay? I thought Jacob had already told you this? You can't just go back and forth through time like it's nothing! I mean . . .' Miss Dinah sigh heavy and her breath hit me. 'I just . . . I can't . . . You need to realize what a dangerous liability this is. The idea of bringing lots of people forwards and back? You being here is a miracle and it's really important that you realize that. Can you understand?' Miss Dinah have a tear in the corner of her eye that peep to get free. 'Obah, I need to know I can trust you. What happened in the past is . . . very, very regrettable and I do want to make amends, I really do, but you need to come to terms with this. Only *you* made it out. Can you be satisfied with that? Because I don't know what the alternative is, I really don't.' Miss Dinah eye glisten bright with her words. 'I can't imagine what kind of an existence it was there . . .' She sigh and breathe out hard before she continue. 'But we have a life *here* too and things are more complicated today, people don't just appear. There are rules, laws, identities need to be proven. You are welcome to stay, but I just can't have any others. And, I don't want you to mention this again. We can all live happily together, can't we?'

164

Me fists have bunched and so me place them under me thigh, pressing them down into the seat. Me understand her clear and me nod me head so that she see me obedience to her, this be her domain and me must abide with her rulings. But, under me, me pinch me skin, hard. Me and Jacob must conduct our deceit. Me feel the pain and the shame of it, but me cannot sit here, living for real, while me brethren dying.

As we enter the schooling building Jesus himself welcomes me with soft eyes from his portrait on the wall. We climb a staircase and more members of the family of God be watching my careful steps in too tight shoes. Me feet complaining, but all here be walking in shoes and I must too. In the classroom, Miss Dinah point me to the other side and get to whispering with the school-house teacher while I look around at the other youth here.

There be about ten of we, a mix of the men and women and me marvel at the colour and shape of all the different faces as them look upon me. Two is white as Jacob and him kin, one with fair hair cropped low. Another youth have skin that be more the colour of parchment and him eyes crease as though him laughing always. Three sitting together have skin not so dark as mine but not pale neither, I blink at how one have thick, tight hair the colour of cooked carrots. Two more, girls, have skin that shimmer brightly dark as mine. We is like a rainbow of people and though me feel a comfort in that, I swallow, ashamed of my backward ways in front of these knowing eyes. I cannot hear them words, but the teacher got both of Miss Dinah's hand in hers and as she lead her to the door and close it behind her, she nod hard with a sad smile on her lip and turn to gaze on me, thumbing her wet brown eyes.

'Okay, class, let's begin. First, let's welcome Obarah – have I said that right?'

'Is Obah, miss.'

'Welcome to St Cecilia's, I'm Miss Thompson.' I blink at the name Cecilia, remembering my mistress at Unity and now me picture her bewildered brow, lined, at the sight of me schooling.

'Obah is here on an exchange trip. I won't force her to introduce herself right now, but I will speak for her and say that a lot of things here are unfamiliar and so there may be some misunderstandings. Dionne, perhaps you could show Obah the ropes at break and lunch?' The teacher pat the black skin girl on the shoulder twice and nod. As the teacher start to speak some more, Dionne turn in her seat, she open her mouth wide and I see what she is showing me. The gap between her white teeth shines with black. I show her mine back. I close my eyes and me see Murreat again.

When my school mistress ask my age, me tell her seventeen, but she don't seem vexed. She don't ask me why me not fixing to start on matrimony or breeding, instead she ask me what me wants to do with my life! Like I's ever had any thought 'bout that before. Me sit still and quiet as the teacher talk, me endeavour to understand her speech, but her accent is even more difficult than any of the High Ostium household and after a time me mind begin to wander away, trying instead to fathom the images she have display upon a large white board. Me have not shed any tear since Miss Dinah did reject my petition, but inside the hurt swell loud. Me tell meself not to be ungrateful, to understand Miss Dinah position, to be obedient, but as the clouds slip across the window, calling loud come another voice, cutting off my reasoning as if the pomander be speaking itself, calling to me, willing me to pick it up . . .

I look about me. Upon the wall is a picture of something me have seen only once from Jacob. Something that did fill me with fear. Water. Me look at the sea, the 'Atlantic' a moving emerald ocean that is so named, between African lands and the West Indies, me consider the size of the water, the distance between the two and me try to imagine that middle passage crossing that my mother did face. How did she survive the three-month journey, floating from her time and place to that next world? Jacob did explain how her journey was slower than mine, her journey was harder than mine. The things she did see on that journey, men thrown overboard into the mouth of the blue to sink slowly and surely through endless darkness before finding rest. She and her sister did survive it together. Them make it to Barbados to work and toil and bear me and Murreat. Me mother survive. Now, here in this new place, as a homage to her, I must survive too.

A bell toll loud and everyone stand up so I push myself away from the table too and watch keen as them move about the room. Dionne have remember me, she beckon me and smile and whisper, 'The canteen's rubbish! McDonald's?'

'Yeah, come and hang out,' say another girl, handsome, with blond many-braided hair. Them both wearing 'jeans' which have tears and holes and me feel a discomfort for them in them poverty, remembering the feeling of shame at my one dirty shift when in Unity. Now, me feel proud of the skirt and blouse me did choose from me wardrobe and sadness for these two who must wear rags. Jacob have say many people here better off, but here is evidence of impoverishment still. Even though my garments bear no holes, me will not exhibit a haughty demeanour upon them as inferior, me have so much to learn from them about this new living world so me nod and me follow them lead. As we walk me ignore me bleating feet and the grey sky that persist above us and try to keep pace with Dionne and her companion.

'So, did you see it?' say the blond girl who have not tell me her name. Her finger apply a sticky substance to her lips and she smack them together to make them shine.

'Yeah, Kian forwarded me the TikTok. Made me sick.' Dionne shakes her head and eyes roll above as if to heaven before more she pour more words as a sign of her vexations.

'What have happened?' I say, concerned at them heated dispositions.

'The policeman who strip-searched that fifteen-year-old black girl? She was on her period for God's sake. Haven't you seen it yet? Here, let me show you.' Dionne tap and stroke her phone instrument until a screen appear and a vision play before my eyes. The screen shake and the colours run hazy. A crowd hold banners and chant 'racist police' over and over. A memory stir . . . that word . . . racist . . . me remember its meaning.

'Can you believe this shit? I mean, fifteen! You can't strip-search kids, especially without a parent or any other adult around! It's child abuse, if nothing else, and they think they can get away with it, just because she's black. Things are really messed up.' The blonde girl shake her head with anger and her braids whip from side to side.

From them demeanour, me think the language them using must include profanity, and Miss Dinah did tell me not to speak, but here me must help them with their delusion.

'But why such worry?' Me tell them. 'Jacob have explain how this is call "acting", the things we see on screens, even though it look real, all is pretence!' Both girls look at me then and it is as though, in my speech, me have summon a ghoul from the grave.

'Obah? That's your name, right? Are you trying to be funny? This shit is real. This is proper footage that someone living in the flats took when the demo happened. It's gone viral. Look closer.' Dionne's hand shakes and the phone wake from blackness, playing the moving image anew.

'Please,' me say. 'What's a strip-search?'

'They made her take off all her clothes. A kid. No one else around, they made her get naked and then they searched her, that's what happened.' Dionne turn away from me to face her friend. 'Seriously. Maya, I'm telling you, people aren't going to stand for this no more, this shit is gonna blow up.' Her eyes are small with hate.

169

'Oh, Dee. It's cause she's on exchange, innit? That's what Thompson said, that's why she don't get it.' Maya look upon me sadly and shake her head. 'Don't worry, babes, you'll learn. Stick with us and we'll look after you, but right now I need my wrap, before I starve to death.'

Both girls turn then and walk off and me watch them walk away. After a minute or two, blond braids turn and Maya beckon me to quicken, but me stay standing still. She shrug and them walk on. Me should pick up me feet and walk after them, after all, me have not knowledge of where I am or how to return to the school house, but me feet cannot move. The image me have seen is truth and not a fiction? How? How can this be in this world? On the auction block, such things does happen, we is stripped naked, bare and shamed for all to see, but here? Do me want to bring Nita, Murreat and Mimbah to here – from one tribulation to another?

Me not sure how long me have been walking. But me know at one point me did sit upon a bench and remove me shoes. It is dark now and lights at the head of tall trees begin to turn on. Thunder rumble and then rain, heavy, beat upon me and me feel the cold water running down my face, body and legs. Me sit on a bench and pull me feet up towards me chest. Rumbling in time with the thunder, a large red buggy arrive beside me and open its doors with a hiss. Many people sit within it and them all look upon me from behind steamed glass. After a moment the doors close again and the carriage continue its journey. Me must return to Unity. Me cannot stay here. Me close me eyes and try to will meself back there. There at least me can be of use. Here, me is an impotent, me can do nothing but watch injustice happen on a screen.

'Obah! What are you doing here?' Jacob step out of him buggy, hands covering his head against the dropping rain and walk up to me. Him eyes is soft but there is grit in him voice. 'We've been looking all over for you! Did you get lost? It's okay, you're safe now. Come on, get in the car.'

Me push him away from me. 'You did lie to me, Jacob.'

'Wait, what?' him say and him eyes flash confusion.

'Me have seen it. Not acting, not a fiction. But true injustice, right here, where we stand. Here in this place called "future".'

Jacob look around him and smile pained at an old lady who me never notice have sat beside me.

'Dionne have shown me the evidence. The people did gather in anger, anger at how a child, black like me, be stripped of clothing and defiled of body, just as them do in my time. You never tell me true. You never tell me that here nothing have change?'

'Sweetheart, it was awful, wasn't it?' interject the old lady, adjusting her trolley to turn her body towards we, her head joggle as if she have not control of it as she continue. 'I saw the TikTok as well. Them police should be ashamed! After all their past mistakes you'd think they'd learn, right?' She readjust her trolley and use it to stand up and crawl slowly onto another large red buggy that have hissed to a stop beside us. Jacob voice against my ear is soft, pleading.

'Obah, we need to go. I'm actually getting really wet here. It's like that old lady said. The police, have their issues, for sure. I hate that this happens, I hate that they feel they can treat people differently and get away with it. But what can I do about it? Let's talk about this at home.'

'Me want to go back.'

'Great, let's go, then! Come on, get in the car.'

'No. Back to Unity.'

'We've talked about this. I'm working on it! We'll go, we'll get the others . . .'

'Not to bring them here. But to help history, Jacob. We can help them rise above. We can make them see the truth, that slaving be wrong, that "racism" be wrong, and maybe, we can help the history to change. Maybe, when we come back to here, this "future" too have changed because of us – do you understand me, Jacob? We two, we understand a truth, that the world can be different but not without help. What happens at Unity will keep on happening here today unless we change it. Will you help me?'

Him look at me for a long time. 'What else can I do?' him say, blinking kindness with the rain. 'Always.'

Me hold him hand and then, Jacob and me, we both look up to the dark, dark sky and blink many times as the drops of rain bang against our eyes.

PART THREE

UNITY PLANTATION, BARBADOS, 1834

CHAPTER 24

The scent of ripe tamarind in the early dusk makes me whole. I close my eye and stand 'gainst Martha, my back sigh against her affection, her strength. I is a part of her an' all of her history; what has passed and that what's yet to come. We breathe together. I whisper my thanks to her with my fingers and turn to take my leave. It's time to find my people.

There's more tree roots than I remember, thickets and tussocks be tripping me over in my haste, burrs and tendrils of green tickle my ears in welcome.

Me almost at the Big House now. I stand under the shade of a pine tree to take in all her looks. The house stares down at me without remorse or shame, her pride glimmering in the dwindling light, like a well-honed dagger an' I knows I is home. Me hold a raccoon in hand, hanging by the tail. Me did hit him with a rock when him back turn. Me have not forgot how much Murreat love raccoon; this will be a welcome addition to our supper plate tonight.

The danger of being here, once more at Unity, make my stomach heave, but there is a strange beauty too. The golden

175

warmth of the sun stroke my brow soft, like a fond memory and me wonder whether this be the same sun that did sometime show her face at High Ostium. As me pass, a cricket chirp the early evening song at me, most times me like to sing with them and me know them watch me, wondering why me stay quiet, but me not ready to reveal my voice, not yet. Me must have quiet for thinking, for understanding what the plan must be.

Last night in bed, me did lay my head on my pillow of cotton begging for sleep, but he would not come easy and free, on account of all the thinking. Me have to lay on my side and gaze out to the firmament of stars. Me notice how the aged window's glass be splintering and cracked a little in one corner and a mossy green sit gentle on the ivory putty, waiting for the growth to come, that sure spread of decay.

Jacob and me, we here, together. We have the pomander, recovered from Miss Dinah's secret chamber, the one that in the attic. Jacob say, him found it with the other artefacts, treasures and letters. Me sorry that we must show her some deceit, but our task, our mission higher than her pride.

Jacob did stop in the old outhouse pass the piglands where grain be stored. Him proclaim to stay near me, no matter what pass, but me did tell him to come only after dusk for me, and each day we will revisit our plan for making all men free. Me wonder how much time have passed in my absence – a day? Week or months as I have seen in the future? Me have put on me old shift, glad now Miss Dinah did wash it with her special rose juice and not throw it into the fireheap as she first suggest.

Now no person but my own self will know where I have been, what I have seen.

When me reach the kitchen me dip me head to glance inside and Murreat drop her utensil and run up to me; me open me arm to return her embrace but instead she grab the raccoon and step back, her tooth gap gaping at me pleased with my catch. Me remember Jacob instruction and using more strength than me realize, me pinch me arm and the soreness hit. All this be true. Me is here, back in Unity. Me stare at her as she grab a knife and start to skin the catch. Without dropping her rhythm with the raccoon she turn to me and pat her head twice as in a confusion. Me reach up and pat me own head and realize the hair on my head still future-braided.

'What? Oh, this? Mimbah just want to play with me hair some! How it look, good?' Me hate the lie, but me smile weak to mask it. Murreat's eye screw small for a moment but then open bright and she nod hard before turning back to throw racoon guts upon the floor. Nita come in then and set down a pail of water, the liquid spill and run rivers between me toes. She look at me once and then turn to set the fire. Me stand silent and waiting knowing she will turn back and look at me again, her good eye graze against me hair and run down to me toes. Her head cock to the left.

'That a foolish thing to do with your nappy locks. That where you hiding yesterday? At Mimbah's? Me have to tell the mistress you is sick. Wrap up now and take care Miss Frida don't take this for evidence you been finding time for idle hokum.' Then she show me her broad back, continuing with her fire. 'She be asking for you, best you get on about her business, Obah.' Me stare at me Nita. She all the same, large, warm and rough and have not any knowledge of how me have changed more than just me hair these past few weeks. Of the strange new world me have seen and how me did wish for her to be with me every day that did pass there. Me reach over to her and hold her to me tight, but she push me off.

'Go on, get! What you playing at?' She huff and point at the damp grey cloth she use to support the weak handle on the pail. Me back away from her lest she give me a kick and pick up the cloth, wrapping it about me braids, gulping back fear, head towards Miss Frida's quarters.

Me realize that me haven't been missed. Other than one dawn, day and night, no time have passed since me did leave for Jacob's future. Inside, me thank the pomander for the mercy, no need to explain me whereabouts. There is a comfort, a familiarity, to being without shoe and me toes curl about the dusty path as me leave Nita and walk towards the Big House. The sun still rising slow, filling the verdant green land with light. Me remember this land, this light, this sweet fragrance of mango and tamarind, and then me remember more . . . all now how it was when me left and cold fear come upon me. Leary's threat, Lizzy's salvation . . . now me must go to face Miss Frida's wrath. Me must tell her that Leary have give me nothing, no correspondence to pass along. How she will chastise me! Jacob cannot enter the Big House, him cannot offer a protection. Me must think how to steer our coming conversation in my favour.

'Girl! Hey, you. Stop right there.'

Me stiffen me leg and turn about to the voice I know can only belong to Leary. Him approach me cool and slow and when him reach me, give me a hard blow to the head. Me fall upon the ground.

'You forget your manners, girl? You are supposed to address me as "sir" when I call! Think you got friends in high places? Well, you watch yourself good because they ain't here to protect you now.'

Me fingers press upon the heated ground, dust flow between me nails and I sit up, head sore and throbbing. Me don't need to pinch meself no more. Me know exactly where me stand now. Now, all memories is back.

'Begging pardon, sir, masser.' Me mumble loud enough what him need to hear.

'You sure? You sure you don't want to call upon someone for assistance? Where is he anyway? That gentleman attorney? Haven't seen or found no trace of him upon the plantation, looked for him all the day long yesterday. Master Cooke don't know he's here neither.' Me don't look in Leary face but me smell him breath against me, me nostrils quickening against the rot that spill from within him. Me shake me head from side to side, three, four times.

'Please, sir. Me never see where him did step to. Me just carry along with me choring, sir. Me never watch where him foot did lead.'

'That so? Indeed.' Leary back away from me and me breathe out a little, pressing me hands together so he cannot see how them shake. Him sniff.

'What is that smell coming off you?' Him eyes screw together. 'There's something different about you, girl . . . know this . . . I'm watching you and I will uncover your deception.' Him reach out him fist as if to strike me again but take it back before the blow land, as if an unseen hand have knocked his own down. Instead he bite the flesh inside his cheek and chew awhile, his eyes fixed on me, trying to find the root of my secret. 'Here. Take this to your mistress at once,' him say as if conceding him defeat. Him press a fold of parchment upon me and me nod, remembering this time to curtsy me thanks at him as I struggle to me feet, and before him can change him mind, me run out of him grip and step upon the Big House. Me laugh a little at my luck. Leary have given me a blow, but him provide me with accidental comfort! Now, me have some letter to hand to Miss Frida.

CHAPTER 25

The smarting against me head stop when me see Mad Lizzy sitting on the bottom stair, sheltering in the dusk light. She venture out about this time, when the sun low in the sky but there still light enough for her to see all about and not be seen by the whites in them hour of repose before supper. Before the evening duties start, she love to bathe herself in the lull of the day. A curious calm come over me as me look upon her solemn figure sitting upon the steps, so small now, so quiet, when before to me she did loom large and fierce. Me have an understanding of her now that I am returned. Me have understanding of how she have suffered, like me, like all of we. Me have an understanding of her strength. How, determined, back straight, she did pull Leary from off of me, knowing that her punishment soon come. How she save me.

Nita say Mad Lizzy born black as me but get changed through magic. I never believe her, but she swear that be the truth. One night, before we settle to sleep, Nita tell me and Murreat how Mad Lizzy's mother have sell her own soul to the Devil Moon to make her baby change to white. Me remember her name, Cadence, the way it travel across Nita's tongue it sound like trickling water in the sunshine; Cadence no want her child to toil and wither away like we common negro. She want her daughter to have a life different to what Cadence live. A life worthy of the breath we give it. Nita say, the bargain did put she mother's mind out of balance and Master did have to sell her off soon after, because of the wailing all day and night and how she walk around naked as her baby, beckoning her arms at the sky as if she talking to it. Nita's story say how, laughing and cruel, the Devil Moon did visit Miss Sun to boast of him power. This vexed Mistress Sun and in her vengeance against him, she put the madness into Lizzy as well as her mother. So, now Lizzy be afraid of the sun and pull down her bonnet hard when she pass through the shine, stepping in other people shadows to hide her pale skin from the wrath of gold. Now, though, me wonder about the story of her and its truth. Maybe, instead of placing blame on the moon and sun, so very far away from what happen on the ground, might there be another explaining to her madness? Might living here, at Unity, be enough?

Mad Lizzy stop her fanning a little when she see me approach and me notice how wide and bright her eyes look at up at me. Most days, she don't mind me when me pass her, she no see me, but today she be watching and her white-black face smile. For a moment, me forget all the troubles with Leary and why me here and unthinking, me smile back at Mad Lizzy.

We have a share bond now, after what she do for me, maybe, that is why she beckon me over towards her with a tap of her tatty fan, a cast-off from Miss Lynette. Me slip next to her and sit down where she invite me, the cool stone of the step sweeping through my smock to send a shiver that I cannot hide. The parchment in me pocket prick me finger, telling me to move along but me no want to rush into the missis chamber; me want this quiet time with Lizzy, to share in our confidence together. Me marvel in her beauty, the fair skin, the green eyes and brown curl that sitting on her shoulder like a pet puppy. She have a straight freckle nose and thin blossom lips, she not unlike to Kitty me think, me and her be light and shade, so different and yet the same. She stare at me too hard, could be she know where me have been? Perhaps me have sit too close for her liking and she bring out her kerchief to place it to her nose for a moment but me know this is a reflex and not because of any stink coming from me.

'Thank you,' me say. How else me can begin to express me feelings?

'Thanks?' Lizbeth cock her head to one side. 'For what purpose you offer thanks?'

'For . . . what you done. What you done for me. With . . . Leary.'

'Is like you speaking French! Me do not understand you, Orrinda.' Lizzy shift back to gain a little distance between us. Me look upon her with a confusion, have she no memory of what pass? Her eye be curious on me, taking in all my looks like me a wonder. I know how she think: me nose too flat, me skin too dark, me wrapped-up hair too coarse – me have too many deficiencies to be a house slave like her, to be her equal.

Me know she feel it true, me don't have her worth.

'Good Lord, Orrinda, you is black! Every time me see you, me shocked how black you be.' She giggle and put out her arm so that it almost touching mine. She line them up side by side inspecting the colour, examining the difference.

'Orrinda, you see that? Why me bordering on white next to you!' She giggle her white giggle-growl and she eyes be looking right into mine. Her eyes be fierce now and her teeth bite me a smile. 'You can see how me so fair and white?' Seem she will not be satisfied with my nod of head.

'Me see it, Lizzy, you pale as Miss Lynette, for true.'

'Me know!' she cry. 'Me more like she than you. Me and you be so different, we no have nothing in common.' In the days passed at High Ostium, Miss Dinah did tell me I is a beauty. Now, once more, me see the lie; what Mad Lizzy tell be true, me too black, too ugly, dark as pitch. Me did forget me true status.

'Lizzy, you beautiful,' me say. And I mean it. She be the most beautiful negro here. Me have a stupid smile on my face looking at her, sitting by her, enjoying her company, me remember the friendship me witness between Dionne and Maya, light and dark, and me hope me can have this with Lizzy. It what me have dream of for so long.

'Then tell me how it have come to pass, Orrinda, that you have a white mister for sponsor you? For offer protection? Me witness how him stand close by you those two days ago. Why him fixate on you? What hold you have on him, hmm? Is it the parchments from Leary that binds him to you?'

Me want to savour this, Lizzy and me, sitting together, being comfortable, conversing, but me know the beauty of it have pass already. Me smile weak and drop me eyes, me cannot think of any word to give her satisfaction.

'Me know you have a secret.' She laugh a little to herself then. 'What pass between them, it did make Masser Leary mad, mad, mad.' She stretch up and stand now, her moon face moving up into the sky above me, like it slipping out from behind a cloud. She close her eye and rub at the top of her shoulder, then she turn herself around and show me her back and me see it, the blood. A strip of blood from her shoulder to her waist, like a little red river flow down it.

'That's what him give me, Orrinda,' she say, her eye dry, not tearful. 'Him hunt me down and find me. And since him cannot find you, him call me your name as him do me this wrong. Him tell me how when the ship come in, and it come in soon, all the troublesome like you will be done away with. Him do me this because of you and me will have a justice for it. You did hide behind Nita yesterday, but me find you today.' She spit then, right into me eye and me blink fast at the venom from her tongue. When me have finish wiping me eye dry with the hem of me smock, Lizzy have gone, taking all hope of friendship with her.

CHAPTER 26

As me enter the door of the Big House there is quiet. Everyone busy prepping for supper so nobody notice me. Me look about the walls of the house as me climb the mahogany staircase, so solid and strong in its own present. Me sense its pride and me itch to tell it that it will not stand for ever, rubbing at the grain of the banister rail, I whisper to it 'one day you will collapse to dusty grey' and me think me feel the rail shudder beneath my hand. Reaching the hallway to Miss Frida's chamber, me unfold the parchment from me pocket and squint hard at the words. Leary's hand is a cat scratching ink but me make out two words: 'shipment' and 'stop'. Me roll it up fast and continue to the mistress' chamber. Me knock twice and push the door on Miss Frida's command. Me curtsy and move towards her putting the correspondence into her beckoning hand. It crackle and crease as she take it from me.

'Where have you been?'

'Madam?'

'Orrinda, I have to say I'm disappointed by how tardy you are today. And yesterday? Nita said an ailment came upon you?

Excused you from all duties for a full day!' Her eyes look up from her note, momently, as the scroll of tawny paper unfolds between her pale palms. Somehow in her single glance she have notice a change in my appearance before turning again to the matter in her hand. 'One could almost believe you to have been off the plantation!' Miss Frida's sighing words are directed upon my person but her eyes fix down upon the parchment as if me not there at all. My gulp come on like habit, but is needless, even I know she cannot have any notion to where I have been, or all that me have seen ahead of her.

Me take in her careful refinement of figure and pose and me cannot help but compare her to Miss Dinah. Miss Frida is all elegance; the pinched cheek of blush to dissemble youth, the careful curls pinned against her temple, the glimmering of the jewels about her neck and person. She be the very essence of ladyness, while Miss Dinah's face holds no colour in its cheeks, sad lines furrow there instead. Her hair, short, stands away from the crown and no jewels other than one thin plain golden band adorn her hand. I smile inside myself, grateful to Miss Dinah, these women are not the same at all.

A sparking sound breaks my comparison. Miss Frida has knocked something to the floor and looks upon me, her unvoiced instruction clear, *gather it up*. I bend down to my knees and reach for what has slipped under her console and as my hand nears it, its coldness makes me shudder and I drop it again. I peer close. It is her pomander. *The* pomander, glinting silver at me from its dark corner, daring me to touch it. How it can be here *and* with Jacob? This pomander exist in both the worlds! It is as Jacob did say, like *Niagara* in Canada and America at the same time.

I look again from her to it, she remains engrossed in her words from Leary and I realize from the length of time she takes with it, she must be reading it over again. Why? What does it say? I glance back to the pomander, and my hand reaches out towards it, tentative, slow, what will happen if I touch it? Could it send me back to High Ostium? Me fingers itch as I stare at the pomander and its temptation, me could leave this place right now. It would be so easy to pick it up, rub against the engravings and wish for High Ostium, away, back to safety, food and comfort. The place where the same sun seeing all, and knowing all shines less fierce. Something tells me Miss Frida did not drop it, the pomander speaks to me, telling me it is here, if me need, as if I am bound to it now. But I shake my head. I have a purpose, I have a mission to complete. 'Me do not need you,' me whisper at the shimmering ball. I glance again at my mistress. Miss Frida cannot know the magic of it, she cannot understand its link between the past, future, present. I pull my hand away, knowing for now, I must leave it where it rests.

'What's this, Orrinda?'

'Madam?' Me curtsy at the address but her eyes stay at the inky message.

'Orrinda. Leary mentions to me a lawyer. A gentleman dressed in strange apparel upon the property today, interfering with his affairs! This *"Someone"* he saw *you* converse with? Tell me at once, where did he travel to, this gentleman?'

'A gentleman, madam?' My voice is high and confused. I must keep Jacob from them both. 'Me not understand well, Miss Frida. I have not any knowledge of any gentleman.'

'Now, Orrinda, Leary is not always the most cogent, but he does not lie. Speak. Who is the gentleman and why has he not been to address *us* here before interviewing the negros? It is most irregular.' Her blue eyes have left the paper and now writhe up and down me looking for some evidence of the change she cannot find. Is it my voice? My too clean smock? My rose smell? Me must take good care to keep my secret.

'Madam, may me speak plain with you?'

'So you *do* have an admission to declare? Good child, know you will always find a confidante in your mistress. I await your confession.' She smile now, her eye blinking soft with benevolence.

'Miss Frida. Me, I, worry for Master Leary. Him has, of late . . . him has level him voice at things that are not there.' Me lean in close to her and use me whispering voice. 'What me saying, miss, is him talks to the invisible spirit of one not living!'

Miss Frida place her hand upon her open mouth, muffling the sound of her high scream, her eyes be twinkling with confusion. 'What in heaven do you mean? What are you telling me, child? Leary consorts with demons?'

'Miss Frida. Me have never been not one to backbite, but me just worry for the master. That is all. I sorry to say this, but he have, in me very presence, speak words to ones not there at all.'

189

I nod twice to colour my words for her greedy eyes. 'Me not sure what you mean by this word "lawyer", madam, but a gentleman from outside Unity have not been here today.

'This "lawyer" must be Master Leary imaginings, me have no knowledge of such a one.' Me shake me head very hard so she will know my next words are important. 'Madam, what gentleman would not first do him duty and attend to you and Master Cooke upon him arrival?' I pause to hide my trembling hands behind my back, lest them give me away, me heart beating loud in me chest. I would say more but I must be careful. My denouncement of Leary, of any white, is punishable by death. The pomander glint from below the table, laughing at my clever lie. Me hate falsehood, but me know what risk there is if Jacob found. 'It is the drinking, Miss Frida. Me have hear how partaking in too much liquor do cause such, erm, how them say . . . hallucinating, Nita have told me so.'

Miss Frida's eyes dart towards the right of the room as if to scrutinize the velvet folds of her chamber curtains then close for a moment as she ponder on what may be the truth. She stroke her chin and me wonder a while, will she prefer the probable falsehoods from my black mouth or the honesty that must flow from a white drunkard? Slowly, in our warm silence, she take her fan and start to patter the humid air against her neck as we stand together in the silence of her room.

Me think that it is the realization that the etiquette has not been followed, that any gentleman could arrive unannounced and not greet her with the formality required that confirms her decision. She turns towards her console looking-glass and the reflection staring at the both of us is sour as a too-ripe yam. The parchment is slowly released from her hand, dropping onto the floor like unwanted orange peel. Her eyes meet themselves in her mirror and her lips draw together in a thin line, so she briefly do resemble Miss Dinah, me think. Miss Frida's continued silence sing louder than the words she does not relay to me. A small line have formed upon her brow. Me nod and turn to leave, knowing me have cast a doubt on Leary's word. Jacob is safe.

CHAPTER 27

Mimbah sits staring into a dim fire when me arrive at her hut after a long day choring. Me put another dry twig upon it and it fizzle, flames dance around in her eyes making them glow with life where there is none. Me so happy to see me friend, me don't notice at first the new tear in her smock.

'Mimbah, is me.' Me touch her scarfed head gentle.

'What you need from me, Orrinda?' She pull me hand away roughly from her person and I step back troubled. Me have not set eyes upon Mimbah for some weeks, but me remember her ways, she have never raise her voice at me before. Mimbah have never use me plantation name neither, she always use me true African name from me mother.

'Mimbah, what have pass?'

'Go along. Leave me be.'

'Me just – Mimbah?'

Mimbah try to straighten, she have one hand on her back pulling herself up, but her mouth screw with pain and she press her hand to her belly before she sit down again with a groan. I take her both hand together and place her firm back down on the stool.

'You no hear me say go along?' Mimbah's teeth show me her white bite and sweat be coming from her forehead.

'Me can't go nowhere, you sick, Mimbah? What happen?'

'Just a little worm is all, Orrinda. A little worm in me. Now, leave me be, me did drink a little nut-leaf tea already, a little rest make the worm soon fall.'

Me love Mimbah and me have missed her ways. Me have missed her laugh, her mischief. Me know Mimbah. She not fooling me.

'All right, me leave you, but me put you back in your chamber and see you is comfortable first.'

'No. Let me stop here, by me fire.'

'No trouble, me have time, just rest your arm on me shoulder here—'

'Me say no! Me sitting here. Me fine.' She firm again. Me never see Mimbah so harsh. Me thinking the whipping night have make her suffer, the sound of Hector's back tearing be haunting her. Me want tell her more about Jacob, about we plans for her and all but me can't say it now, not with her anger so.

Me don't mind her complaints and walk over to her cabin. The bent wooden door swing in its too-large frame, banging at me as me draw near. Inside is threadbare, like all negro huts. A bit of cane trash upon the floor and the hessian bag where she sleep be a little further along. The light from her fire be behind me and it take a while for my eye to adjust to the dusk. The air is thick with the smell of sleep and sweat and something else me can't place, a dewy sweetness. Me see from the shape of the folds that the shawl she wear be laying on her floor. The light behind flick strong as me turning to leave, like Mimbah have place more wood, it stream in through all the gaps in her home and break upon the floor, showing me a shiny something bathing there. I walk to it and pick it up, cold and heavy with menace, me know what it be. Me have seen this thing stare at me before, a brassy eye piercing mine, this here be Leary's buckle. Him have been here today. Him have give her the treatment he did plan for me.

This be my fault.

Me roll back my shoulder bones and my chin press forward. This is my purpose, this is why me have come back, Leary have hurt Mimbah for the last time.

Me step out from the darkness into the golden light of the fire, angered and ready for shouting. When me reach Mimbah me place the shawl about her shoulders. Them shake silent with the tears she cry. She body rocking forward and back, her white eyes closed and her arms wrapped around, hugging herself, trying to seek some comfort. Me put me arm around her then. Pull her close to me. All thought of the scream me did summon have gone.

'Hush now, Mimbah. It be all right.' I say, rubbing her back and letting her wet face muzzle itself into me dress.

'No,' she say. 'Never. It never be right.'

'Nasty Leary done it? Again?' She stiffen at the mention of him name, digging her fingers into my thigh.

'Me did see him buckle, it did drop off when him whip you. Mimbah. What him whip you for this time, hm? Why him do you like that?' Me trying to make me voice mature, like Nita; me trying to sound like me can assist. Like me can help her ease the pain of it. We both know me lie.

'Whip me?' Mimbah, hiccup now. 'Yes . . . Him whip me.' She sob some more. 'That's what him do.' We both of we know he do more. But we keep up we game. It a comfort. Just like when we have play at ladies. It help her and it help me. Me wipe off me secret tears that she cannot see falling with hers.

'Mimbah, sometimes, me imagine there be a place where we can walk free! Where all of us no need to fear the white man. Where we have right to live fair, free, just the same as them.'

Mimbah look up at me as if she can see inside my soul and a clear tear fall from her white eye. There is an empty moment between us, filled only with the faint crackle of her dwindling fire.

'Well, me don't know what Leary play at, beating up a' innocent; a poor and a blind. Me will tell the mistress.' Both of we know me can't do that, but the game continue because that's how me and Mimbah be, together we be playing.

'The missis . . . ? Miss Frida?' Mimbah say. 'You will do that for me, Obah? You report him for me? Report him offence? Me know you have her ear! You will bring me the justice?'

'Mimbah, me have her ear, real close, she love me like me her own pickney! Me will tell her, me will plead and beg for you. We will gather up our rightful justice, like cane harvest. What kind of world we living in if we can't get no justice?' She nod into me, pulling me closer and me rub up her back some more.

'It no right what him do. Him a . . .' and me stop me talk. Me never curse. Nita say only coarse negroes or men can cuss so me hush up now, me can't say the word me want to say. But, even

195

if me did, me know the most loathsome word me can think of is reserve only for black, like we.

'Now then, Mimbah, you must stay out of his way for now. Until we have arranged amends for you, stay close to your chamber. Maybe the weaver women, Anna and Rosemary, can lie with you this eve? Me go ask them.' Me surprised at how strong is my voice. Mimbah stay alone at night, all of we know that, but these ancient ladies, the ladies who have seen all at Unity and dip and wipe the rag on broken bodies, them present no threat, surely them would come if asked?

'Me no need no one.' Mimbah straighten up herself, her eyes cloudy as she wipe her nose with the hem of she sleeve. 'I better off alone. Me no want him to beat Rosemary or Anna on account of me,' she say.

Mimbah tighten her hair kerchief in place and put herself in order, the hiccups start to drop off. We share every inch of the sadness; it be mine own.

'Mimbah, you did say once that me have a *"friend"*, you did see him in the card, the two of us together, you remember?'

'You did find him,' she say.

'Yes, Mimbah. Me and Jacob, we two, we have a plan for Unity. A plan to fight back. No more will one of us have them back drip up with blood. No more will one be forced to lie with bucks who step off boats. Things going to be better here. Me have seen a different way for us. We taking the plantation for us ourselves.'

'Me see it, Obah,' she say and she smile soft in the firelight against me. 'Me see your destiny.'

CHAPTER 28

Leaving Mimbah, me march hard and hot towards the piglands as the small shadow of dusk fades behind me to blackest night. *Leary*, him have hurt Lizzy *and* Mimbah in my absence and both of them *because* of me. Jacob's intercession with him have caused more anguish, not less. This be my responsibility.

The piglands are not far and me can make me way to them even in the dark but I need not venture so far, as me find Jacob on the path from Mimbah's hut. Him face is worn and tired as if him need sleep and there be a trace of small hairs growing on him chin that did not travel from High Ostium. I turn about me to make sure, but there is none there to see as we enter the cover of the trees.

'Jacob?' Me reach out to touch him face, grazing me fingers against these soft hairs that look like darkened grasses growing soft. Jacob step back at me touch as if me have burn him and me hand fall away to hang beside me.

'I sorry,' is all me can think to say. *Friend or foe, how you can lay finger upon the gentleman, Obah? You forgot who you is?*

'Sorry?' Jacob step forward one step, but pause there, shaking him head as him look me up and down. 'You're sorry? Jeez, I'm the one who should be sorry, I'm useless here – I can't *do* anything.' Him step forward again and this time, him hand is on my chin, pulling it towards him gentle, him turning me face left and right, eyes peering close to examine me. Them soft hairs upon him chin is so close to me, him breath blow sweet against me and him lips so close that me wonder what it feel like if them brush against mine own. Me close me eyes and feel the air empty about me as Jacob step back. When him speak next, him voice crackle like fire. 'I've been so *worried* about you, waiting here out of sight – I won't do it any more, I won't wait out here . . . hiding, while you fight. What if you needed me? I'm here *and* I can help. Let me.' As him cross him arms against him chest, we each regard the other.

'Jacob. Me know you want to help but me must do this alone. Leary . . . him have . . . It is me who must fix this. You cannot assist. Not now.'

'But we *know* what they're capable of. From now on, I go where you go.'

'No. Jacob, you must listen. Me have a plan. Me need the men to back me, to help us take this plantation for ourselves. But, for it to work, you must stay in the shadows. I have told Miss Frida that you is an imagination, the duppy that me did think you were before! I think she believe it to be so. Anyone who chance upon you, with your dissimilar apparel and voice can but think you is an apparition and them will run from you in fear! You do not speak to them, you do not stare into them eye. You must *do* nothing! Go home. Take the pomander and return to Miss Dinah. Niagara remember? You will know if me need you.'

'No, Obah, that wasn't the plan!'

Me offer him my hand and him place him fingers in mine, just like him give to me when me arrive at High Ostium. Jacob want to save me, me know, but I can save me too.

'I need you to go, Jacob. Leave.'

Me resting up, Nita beside me, sleeping with all of the burlap pulled over her thigh as usual. Tonight, me don't mind that she have it all, me don't mind that she leave me cold and shivering in the darkness. Me warm anyway, glad of her, content to feel her big and broad shape next to me. Me can't sleep for the pain of the hard floor beneath me, but her snores be like growls, protecting me, keeping me safe from the thoughts haunting me in the night, me wish it can protect me from the trouble that coming soon. The responsibility me have here, the job me must do. Me stroke upon the red ribbon, reminding me of Jacob waiting in the shadows. Me put it under my neck, loving how it feel against me skin, so soft. Like how it did feel when Jacob hold me face before, him thumb brushing against my cheek.

Murreat is awake like me. I tell her to sleep but she don't pay me no mind, she turn to me and slip she finger in me mouth, pressing on the gap me have between my front teeth. The gap is not large, me have all me tooth still, but she love the gap, she know how both her mother and mine did have the same. She press it, rubbing her finger from the gum to the bite and she smile, showing her gap to me. Me let her carry on as me know how it comfort her some and me have missed her baby touches. I bite her finger gentle when me had enough and she stop. She lay herself out as if to sleep but her eyes don't close, instead, them keep staring straight up at the roof, like she know that somewhere higher, above we here, there be a life.

'We can live better, Murreat. Just like we mothers did, we too can taste freedom. Me will make it happen soon-soon, me promise. We taking the plantation. We taking it for ourselves.' Murreat regard me for a while and then settle her grey gaze back upon the ceiling again, as if she think my words are an empty ministration and it be the timbers above our head that contain the truth. Me fetch the ribbon from under me neck and place it between us, so we can share the softness of it. She show me her gap as she smile upon seeing it. She bring it up to her mouth and finally, her eyes close as she let the gentle ribbon kiss her over and over.

My body ache from the cold of the floor in Nita's hut when she kick me to wake up and I reach above me head to stretch away the pain in me shoulder. She raise her eyebrow as me smile at her and she shake her head and mutter curses at my laziness. Me have missed her chiding. I did toss and turn so much between she and Murreat in the night, but neither one of them did mind my movements, both dead as rocks beside me with them fatigue. I blink about me at the familiar unfamiliar, the hessian square have scratched against my leg and me rub at where it chafe. My soft bed at High Ostium is welcome now.

Me think of Jacob resting there, now me did send him back. Me hope him have done as me did instruct. Nita give me a cup of brew for Hector and now be my chance to seek him for his overdue forgiveness, me need him on my side. Readying meself to leave, me hear her voice, soft.

'Sometimes.'

Nita is speaking just over my left ear. 'Me wonder where them be. Or even if them living at all. Me don't have a yearning to know if them happy, just if them living still.'

'Who?' I look at Aunty Nita and find she be closing her eyes for a long moment.

'Me pickneys. Me did have a boy-pickney here with me, but Masser did sell him off before him reach Murreat size.' Aunty Nita turn away and with a heavy grunt set the kettle on the fire but even though she speak towards the wall me hear the whimper in her voice. 'Me shame to tell, but him face dusty in me mind now. Me would never know him if me see him today. But if him was here, Obah, me sure him would fight, me sure that after what we see them do to Hector, he would raise him arm and look for a way, a way to stop the terror, a way to redeem us all.' Nita's cry cuts through to my core and just as me move towards her back, the wailing dwindle and the set of her heaving shoulders hardens again. Like dried pighind, there be no way to crack it.

Me know she have finished with talking. I want to hold her to me, stroke her tears away, tell how all will be well, how the new life me planning will be, but me know Aunty Nita, she will kick me with a hard foot if me try. Instead me wipe me own tears into my smock hem, turn about to make my exit but me stand there a moment and look upon her frame. Me never know Aunty Nita did have a pickney. Me cannot vision her to ever be young, seem she always been aged, lined and grey. Me not sure why she thinking of him today. Maybe, she telling how we both have suffer loss. My mother run from me, but Aunty Nita's pickney been taken from her and me don't know which of them be worse. But Nita have give me hope, the men here, them does feel the same way as her pickney, them will fight with me, it is time for us emancipation.

Before me press on towards the men's cabins, me spot the baby, Benjen, him playing alone in the red dust, by the trough, twirling round and round in circles as it cloud about him, making him cough. Me stop and place down my cup as me regard his small form and wonder what him will be like when him is grown, *if* him will reach full grown. Me wonder if him did understand what him see, amongst the gathered crowd, when Hector get whip. Me wonder if him ponder on the life before him. At High Ostium, there would be medicine to help him with the leg him drag. But not here.

Me bend to pick him up and press my lips upon dry, hard and dusty hair. Benjen, another one of we who have no mother to hold. Him black eye is rimmed red with dust as him reach out him small-small hand to me and stroke me face, gentle, reminding me of another who touch me face like this. Me hold him against me once more and swing him against me hip from side to side, ignoring Nita's cursing at my back to put him down and get to work. Benjen stay still in my embrace, him no writhe or wriggle, unaccustomed to a warm hold him stay motionless, accepting the new comfort, him brow warm against my breast and me realize, this is what me here for, nothing else. Me place him down and set back me shoulders against him cries to pick him up again. But me walk on. Me have no time for caressing, me have work to do. Me have men to rally. Me must speak with Hector.

As me walk, me stare at the cup of brown liquid that me must hand to Hector – the leaves did steep for some days and there be a little foam riding the top that me hope is medicinal. When I did sup it to test, the taste be so bad me decide to put in a little of Nita's molasses but it still have a bad-bad taste, like her own wine. It not rum, but at least me can show him something apart from me empty hand.

The men's cabins is at the back of the piglands, past the mill house. The smell of the swine be strong today, in the pen a lot of shining sucklings be clinging on the sow. Them lucky, me think, cleave upon your mother tight. Never let her go.

Hector be up already, pouring cool water over his outstretched bad leg and me wince as me call to me mind young Benjen. His hand stop in mid-air when him see me.

'What you do here, Obah, seem you just like your mother? Never rest, always up to some scheming or other.'

'How you feeling today, Hector? Me bring you something.' Me press the can under him face. 'Me and Nita make it for the pains,' I say.

203

'Me pains? You really be trying to kill we?' There is no smile in his voice and the two teeth in him mouth stare out in disbelief.

'No . . . ! Hector, me so sorry about the count. Me know you did take blame for me and me did not deserve that . . . But what you said, before . . .'

Opposite, from the open door of Apollo's cabin, his wife and pickneys all look at me with blank faces. Them sit quiet on the matting them share, the older boy be whittling something with a blunt knife, he hold it in front of the little babe, waving to and fro. The babe reach out for the dancing stick, kicking his foot against his mother's lap, struggling for freedom against her hold and chewing hunger on empty gums. Them the only family that have mother and father and childrens living together. Only ones that have survive Unity in one unit. Me think them faces should be happy, but me see how them all scowl same way and me grieve at the family sharing Hector's pain.

'Me never say nothing, Orrinda,' him say, eyes fall downwards like him musing on the spider that crawl slow upon the ground.

'But you said me should . . . me should find a way out, you 'member it, don't you, Uncle?'

There's the sound of the toil bell, the ring harsh against my ear as the tin echo about us. Hector hand still grip the can, tight, though it look like him have no intention to drink. 'It was the pain that talking. Me did take the beating and now we is even.'

The other mens is starting to mill out to them labour, faces blank upon us as them step forward to carry out them business.

Me want to ask him what him mean by 'even' but time press against us. The toil bell finish and me know me must speak fast and plain, Hector have work to do same as we all, stripes or no.

'Hector, me did listen to you. Me *did* do as me mother. Me find a way out and now, now me want for all of we to feel that freedom! To make this Unity the place where we all live free.' Me voice shake a little and me realize that this be the first time that me say these things out loud for another at Unity to hear. As me speak the words me see the reality of it. The danger of it. What me be asking. 'Me have a plan. But me must enlist your help.'

Hector shut him cabin door.

'Let me tell you about she.' Uncle Hector face me square and me feel him eyes in me face as if him bore holes, such is how him watch me close. I know me resemble me mother and him look at me now as if him seeing her, smiling when he never smile and considering the pain him in, the smile is stranger still.

'She proud. She stubborn. She never listen. And she have make her daughter standing here the same way. The same heart, that same fire in the belly she have. Me see it in you.'

Uncle Hector pause then and me breathe in deep as if to hold on to him words. Me don't fill the silence with any voice of me own because me want him to go on. Me need him to tell me what him know.

'She and she sister, the one that make small Murreat, the two of them same-same. No one can tell them 'part, them like cane stalk, 'cept for one tiny mark upon she finger, here.' Hector lift up him hand and stroke where his forefinger meet knuckle.

205

'Just here, like a ring have burn its mark.' Hector pause then and him look beyond me into the corner of him hut as if trying to see something small that lie far away from where we stand. 'It my fault that she did up and gone. No one know where. Not till this day.' In him moment of dreaming, my mind's eye dash to silver lines. To the pomander. Could she? Could my mother have travel away from Unity? Same way as me?

'What you mean, Uncle? How is any fault lie with you?'

'She did answer to "Occo",' him say, and him cannot see me now. Him in a place where we is not and shake him head from side to side. 'We call her "Occo", her Africa name, not "Triphena" that them give her . . . she did say where she from.' Hector close him eye for a time and tap him finger against him mouth. '*Akan*, yes. That a place, you see? Inside Africa.' Hector smile then and seeing me again, him few teeth sparkle at me. 'You know what strangest thing about them two? Both she and she sister answer to "Occo". Same face, same name. Ha! – yes, me remember now, you call one and you get two!' Hector's laughter stop abrupt. Him close him lips together and he wince, remembering the pain of him sore back, remembering him troubles.

'Your mother, she come to me one day when the rain fall hard and even we must stop work till it pass, she come through the rain, here, wet through, carrying you against her back. She did ask me for help. She have enough words then. She speak for the both of them, she and she cane sister. She say: *"Brother?"* That what she call me. *"Brother, Hector? Help us? We must to go home."*

She never place you down upon the wet ground but keep you tied in that knot at her back and you tip open up your mouth to drink the water coming from the sky. She say, *"Brother, you watch over my Obah? She small. You watch my babe. Occo go home."* And the rain did fall, and we both wet through as she plead with me. She face twist and wretched, water running down, me remember it still.

'Me look upon her, same as me look upon this face me see here and you know what me tell her? When her eyes shine at me, black as Nita molasses, me tell her, *"Yes, me helping."* So, Obah, child. That is why we even now.' Me fight back the tears that threaten as me realize what him saying. That when him agree to helping me mother escape, it means I have none; no mother, no more. And him taking the beating was a penance, a gift to me for him promise to her. Me wipe the tears that fall and sniff quiet. There is a sound from outside the hut, a voice.

'Hector? You in there? I better not have to drag your black behind out.' It is Leary. Hector move to pass me but me block his way for a moment more and whisper in him ear.

'Uncle, listen. You not to blame. But you can help me, *help we*, me want a redemption. Me mother seek a better way. Now we need to seek the same thing, but for *all*. Me have seen a new way for living life. We have understand that freedom possible for all and we not resting, we not satisfied until we have it. What me saying is, me need your aid again.'

'Hector? You're not using that whipping as an excuse to miss a third day! Step out now!'

Me peek through the rafters and Leary stand hands upon his hips. Behind him, Apollo and him older son look at each other, them scowl at Leary's form. The sadness from before is anger now and me glad to see it.

Hector prise the door open. Pressing him head out. Me stay upon the shadow of the door and hold me breathing tight.

'Me coming, masser, just bringing up the tools for hoeing, sir, them a little heavier for me . . .' This seem to satisfy Leary and him turn about, coaxing and cursing at the other men to move towards the field. Me petition him again.

'Uncle. Just as me mother did ask you before. We need you to gather up the men. We must fight the master and tear down this house, then claim the plantation for us ourselves! Him cannot fight all of we if we unite and work together. Uncle, talk to the men. Beg them come to Mimbah's hut this evening and we will tell of the plan for redemption.'

And for the first time, Uncle Hector look me in the eye and nod.

CHAPTER 29

While me shelling peas with Nita, Murreat come back with another pail of water from the pump, me help her to place it down from off her head upon the floor and Nita tisk when some spill. Murreat tug upon my skirt and point her thumb over her shoulder outside while Nita back turn. Me slip out quick. Uncle Hector stand there looking left right and all about himself.

'Me can't be here.' And me see the sweat upon him head not coming from the heat about us. 'Them will listen. Apollo have a task in the mill house say will keep Leary occupied for a small time. You get only that one chance, Obah. Just one. Mimbah's hut, after toiling done.'

'Thank you, uncle. Me won't let you down.' Me hope inside that this be true.

A crowd starts to gather around me in Mimbah's yard, small at first, but the assembling black drops soon make up a band. She did agree for Uncle Hector to send word to all to come by her cabin and they are here. All have a respect for Mimbah, for the blindness, for what she went through. All have a respect for

Hector too, them see the beating Cooke did give. They know that time is not on our side and soon others will come looking for them. Hesitant and watchful, one after one, my half-naked brethren comes to hear if the rumours is true, the whispering talk of uprising. Limp and fatigued, they are muttering low to express their disquiet at the gathering, the danger it brings, the fallout to come. I hear my name cursed and I bite my lip, what if them is right? What if it doesn't work?

From the corner of my eye, I see how them tense, the knuckles shining strained; them ready to start the scraping, bowing, obeisance just as soon as white skin shows itself and starts giving instruction. Aunty Nita here too, her back upright and strong and me gasp at the sight of her. Me did not tell her to come, but after the confession she give this morning, me know why she stand tall. Her dirtiness shine with love for me, but I see it still, the poverty, the degradation of her, the stray of her nappy hair beautiful in woe, peeking from her bitty scarf. And me want a better life, for her.

'Family,' I say in a quiet voice and Mimbah presses her good hand into mine, squeezing my fingers to let me know she is standing right beside me. Is Mimbah who bids me talk, who makes me speak my truth. Me open mouth close as I spy Mad Lizzy, watching me from a set distance, she don't come too close, but shelter under the pine that's there. Me cannot tell her thoughts. Will she rest here with us or will she run to tell Cooke? She got a length of twine holding up the waist of her pinny and she clutch the extra rope end tightly in her fist, it

210

loop into the shape of a noose and she swings it gently back and forth. Mimbah push me forward in the small of my back. I cough once, twice, my voice is small.

'Evening, brothers, evening, sisters. Me thank you for coming to hear me short address. Me name be Obah, daughter of Occo who is run off.' The crowd moves restless and a woman spit upon the floor at the word 'Occo'.

'Speak up – why you call us here?' shout one.

'Come on, what this for?' scream another.

'Let the child speak!' say Nita and the grumbling stop.

Me gulp. 'Sure, you know my face. But you have never hear me speak before. What me have to say is . . . is . . . Here, where we stand it is always winter, always winter but never Christmas.'

'Winter?' Hector shake him head at me and me know me losing them, me must to try again.

'What me saying is . . . the year is 1834. What difference that make? Don't every year be the same for us? Every year pass, and what does we get, but older, weaker, closer to death. We *will* the years to quicken, to hurry, to deliver us – deliver us out of this evil. But there is a truth, and all of us must know it. Each passing day marks our future and our children's future.'

Lizzy look over her shoulder then back at me, forward and behind with unrest, confused on if she should listen more to my voice and the spectacle before her or the invisible, powerful white one calling to her from beyond. She so used to hearing it call, she hears it when it don't. She drop her noose then and me know her choice is made as she slip away from the crowd.

211

I breathe in hard. My time be up. I need to start speaking, need to tell them what I come to do.

'You is not Obah, you be *Obeah*!' cries an angry female voice and a stone blows a soft kiss against my ear, I hear it thud onto the ground. The jeering grows in strength and some begin to walk away. Mimbah steps in front of me, protecting my body with hers and the stoning stop.

'Listen!' says Mimbah. 'You none of you know the true meaning of Obeah, it nothing close to any evil, Obeah not about witches and cursing, it *good* magic. The magic of our ancestors' voice.' Mimbah steps to the side of me again and I take a deep breath.

'Brothers, sisters. I beg you hear me with a mind that's open. This world is changing. There is freedom coming, ready for the taking and it must start here, with us. We taking Unity for ourselves. We taking our freedom. Tonight.' The faces stare out at me impassive, not registering my words. I want to try again but there is a shrill cry from the back of the gathering, it so wrenching me feel it coming from the deep gut of within. But what it say confuse me something terrible.

'Fire!' she cry out. 'The Big House, it burning red with fire!'

CHAPTER 30

The crowd divide and scatter like cotton seed in the wind as all run towards the Big House. Me beg Mimbah stay back where it safe and she nod but she touch my ear between her few fingers to hold me from leaving and whisper urgent.

'This fire. This burning. It what me did see in the card. Obah, please, you must take heed! Remember, me did see death!' Me nod, hugging Mimbah close.

'Mimbah, me promise you, all will be well.'

Me see him then, Jacob, standing in him strange apparel at the side of Mimbah's hut. It is as him say, somehow we is connected, him know when me need him and when him need me. Me wait until the last of the crowd have gone and then me reach to take Jacob outstretch hand and together, wordless, we run to follow upon the panic and noise.

The smell of roasting wood bite us and we start to coughing as the black smoke filter all about. Flames cackle fierce, snapping like braces against skin, the hungered fire crack over and over against the air as it consume the Big House and the burning be rising gold and glowing orange. Me feel the heat from here, hotter than our daytime sun. Me feel as though me feet cannot move, seem the fire have start in a upstairs bedroom. Everybody be screaming, the mens them be shouting orders for water to come, the dogs them is barking at the stand where them is tied, straining at the rope for freedom. Miss Frida stand outside looking up at the sight, she shake her head and press her kerchief to her nose, desperate as Mungo block her path to entering.

'Get out of my way, Mungo! Husband! Husband! Oh, God in heaven! Save our daughter!' Miss Frida wriggle and beat a small clenched fist against Mungo's arms.

'Masser tell me to keep you safe, missis, that's what me do. Me not letting you in.'

Me look around, Miss Lynette not outside, she not standing here wringing her hand or fanning herself beside her mother – where she be at? Is the masser with her? Me feel me lip tremble as me speak.

'Jacob, listen. Miss Lynette, me can't see her. Me thinking she the one in danger! Someone have left a fire burning to come and hear me speak, this be my doing! Me need to aid her now, me need to find a way to her room.' Jacob eyes widen as him look up at the flamed roof. Him take in a deep breathing.

'All right, okay. I can climb that tree at the back and try to get in from the attic. I'm pretty good on the climbing wall, this can't be too hard – well, apart from the crazy heat, of course!'

'Jacob, please, take a good care. It look like dangerous.'

'I'll be fine! See you in a sec,' him say and letting go of my hand, he turn and run towards the side wall, slipping between the many bodies without fear and me feel me chest pain a little at the sight of his running back. Me glad him did sense me calling in my mind. Glad that he is with me here right now, it make me feel like we should never be parted.

Biting my lip, me start to head towards the door to join the chain that have formed to send water pails back and forth when a rough hand grab me by the scruff of my neck. The hand pull me round to face the bile and evil that is Leary. Him black eyes squint small as him box me face, once, twice and me fall to the ground gasping.

'You! You again! Is this your doing, Orrinda?' Me feel him kick me in the side and when me cough, blood appears upon my finger.

'Lizzy seen what you up to. You and that "lawyer"! Got some nerve telling the mistress you think I'm seeing things! You know I seen that fellow as clear as I see you.' Him shake his head from one side to the next then bend his head down low so me can hear his words clear against the crowd cries. 'I got a boat coming in soon with fresh meat – niggers who will be *grateful* for a whipping from me after that passage over the sea, niggers who ain't spoilt through with coddling, niggers who know their place. At that auction, we're gonna add you on the block. Maybe, just maybe, I'll see what I can get for that dirty race traitor too or better still have him sent to gaol for his miscreancy!

'Lord, I am sick to death of your troublemaking and I've finally convinced the mistress it's time to cash you in.' I close my eyes from Leary's words, trying not to picture his threat but it no good. *I see myself on that auction block, me feet burning against the hot wooden stage, me face and arms shiny, dripping with butter for the show. The sun bear down too strong and make me blink, but me can't lift my hand to shield my eye, them shackled to me feet. I wary of muttering from the crowd, voices raised and frenzied cries. A white hand strokes my thin breast, a thumb folds back me lips, rubs the gap between my teeth, presses my gums, my tongue . . .* Me wince in pain at the future Leary want for me and Jacob, against the one I want for all of us. I open my eyes and in the haze me spy a figure have come to stand by Leary's side. Is it Mimbah? Me blink again at the figure. No.

'Yes, sir, me see *her* do it. She did light the fire that cause this blazing!' Mad Lizzy now stand beside him and cross her arms about her breast. I remember her face under the pine tree, the panic in her eye as she did hear me speak and how she leave before me can finish.

'Please,' me say, quiet. 'Please, Lizzy, tell him the truth. Me never start no fire. Me never hurt none. We have to save the house, we have to save the masser. Any argument between we, we finish after, we cannot stay here idle and let them perish.' Lizzy giggle.

'Oh, Obah, my fool-fool sister, what you gone an' done? You put the masser *and* the Miss Lynette both into a dangerous peril? Masser gone inside to get him child, as him no trust no slave to save her, him must do it himself!' Me hear the dark laughter in her smile when she speak and me wonder how Leary can't spot it too. Mad Lizzy smiling make me want to empty me belly. Leary have me here on the ground, the blood pouring from my lip but she the one who have start this fire! I know it then, like me know my own bones within me. Her actions is threatening the life of two. But what about Jacob? What if Mad Lizzy is killing three?

There is another scream and we all three look towards the house, me see Jacob then Miss Lynette on him arm and Masser trailing behind him. Him place her down upon the porch with trembling steps and all three bodies become as crumpled parchment. When me sigh deep at Jacob return safe, my rib burn from Leary's kicking. Miss Frida rush towards her child and be stroking her head gentle, begging her to open her eye, to speak. Masser Cooke coughing stop his voice from asking questions, but him hold upon Jacob arm, a strange look upon his face as if he cannot fathom who he be or where him from.

Leary run towards the porch now and me summon up me strength to stand but me cannot summon energy to follow, the pain pin me down, *me cannot let him get hold of Jacob.*

'Well, well, if it isn't the *"lawyer"* and him just happening to be in the right place at the right time?' Leary sneer at Jacob who have place him head between his knees to capture his breath. Master Cooke wave his arms and pat the back of passing men who rush into the house. Over him shoulder he shout, 'Apollo, Artemis! Water! More water! Get here, quick.' He splutter and cough to get him words out before recording what Leary have say. 'What lawyer? What are you saying, Leary?'

Leary turn to point at me. 'That's his accomplice. Orrinda. Now, I don't know what they are up to, but she and him have started this fire. I got a witness here! Lizzy see them doing it with her own eyes. These two be here to sabotage your endeavours, Mr Cooke!'

Masser Cooke cough hard into his shirt sleeve and rub against the soot in his eye.

'What? But? How? This young man just saved me, saved us both! We owe him our lives.' His coughing stop more words from entering the debate.

'Cooke, it doesn't have to be this way. You can be better. Do better. We all can.' Me hear Jacob's voice, his strange accent taking all by surprise.

'No, no, no!' Leary shaking his head and I see him take his whip from out of his belt. 'Sir, do you recognize this fellow? How'd he even enter onto the plantation? This so-called white is a traitor, he's the one masquerading around here pretending that he's a man of law! He is in cahoots with this troublemaking slave, they caused this fire. The both of them must pay for this wild act.'

'It's true, masser!'

Mad Lizzy step up to stand beside Leary, her bonnet awry, she press dirty fingertips against her apron to smooth it down. 'She saying she want us slave to uprise 'gainst you! She plotting, masser, just like Masser Leary say!' Lizzy turn to look at me and her finger point too at me squatting in the dirt.

Jacob eyes meet mine, his head shake from left to right and I nod in understanding. Him run then towards me and I hear the jeers of Leary from behind as him set chase.

'Hey! Stop!' Leary's whip is raised and he kick the small child that have crawled by his feet out of his way in his eagerness to get close to Jacob's rushing figure. Jacob nearing me now and though me struggle to balance on my knees from Leary's beating, me press against the floor to standing. 'Now, Obah, now!'

All is over. As we runs I feels that freedom lift me already, my body leave off the ground, a lightness spread over me, and I go forward, riding that wind under me like a nag. There's a dim barking in the tamarind trees, I don't need to turn my head to know that them dogs is on my scent. With my eyes closed, I see their drool flying off them wet muzzles, I see their black eyes squinting concentration through the dark, leaping past saw grass and fens, noses twitching with rage to get me. I know they gone be on me soon, then they go kill or maim me. Jacob cry out and me see the glint of silver shining brighter and brighter and me grab onto his hand. Me taking my leave of Unity for the last time, like my mother.

PART FOUR

SOMERSET, ENGLAND, PRESENT DAY

CHAPTER 31

Me open my eyes and then breathe out slow. Looking up at the ceiling me see small suns. The circles of light that shine down upon me is familiar and I blink at the brightness. This is not Unity. I reach out and touch the crisp linen that pins me upon the soft bedding and I turn my head to the left, thumbing away the wetness that fall against my cheek. Me finger move towards my bottom lip and press where it puffy and tender. Me rub me hand against the strips of bandage that bind my chest and remember the darkness shrouding Leary as him did kick against my ribs. Haply, all me can bring back from Unity is discomfort, of body and of mind.

The young new branches starts to tap at the glass to keep my thoughts company. I answers their call and push myself up to sit before the window, pressing my head against the cold pane. From this here spot, there is no Martha, no Big House or Unity, but I sees Miss Moon, even though she just as far away. She no ball of sugar like me used to think. Men has walked on Miss Moon's back and told how them spots of grey she got marking her complexion, they be her craters, rivers, hollows and hiding

223

places, just the same as here. I come to reminisce; if I is here, then maybe, up there and looking down, there be a girl like me, another walking stranger wandering lost, alone in a place of mystery and wonder. Trying to find a way out.

Me turn away from the moon and seat myself back upon the soft bed. There be nothing I can do. I have failed and them have won. Leary and the Cookes have barred shut the door of history upon us. We won't never be free. Not there, not at Unity. Must my brethren wait for death to know how freedom taste? Will only I see justice while me living?

There be a knock on my door, and then me hear my name whispered soft from Jacob's lips. Slow, I step away from the bed and make my way towards the knocking, the calling. I press my forehead into my shut door at the sound that rattle against my skin. The cool dark wood press on me like a casket top, heavy and firm, pushing out me air as me sigh. I feel the joy of it, the liberation. This be where I belong, buried six foot under with my brethren, with my folk. I feel as though not Jacob, but me now, is some kind of walking dead.

I turn myself about, away from Jacob's voice, pressing my back into my door now, feeling this coolness against my spine. And I am there, finally, my body in the box, in the grave. I part my lips and I taste the heavenly dirt as it fall and cover me up. How sweet it taste.

I am in the future again. And this means my family, my friends, them is all gone. Me could not save them. In my closed eye I see them. Aunty Nita, even with her deathly pallor she be she shaking her head, Murreat and Mimbah be with her, all of them lined up against my bedroom wall, looking on me, grey-sad, but sounding no words. Me don't want them to open they mouths, I don't want to see the creatures crawling on their tongues when they speak, the living things that walks on the dead.

'Forgive me!' me whisper. 'Me sorry.' The three of them stand there quiet, watching. But there be one more. Another me never noticed at first, a shadow face, standing plain behind Murreat. Can't see her clear, but I know her just the same, we the same blood that is why. 'Mama,' I say, 'Mama, where you be?' But she turn about and as me watch her back grow small my tears fall fast. Me have failed and all of them is ghosts now, all dead. All except me, the one floating like a hummingbird stuck between heaven and earth.

'Hey, you up? Dinner's ready – we got a delivery from the pub, your favourite, a proper roast!'

Tap tap tap come the sound again, like nails upon my casket. Why Jacob can't let me be? Me look again at my failed face reflecting back from the looking-glass and wipe my eye dry. Eat? Why should I eat when my kinsperson have none to fill his belly? I don't deserve to eat, I don't have the right. Me tummy growl in disagreement and my hand pat to quieten it but the noise persist, telling me she have no memory of my last meal and Jacob is offering roast meat! My body betrays me and I turn about and open the door where Jacob bear his shy smile upon me.

225

'You've been asleep for two days! Mum said to leave you but you must be starving by now!' He step towards me and gently, him brush against my brow with his hand, once, twice, me feel the softness of his close breath and me tummy jump with something that is not hunger.

'You had this weird thing stuck in your hair. A feather, I think.' He step back then, regarding me and his breath jump a little when him talk. 'You should have seen Mum's face when I told her what happened. That bastard! He has to pay for what he did. I should go back there and . . . !' Jacob punch his hands as fists to the wall.

'Go back?' I ask urgently and stare up into Jacob's eye.

'Obah, we *can't* go back there! You know that, right? He was going to have us both killed! Mimbah and Nita would want you to stay where it's safe. We're not perfect, for sure, but you're not likely to get *killed* by a psychopath here! Maybe we can get a kind of justice by you surviving and being safe. Don't you think?' His voice be pleading with me now and there is a tremor that beat soft against his brow.

I nod submissive. It is as I feared. The fighting is over and we have lost. The battle for Unity can never be.

At the table I cannot lock eyes with any person. Not Miss Dinah, Kitty or even Jacob. We eat in the empty hush, them is waiting for words from me that cannot come. Here as in Unity, a day have passed without my presence. How is it that however long me be gone in the other place, it is always a day left behind when me travel across time? I press my fork into my plate again and again like an automaton. I swallow down the roast meat and wonder why today, despite the warm, rich and flowing gravy, the meat on my china plate taste dry.

CHAPTER 32

Pushing myself from the bed, I scratch the itch at the nape of my neck and leave the room. Water. I must quench my thirst. I am walking down the carpeted steps, my hands stroking the wooden handrail, feeling its warmth, its breath living still in the knots of it. The jacquard papered walls are the same, not new, but much confusion and many thoughts roam in me. Am I here or there? May I speak or must I stay silent? I listen, approaching the last step and start to work my padding feet along the corridor towards the kitchen. This time, the voices are not mine, but they speak loud in their quiet whisperings. Miss Dinah's voice hushed. Jacob's voice too. Them words softly-softly bounce against the cool tile and me hear them conversation clear.

'You had no right, Jacob. No right.'

'Mum, I don't get why you're still going on about it. It's over, it's done. I had to let her try, at least! And she had every right to try, we owe her that!'

'You put her in danger. You put the both of you in danger. Don't you understand what it is we're trying to do here? I need you to keep her safe! I don't know why I thought I could trust you.'

'Look, she's back, we're back, okay? Nothing bad happened – that ball, the pomander works, you of all people should know that! Just because *you* didn't try to help when you had the chance, doesn't mean that this is wrong.' There is a moistness now inside my throat that was not before. I gulp it down. What Jacob saying? Miss Dinah could have known *how* the pomander was working before Jacob find me?

There is a sharp breath taken, me feel it is from Miss Dinah.

'Jacob. This isn't a game. You need to promise me, right now. That's the end of it. You're never going back. Never again. If I could throw that thing away I would.'

'Yeah, but, Mum, you can't. We both know it doesn't work that way. You can't pretend. You can't just ignore things that inconvenience you. You tried that once, it didn't work. You could throw away his money, though. That would count for something, wouldn't it?'

'You know it's a condition of the estate; we have to live here. I hate it, but what on earth was I supposed to do after your father left? I would never have brought us here if I wasn't desperate. As soon as I'm back on my feet we're moving. You must know that!'

'I don't believe you. You've been saying that for five years. You're stuck, Mum, stuck in the past and you know it!'

In the silence that they make, I enter the pause of it and the four sky-eyes turn to look at me.

'Miss Dinah, Jacob. Me bid you good evening.'

'Obah? Can't you sleep? It's so late! Did you want a drink of water or milk, or something?' Miss Dinah's face smile is not within her words. She step towards me and her hands have knit together, the fingers pressing into each other like vines.

'Thank you, miss, me have thirst.'

'And something to eat? A piece of toast?'

Miss Dinah walk across to me, place her arm about me and squeeze me carefully. Me feel her warmth against me and no matter how many times she do it, it stay unusual for me, the warmth of a white person.

'You poor girl. What they did to you. Did you have a nightmare?' She turn then and take the carton of milk out from the shining refrigeration door and begin to pour. 'Warm milk's good for that.' She place the cup into the magic box above the oven and turn it on. We wait, silenced, all of us eyes on the cup turning circles in the box like a dancer on a silent stage. The box cries out that the milk is warm and I jolt at the sound as if awaked from a sweet sleep. Me survey small smoke rising from its mouth as she hand the cup to me. I sip slow, enjoying the heat hitting the roof of my palate. The eyes of Miss Dinah and Jacob are quiet as them watch me sup, waiting for my move.

'Miss Dinah, me have a question.'

Miss Dinah turn her head towards Jacob and them eyes meet, she bite her bottom lip and lower her chin before she turn back to me.

'Of course, anything, Obah.'

'Thank you, miss. Before me ask, may me request one thing more?'

'What's with such formality?'

230

'Me need your answer to be the truth.' A boldness have rise in me.

'The truth, Obah? What do you mean?' Miss Dinah dart a quick look at her son.

'Me did hear Jacob, just now. Please me must know, miss, did you visit to Unity with the pomander that belong to Miss Frida?'

Miss Dinah look at Jacob again and me see her swallow. She sigh hard and this seems to help her move her feet. She pace away from us and then back again before finally stepping to open the cupboard under the sink and pulling out a bottle of clear liquid. In silence, Jacob and I watch as her shaking hand pours a tumbler's worth and she begins to drink it. It looks like water, but from the relieved expression on her face, me know this is liquor.

She pour another but does not drink it, she stares at it for a while, as if asking it a question that has not an answer. Instead she carries it to the table, adjusts the sleeves to her elbows and sits. She pushes out the chair next to her with her knee and beckons. 'Come, sit with me, Obah. Let me explain.' I stay standing in my space, stroking gently at the elbow scar from Leary. In my quiet silence Miss Dinah's fingers move to working at the chain about her neck.

'My great-great-grandfather was the son of the girl you call Miss Lynette. The one you share a birthday with. Do you see?'

I shake my head. I do not see anything. What do Miss Dinah mean by this?

'Lynette inherited the pomander from her mother and hers before that, I suppose. And I guess, it's been passed down the generations. Have you ever examined it properly? I mean, really taken a careful look at it, all of its engravings, the way the sunlight plays on it . . . If you look, really open your eyes, you'll see the inscription. It's faint now, but when you're at Unity, when you're in the early years, you can read it clearly. It says: *"For Agatha, Wherever you travel may love follow after. Your Papa."*

'I never wanted or needed this home. I knew the family connection, the history behind it and I didn't want anything to do with it. But then, our circumstances changed, and well, I felt we *had* to come here. My husband left us and we fell on hard times, I'm ashamed to say it, but I had to swallow my embarrassment and we had to move in. I couldn't sell, it was a condition of the estate.'

Jacob clear his throat and I stand mesmerized by Miss Dinah.

'The first time I saw her, we hadn't even finished unpacking! Dressed in velvet and lace, a floppy bonnet on her head, looking around her like she was in some kind of historical TV show. I was standing right by this window and I saw her walking about in the gardens. I went up to her, to ask her what she wanted, why she was here. And the fear in her eyes, I'll never forget it! She stifled her scream, she reached down and pulled out this strange silver ball . . . she actually opened it up and took a pinch of something inside it, a powder that she sniffed with her eyes closed. When she opened them again and saw I was still there, she fainted!' Miss Dinah almost smile at the memory.

'I managed to help her up and sat her down on the sofa. I was about to call for help when she started to pray. "Lord, deliver me from evil! From these heathen instruments of Satan!" I would have laughed, but it was *how* she said it, the *voice*, the *whimper* in it and I realized then what she was. A ghost! And all the while, from her hip, this ball gleamed and shined, winking at me.' Miss Dinah shift her gaze to the left of her, at something unseen standing by.

Miss Dinah have given up on the beckoning for me to come close and lift the glass to her lips, she drink from it twice, slow.

'Before I knew it she was gone. But I wasn't afraid, just curious. There hadn't been anything malevolent about her and I'm an open-minded person. I've done yoga, crystals, meditation, you know . . . I just thought we'd had a visit from the other world and I wondered if she'd come again. And then I remembered I had seen that ball of silver before somewhere. I rummaged through the things in the inheritance box that had gone straight into the attic and there it was! The exact same silver ball, the pomander, that had been sitting at her hip. I remember looking at it carefully, rubbing away at the engraving to read it better and then . . . I was . . . there.'

'There?'

'There. Where you were. Only . . . you weren't there. I mean, not as you are now.' Miss Dinah pause and cover her both hands to her face.

'Not as I am now?'

'I saw it all. I saw the pain, the heat, the torture, the sun, the suffering. Children, bellies swollen with hunger, mothers whipped at the post, men wretched with bent and broken backs . . . It was . . .' She swallow the drink again. 'I wish to God I'd never seen this for myself. Once you've seen something as heinous as that . . . it's impossible to unsee it, as of course, you know.' Miss Dinah's mouth have twisted into thin rope. She look up to the heavens that are not there and standing, push away from the table, starting to move towards me as she speak.

'And then I saw her, the woman from before, the owner of the pomander. She was sitting and being fanned on the steps of the house. Frida. My grandmother many times over. Do you want to know what's truly strange? Stranger than even the *thought* of time travel? She recognized me! Smiled at me, even. I knew what she was, I knew what this meant then and I was so . . . ashamed . . . All I could do was close my eyes against the cruelty and wish for home.

'Obah, you must believe me. I never understood, until then, exactly what had happened. I mean, the history, in general, I knew of course, but . . . I didn't know how close it really was to *me* . . . does that make sense? I put the pomander away. Maybe I should have thrown it away, but that felt wrong, like a lie. So it went back into the attic and I tried to forget about it. I didn't . . . I couldn't *do* anything, could I? I'm ashamed to admit it, but I thought I could just try to carry on as best as I could, bring up my children to know that hate and prejudice is wrong. What else could I do?'

'You could have done more, Mum. You could have challenged them, spoken to them, told them to stop! Why didn't you?' Jacob have raised his voice now, fury and rage at hearing this revelation.

234

'I don't know. I don't know. I'm so sorry.' And Miss Dinah's tears flow then, hard and fast and me beg Jacob to stop him interrogation. Slow, me rise to me feet and leave the room to Miss Dinah and her regret.

CHAPTER 33

Today in school we be studying history. History mean things that did happen before today. It make me realize that 'I' is a history. My life at Unity is now put behind me. I am one of the people Mistress Thompson show us in pictures. My sadness grow each day, as the history grows further away from me. Replaced with the knowledge of the here and the now and Miss Dinah's deceit.

Miss talk about when Britain have had an Empire and how this country is small but so great it have a control in its small palm of nearly all the world. Me heart did pound heavy when me see the image of the gentlefolk, them wearing the same silk bonnets, skirts and stiff breeches of the Cooke family! Them hair set in the curl fashion that me did make for Miss Frida in the mornings and them skin is both pale and rosy like them hide from the sun. I did fear that it was them that lived at Unity! Masser Cooke, Miss Frida and Miss Lynette, about to step out of the board, grab me and pull me back to history!

'So, as you can see, women in the nineteenth century were the property of their husbands, their job was to bear children and in the meantime, look after the home. They were not expected to express opinions on either politics or business. So, who can tell me why this might be?'

Me listen with care when Miss Thompson talk because her sound is still hard for me to understand each word. She have say that women is controlled by men in my 'history'. I think on the question she have ask and Miss Frida's shape appear in my mind, I watch my hand slowly raise itself up.

'Oh? Yes, Obah?' Her voice is high and one of her brownish-red eyebrow is raised.

'Mistress Thompson? May me give answer to your question?'

'You're welcome to have a go, yes,' she say and her eye glisten a little.

'Gentlewomen is strong in history, not weak. The white women, I am meaning. Them control all aspect of business, and husbands, them must observe them. These womens is most clever with them . . . their . . . strength, them hide it behind coquettish ways and tears.'

'Erm . . . strong you say? Well, that does go contrary to the narrative *we* understand, but why do you say that, Obah?'

I feel the eyes of others on me, but I use them energy to raise up my shoulders and continue my speakings.

'When I see history, I seen women wrangle with their men, like always. And, at the end of the quarrel, the men must give to them all they did request! Why? Because them not like to see her weep.' I shrug, it seem so easy and simple to me. Mistress Thompson's head twist to one side against her shoulder, ask

237

Kryztof to put him phone away and then she blink slow.

'That's . . . quite profound. So what you're saying, and perhaps you're right, is that a woman could truly hold the upper hand through manipulation. How interesting. Who else has an opinion on nineteenth-century women?' She eye my classmates but as usual, silence talks and none stir. My hand go up again.

'Obah?'

'And when it come to slaving, miss. Then, the mistress in "history", she has all the say on if a baby should stay with him mother or who to sell and what name them should have too.'

'Slaving? What do you mean? We're talking about British history, the history of the Empire.' Miss Thompson give a sad sigh at my ignorance before she turn her back and a new image appear on the board, another family from my 'history'. 'Now, during these colonial times . . .' she continue with her teaching but I hasn't finished with my question.

'Please, miss. Is "colonial" meaning negro slaving?'

Mistress Thompson very quickly show me the palm of her hand like a shield to ward me off. 'That is unacceptable language, Obah, be sure never, ever, to repeat it.' She give a long sigh and wring her hands together in prayer. 'Yes, enslaving people *was* a part of British history, but slavery happened in lots of countries, all around the world.' Miss Thompson smile, now that she have help me understand.

'It have happen here, miss? Does Britain enslave her own people?' Me curious to see how she come back on this. Me think of Miss Dinah and what she too ashamed to admit.

'Well, perhaps not quite in the same way . . .'

'Yeah . . . I think instead of slaving them, didn't they just send them to Australia?' Say Frimpong, wakened now in him chair and turning him head towards Miss.

'Well –'

'Actually, they treated the Irish really badly too. My foster carer says they starved them in a famine, like I think half the population died!' Maya sits up now too, flicking her blond braids over her shoulder and showing everyone the gum she chewing.

'My great-grandfather was Indian, he told my mum that the British did the same there, let people starve and die, just to keep them controlled. Man, that's messed up.' Munir, whom me have never heard speak before, call out from the back of the class, him brow furrowed at this new awoken memory from his family.

'But the fact is, that histories are complex things, aren't they? We learn from history and hopefully, we don't make the same mistakes. Is it really fair to judge the people living today by the actions of those living in the past?' Miss Thompson have spread her hands wide, embracing all of us in her perspective.

'It is, if they have not learned anything!' me call out, me voice ringing in the classroom air like a cowbell. 'Have all things changed, miss? Or must there still be work done?' I am standing now. Munir is nodding and Maya slap her hand down on her desk.

'Sit down, Obah. It is a passionate subject but we must move on.' Miss Thompson smile is thinner than when her lesson started, her cheeks is stretched and grey as if all them questioning have aged her.

239

My ear cannot hear her any more. Me raise me hand and take her nod for permission to exit.

In the bathing room, the cold water flow free for a moment and I cup my hand and splash it to me face. What Miss Thompson have say be true, me do not blame people living today for the past, for my history. But have them *learned* as she say? Have them learned enough? Not yet. Nearly two hundred years have pass and them still treat we black with the same 'racism'. Me see it with the child who is searched as if she an adult criminal and me hear it in the testimonies of my classroom brothers and sisters. Me bend, splashing more water across me face.

In the looking-glass me eye seem darker, older. My teacher cannot teach me history because me have seen it all already, what is more, me has lived it.

CHAPTER 34

Rose arrived at Unity one afternoon on the back of Masser's old wagon, pressed in a corner, and weighted down with the other provisions. She old, all of us can see it, I figure she nearing a hundred, but might've been the dust she pick up from the road that make her look like she already dead and buried. He never purchase her, him say, to no one in particular, he 'won' her on a game of cards when he took refreshment in an inn of disrepute on the way home from visiting some farmland with good prospects. Masser did jump off the wagon and shoo away Old Jeremiah, fixing instead to tether the bushed-out horse himself. He turn and grunt at this old Rose, bid her get outta the wagon, and point she in our direction, tell her to make herself acquainted with us that manage the vittles. Aunty Nita weren't happy about that at all. Not at the first. Later, she woulda wish to have that Rose by us in the kitchen many a time.

Rose take a while fixing to get out of the wagon so Jeremiah have to help her down. She shuffle up the side of the house slow, both legs gamey and bad, face like beaten leather from all them crushed-up hopes. She hobble with a stick, hardly able to walk one leg in front of the other, a little track of wet done line the ground where she walk. Rose have her mouth all bunch up like an angry fist on account of the no teeth in her head, but she got on goodly garms, I 'member that, skirt and blouse, a full pinny and a cap of cotton trimmed in lace.

Rose sit herself down on the stair to the house, looking 'round with eyes that living but dead. Eyes that would not meet any of us eyes looking on. Miss Frida come out the house then and see fit to laugh when she see her sitting there, 'What's this old, crumpled nurse?' she say. Masser stick his thumbs in his belt and set his shoulder. He get to telling Miss Frida all about how she been poor pickings. 'My dear, my card companion was unfortunately outwitted and this, I'm afraid, was the only payment he could proffer.' He shrug a little and tell Rose to sit up straight when him talking. But to us surprise Miss Frida don't say nothing about that – don't give Masser none chastisement about the cheating and heathen card-playing. Instead she pout, peer at Rose from where she stand.

'Husband, I cannot say I like her looks. She's as dried up as tobacco in the sun. Is this economical? Can we not pass her on to Mr McDougal? In exchange for a mule maybe? Think on it, would you?'

And she open up her fan and swing herself back off to the veranda and on into the cool of the house. But she turn just before and as if in afterthought she say, 'Meantime, call her Rose. Since she is anything but, it will be a pleasing diversion!' And with a light laugh and step she vanish.

Rose sitting there said nothing, she sit and play with her gums, clicking them with a rheumy rhythm for a time. Masser stare at her a while, then shaking his head, he step pass her, heading on into the house. Nita step out then.

'Come on now, Rose, be getting cold out here, come on and sit by the oven.'

But Rose don't even look at up. She sit face set, clicking them gums, back and forth, back and forth like a feeding heifer.

'Such things happen to the likes of us. Mustn't take it to heart. I's sure you seen plenty change in your time,' say Aunty Nita as she place her arm on Rose, gentle. 'Rose ain't such a bad name, neither. I is Nita and these pickney be Orrinda and Murreat.'

But Rose don't say nothing. Don't even turn and look on Nita's hand pressing on her shoulder. She don't look at us half-dressed bitty ones, neither. She sit there, gums moving but no sound coming outta her mouth other than that. Aunty Nita beg her to get up, but she don't. Like she don't hear what Nita saying at all.

I figures her skirts and petticoats must be keeping her warm and full besides, 'cos she don't come in for mush, not even later neither, when dark fall and every one of us be huddling up to take sleep. We hears the rain tapping on the cabin and Aunty Nita get up, but Rose still stay out on the step. We looks on us each other, we knows how even all them heavy garms she got on can't keep off that wet, that night cold. Nita fretting over it, she look out through them shutters at Rose on the step, but Rose don't move at all. Her shadow bent and black under the moon. Aunty Nita curse low, but me and Murreat hears it anyway and we looks upon each other, then at Nita but she don't move to 'pologize for it.

Seem like Overseer Leary never full done his rounds, for surely if he done them, he would send Rose inside, him would never let her keep herself sitting out all night on that step. He would have thrashed her hard and full with the thresh till her skin so raw she gots to move. All me know is Old Rose didn't live till morn. The cold and damp got her, they says, on account of the sitting out all night. But I reckons something else, I reckon Miss Frida bad enough inside to tell Leary to leave her be. To let the Rose be watered by the night rain until the morn bell come. That how women in history be. Them stronger than Miss Thompson will ever know.

CHAPTER 35

This morning I did wake up to glowing, as if me whole room is bathing in sunlight even though this is the wintertime and the air is chill. Here is colder than the icehouse at Unity where we did store rabbit and beef. In this wintertime, any skin open to the sky feels its whipping sting and so my toes insist to be covered. The moon have move into the sun's place and touched her with its whiteness; she is no longer golden but pearl. This morning, the light, the glow, appear instead of the darkness, so in curiosity me rise up and pull back the curtains to see what is happening. Me see a blanket of white cotton spread over the whole of the grounds. It have covered everything living, every tree, every leaf, every blade of grass, the little outhouse roof have a thick layer too, like the icing them put on top of the cake. Me gasp. Everything look like it sick, it look trapped, suffocated like it can't breathe. Me clutch at my neck as if the white dust have got into me and stop me too from drawing air. What have happened to this world?

Kitty approach my door with a soft knocking before she push it open from the other side. Her nails are shiny and black as they press against the door frame. Half dressed as is her custom, a dull light flicker by her side from her mobility phone and her skin glow porcelain in the dim light of the hall. Musket slip soft through the cracked door into my room, not waiting for summons and settle himself upon my bed. Comfortable he nuzzle on his paws, one eye open as he survey the encounter between me and Kitty. A cup of hot liquid is smoking in her hand and she hand it towards me.

'Hey, hot chocolate, your favourite!'

'Thank you, Kitty.' Me sup from it carefully, trying to stop the shaking in my arm as me stare out at the whiteness that cover the ground.

'Oh, your face! You've never seen snow before?'

'Snow?' Me gesture to the thick whiteness outside with more alarm and spill some of the hot chocolate upon the tapestry floor. 'This the snow like them say in Narnia?' Me place down the cup and my fingers tremble as they press down on the cold metal handle of the window to look closer, me turn it to opening and feel the bite of the frozen air. The shapes of trees seem sinister and vicious without the green and me think of the White Witch.

'Always winter, and never Christmas,' me say and with a shiver, me close the window too.

'You okay?' she ask. 'Do you need me to get Jacob? You don't look great.' Me hear a sincerity in her voice.

'No, no.' Me do not need him to coddle me.

*

246

Outside, the air cracks as I step into it, shifting about me, I place one foot down onto the white carpet and feel the crunch beneath me, it rises up my leg and into my body. The next foot goes down and the same thing happens, although it looks like the floor has gone, it is there, under the snowfall. I step off the back porch and onto where the grass is covered, lifting my foot and I see that I have left my mark here! I walk about in a slow circle then stop and check how my footprints have made a pattern, showing the path I have trod. The crisp crunch continues, my one left foot squelch in a cold wetness in the too-big wellingtons that Kitty has given me. I think there may be a hole in them.

I try to lift my foot but it is stuck, the snow hold fast about my ankle and I panic as I pull hard. I fall, landing on my back, my fingers feel the soft cold bite as I gather the snow at my sides. I look up, blinking at a sky that is white too, this is all I see, whiteness, it seems the whole world is white. The tiny particles fall upon me faster, like manna from heaven, blown by the wind, so many tiny white flakes shift into my eyes and I blink with the confusion at this white world. I see myself from above, slowly buried in whiteness and even though I am already down, I feel myself falling.

'Never Christmas,' I whisper.

Kitty is back in my room again today. Me smile at her returning friendship, which is warm and welcome in this winter scene.

'Well, I'll leave you two to it! I'd better do some revision anyway. Shout if you need me, Obah.' Jacob get up from my bench where we have been reading together and wink upon me as him leave. Kitty have brought me another hot chocolate drink. Me have taken its warmth into my hand to start my grateful sup again when she stand and go to the door, open it and stick her head out for a moment before closing and sliding across my bolt. Then she pull out a black stick and place it to her lips. Kitty inhale deep and then like a kettle boiling, she blow a piece of steam from out of her mouth. She look at me with one eyebrow raised before offering the black stick to me. Repulsed, I twist my head away.

'Look, O, you've got to stop being so boring. It's not like I vape every day, just once in a while, and that's not going to kill you! But *don't* tell Jay, you know how lame he is.' Kitty move to the window, bite her lip and struggle with one hand to twist the handle to open it. Eventually it bend free from the frame and the wind moans in a lamentation through the opened gap.

Although the smell from her fire is sweeter than the tobacco that Leary did chew and Masser Cooke did sip from his pipe, I cough and bat the smoke away as she suck back on the stick.

Me have never know a woman of high standing to use tobacco before and me wonder where the pleasure come from, when food and even better, the hot chocolate drink, is in abundance.

'Yeah, anyway. Listen. I was thinking that we should hang out more, go shopping. Cheer you up.' Musket have curl up at my feet now, the warmth of him pressed against me and my hand get to stroking him some.

'Hang out?' me ask.

248

'Look, Obah, we know you're sad. It's awful seeing you this way and I want to help. Mum says you have PTSD. Let's get the bus to the shopping centre.'

'PTSD?' Me eyes widen.

'You know . . . trauma, like when you have bad memories for something that happened in your past. And it still affects you so you can't get over it.'

'Trauma.' Me try out the word on my tongue, it feel heavy, leaden. It speak to me of Mad Lizzy, she have this, this PTSD. Maybe we *all* does.

'D'you wanna go? It'd really help me out?'

'Yes,' me say and give her my best smile with teeth.

'O.M.G.! This is the one, you have got to try it on!' Kitty press a garment into my hand that shimmy-shake with silver and then she stand back, hand upon her hips regarding me. I smile back at her nervous, the smiling hurt, but me do it anyway.

'The fitting room's just here, it's *the* one, I promise you. You're gonna look so freaking hot, I can't even!' As she run ahead, she pull me behind her like a pup upon a leash and we enter a room where ladies are standing circled in undergarments. Me gasp and turn to leave but Kitty have me arm still, so me avert my eyes down and begin to beg pardon, wondering why them women so exposed, and what kind of place she have brought me to. This be no auction, yet women stand here baring all! Kitty drag me on and pull aside a long grey curtain; we enter both into a smaller space that just about fit we two. She step back and look at me with expostulation but I don't understand what me have done. Her eyebrows raise and she thrust her chin before me and me blink back at her form.

'Obah? What are you waiting for? Take your top off, then!'

I put my hand across my blouse and press the cold buttons against my flesh.

'You want me take off me garments? Here?'

'How else are you going to see if it fits properly? Okay, look, I'll wait outside, all right, not that I was gonna check you out or anything. I mean, whatever, it's fine. Just step out or pull back the curtain once you're in it, okay?' and she jump out of our small space before I can speak.

I look about me at the two tall walls that press against me from left to right. The garment sit upon a hook, twirling about in an invisible breeze, impatient as Kitty for me to try it on. Before me stand myself, mirrored in the wall. I remove my blouse and skirt and stare at the garment in my hand with its missing lace, missing petticoats and missing velvet. This is not any kind of dress me did imagine wearing when back at Unity. Me pause momently to see how the curves of me body is reflected in the looking-glass, how me is not so lean as before, then pull it over my head. The robe hardly cover me up and me think that Kitty have given a child's size in misplay. When me mutter my thoughts through the curtain she say, 'It's the right size, it's supposed to be short. If it goes over your bum, it's a fit. Come on, let's have a look!'

I pull the curtain open a little, and even though the

discomfort present in my eye, Kitty grab me and pull me out, placing me among the many half-clad women. I do not like this place. Me feel naked, me feel dizzy. Many of them wearing just underclothes, many in garbs like this one, where them twist and turn to look upon themselves in the mirror, unseemly and unclothed in clothes! Me is so glad that Jacob have not accompanied us as him declare him 'hate shopping' and it good for me and Kitty to have 'girl time'. Me would be shamed for him to see me dressed as this. Me know me not lady enough to expect lace and ribbon, but why must me adorn myself in such ungodly apparel?

'I knew it! Stunning, it's perfect for New Year's! Let me take a pic.' She hold her phone before the two of us, her head tilt left and her lips push like she kissing the air. There is a flash of light and then she examine the phone close.

'Miss Kitty, this not any type of respectable garb – this hardly cover me, this be for a pickaninny of three or four years, please, fetch me the proper size.' I cross my arms across my chest where the top of my bosoms are showing and shiver at the cold against my bare legs. Why Kitty want to dishonour me so?

'Seriously? Obah, you need to trust me! I know what works, okay?'

We walking back now, shivering against the cold, towards where the people bus wait to return us close to High Ostium. Kitty have help me with the phone to call Jacob and him have say him will meet us at that place where the buggy . . . *the bus* stop with the *car*, so that we do not have a long walk in the darkness. The phone is an easy object, me understand why Kitty love hers so! Me just see Jacob face and press upon it and then me can hear him voice, and see him face, wherever him be!

Kitty swing the bag that have my new garment inside. She have purchase it from the tailor even though I have swear oath me will never wear it where others might be present. She seem happy now and me feel as though me have been of some use to her. Before us a man with his clothing pulled over his head walk, arms bent into the shape of open shears as if to ward off those who would walk too close to him. From his person drop a bright-coloured box that start to bounce in the wind and me pick it up and run to him, not heeding Kitty's call.

'Sir?' Me tug upon his bent arm. 'Sir, you have drop this!' Him turn and look at me then. Him see the object in my hand that did fall from him and shrug me off with a wild waving.

'What you doing, man? Get off me!' The sound of the youth is angered at my touch.

'Hey, hey, leave her alone, all right?' Me hear Kitty from behind me, a plea in her voice.

'What you touching me for? That's proper rude, man.' The youth step forward, him gaze hard upon my own, and as I step back, I slip against a patch of ice.

'We're sorry, okay? She gets confused, she didn't mean anything by it!' Kitty is at my side and she pull the box from between my fingers and throw it back upon the ground, me watch, confused as the wind begin the toss the box about and the smell of the meat inside whip about us. The youth have skin as dark as mine and we look at each other mirrored in black. I smile at him, recognizing my fellow brethren, but his eyes dismiss me and move back upon Kitty.

'Tell your friend, yeah, she needs to watch herself!?' The boy make a sound with his lips and teeth and then pick up his speed and move on. Me feel Kitty breathings have stopped as we watch the back of him grow small.

'Seriously?' sigh Kitty. Her eyes is round tea plates as she look upon me. 'What are you playing at?'

'But . . . him . . . don't want his meat?' There *was* a meat in his possession, even if him comportment towards me suggest otherwise. Me could smell it strong – so why him discard it so? Me think of Benjen, Murreat, all of the children living in want of meat at Unity and the sickness rise in me as me realize what have happened. This man do not care about his meal. Me want to explain myself but I already know what I have done is in the wrong. In this place, my new home, I am always in the wrong. Have I really travelled so far?

'Kitty?' me ask and me take her by the arm so her eye can find my own.

'What?' she say.

'The people here, them must believe in something? What is that?' me ask her urgent, me must know the answer.

'Believe? No one believes in anything! There's no such thing as a god if that's what you mean?' Kitty stroke my back gentle, as if to comfort me with this new news.

'Then how them can have hope?'

'I guess there's none of that, either.'

Sleep have not come for me tonight. Too many times, in my mind, I did see the walking back of the youth with the covered head. From each of his hands him have a string trailing meat behind him: chicken, ham, turkey, beef . . . following is me, hand in hand with Murreat and Benjen, sniffing the air about him, us lips dripping water, barking after his scraps like dogs. I open my eyes. From the window glass I spy the moon, full and pregnant with light.

Me wish to be there again, at the Martha tree's feet. *Me imagine how she look down on me, her face withered, whiter now than grey. Her hair wild and curly, being messed up the more by the night-time breezing. I settles down by her, I feels her breath, warm on me and I don't feel the cold no more, her sheltering arm dry me from the rain. I press my body into her roots, curl myself into her affection, she always been the one to protect me. And it is here, here that I finds my bed and soft blankets, finally, I sleeps.*

CHAPTER 36

'Merry Christmas, Obah.'

At Unity, Christmas was a big and fancy occasion and we work ourselves full hard. The Cookes love to have a fresh and steaming hog roast and plenty of corn, yams and potatoes all to share upon their table, resting against the glisten of the white china plates, so Aunty Nita and me have to bring another two into the kitchen to help with the choring.

Christmas is when the three of them Cookes does make us wash and dress up in a costume them keep in a box so that we looking very fancy and particular to wait at the table. Them dress themselves up in more than them usual finery, with clothes from the big chest and sit at the table with a flourish and a bounce, stinking of camphor. For drinking them have a wine in the sherry glasses and them always make a longer toast to the health of the King of England before them start the cutting and the slicing and the putting into mouths.

At the end of dining them tell us to sing and play a music for them to dance. The fiddler boy did come in from the field and play as best as him can and me and the weaver women Anne and Rosemary did sing along to him tune. Them try to teach us a sad tune that them say come from England and be about two women call Holly and Ivy but when we never catch on good, Cooke wave us to stop and so we continue with our own local song. At the end of the Christmas day, our feet is sore, our backs creaking and our bellies rumbling, but oftentimes, there is a little leftovers that Nita let us share to stop our bodies' complaints. We sleep sound.

Kitty is more excited than me as she count the boxes. Miss Dinah must have come into my room while I sleeping because there is so many boxes scattered around and me never hear her come. When I wake, her warm white face is over me, gently pushing me shoulder to pluck me out from me dream in Unity with Mimbah and Murreat and bring me back into this world. 'Merry Christmas,' she whisper, her breath sweet. 'Look what Father Christmas has brought!' And I turn to sit up from my bed to see the boxes, them looking so beautiful, the shine of the red, gold and silver paper catch the light and them seem like jewels from a Aladdin's cave is here in my room. But I don't want to know what is inside.

Here at High Ostium, the Christmas I am facing be a different kind of toil. Nobody ask me to do anything, no sweeping, dusting, cooking or singing. The white folk here be giving *me* the gifts to open. Them stand and want to see how me react as them throw coloured boxes at my feet. There is something rising in me, a sickness as I see this pile at my feet. I know that inside are things that will be pretty and joyous to see,

256

hold and touch, but I don't need them. I have running water, a warm bed, clothes and food to eat and people who treat me kind. I have everything I need, all except the family me leave behind at a burning Unity and me sure not one of them boxes have *that* inside. I don't understand how there is so many parcels for me to open and although I know it will bring Miss Dinah a smile, my fingers cannot find a way to tear the paper.

This is not as when Jacob did give me the book at Unity. There, I did have nothing and it was like dreaming to have a gift of me own, but these things? If I didn't need them before I peel off the paper, why will I need them after the paper is pulled away?

Jacob say, 'Open this one, please.' And because it is Jacob, I do so to find a journal, in soft brown leather. It is engraved with my name. Thick, empty pages of ochre paper stare up at me and I smile, I cannot wait to fill them with my careful ink pen writing. This box is enough for me.

After the dinner of turkey and goose, vaguely, I wonder how it is that two fowls I have never partaken of before still taste as like chicken. We sit down by the fireplace and Jacob struggle with lighting it, so I crouch down beside him and look for a hot coal to start the fire up, but there isn't one. Instead, him use a special lighter, like a long finger with a flame at the end and the sparks catch to set the fire ablaze. I stare into it as it grow, it is beautiful. I have missed the feel of true flame stroking my cheek with its heat. Jacob pick up the poker by the side of the fireplace and I shrink back from him. What him planning to do with this? I crawl backwards to my place on the sofa, watching him carefully as he prod the coals. I cannot stay near him with this tool of violence in his hand.

'Kitty, can you pass the chestnuts? They're on the counter,' say Miss Dinah. 'Obah? You wait, these are so delicious roasted. It's one of our traditions,' add Jacob.

But my mind has gone back to revisit another Christmas tradition from Unity, when a poker was dipped in flame. The year when everything changed. That year, them did call for Mimbah, when all of them was seated and drinking port in glasses for to satisfy the end of them supper. Happen she did come into the room where all of them is seated and look around at the pale faces that has grown rosy with good food and wine. Poor Mimbah, if only she could turn and run at this point, before the wicked act took place! It has happened that morning that Mimbah did not bring in the madam's ruby-frill dress in a timely manner, she did have a dress that she must take out at the waist because Miss Frida have grown a little around her middle. Miss Frida give it to her the day before Christmas and tell her she must have it ready.

But Mimbah also having other chores at the house and must finish up tailoring the jacket of Masser Cooke so even though she work till late, when the sun have finished, she cannot see to work and did start to make work on the waist of Mistress's dress on Christmas morning early. But Miss Frida is angered that the dress is not ready and that she must wear the emerald lace instead of her ruby. Some did hear that over dinner, she have complained to Masser Cooke at how it is a shame she did not have her proper dress for Christmas dinner and how it have ruin her day. Mimbah arrive with the dress, but late. The dinner is over. Masser Cooke pick up the poker from the fire, him tell Mimbah to kneel at him feet and look up at him. Then him press the hot metal to the corner of each of her eyes, brief and gentle. Them say, when he do it, him wish her a Merry Christmas.

As I pass Jacob him chestnuts, I pick up myself from the floor and tell how them must excuse me as me tired and feel a need to rest. Them eyes is all confusion behind me as I leave them to them Christmas.

That night me dream.

The cool water be washing me toes and the sound from the brook is the soothe lapping of a thirsty dog. The water sit dark with rushes and grasses and mud, little wrinkles be moving on the surface like the creek be cooking something inside it. Me did swim and bathe here when me was a pickney, but none come here now, the land fallow for rest, even the washer women use the small spring for the linen, not the creek water.

Before me realize, me start wading into the creek and soon, me lying on me back. Water feel cool, like I remember. Right here, I can find my stillness, can be empty of all my trouble. I look up at the little light but there's something I spy sitting there that is not the sun. It be too early for all the stars to be out, but this one be impatient. It so bright, glinting like saltfish in soup. I close my eyes to the light of it and then, a new dreaming start.

As me floating here, me see the image of a woman by my side. She a serene beauty, black as ebony, with a serious aspect but a warm eye. She have something in her hand. It blinking at me and me realize she have plucked the shiny star from out the sky. The silver of it gleam, me recognize this jewel, the pomander of Miss Frida. How she can have that? Me want to ask her, when she start to sing, her voice be a shiny syrup flowing in me ear.

'Yen co fie, me bah

Yen co fie, ayeh enye, ayeh enye

Yen co fie, me bah

Yen co fie.'

My mouth open and me cry out, I know this melody, this voice. These the African words me mother did sing to me; them say, 'let's go home'. I let the words wash me like the water.

CHAPTER 37

At my bedside sit my unlit candle, I pick it up and bring it to my nose, it have a perfume – how can that scent stay sweet when this life sit rank with injustice? Against the wall stand the bureau with three drawers, the chair painted ivory cream slid under it, neat, orderly. The window stand open and I shiver against the cold. From the world outside, a thin-finger of russet ivy reach in and tap, silently, on the sill. Below it sit a laptop, a phone, a vase with the dried rose posy – some of the petals have fallen off and sit upon the table, shrivelled and curled. All of my things. All 'mine'.

'*Mine.*' I open my mouth to say the word loud but it don't come. I try again, '*Mine.*' It is painful, wrestling with my tongue, fighting me, as it knows, like I do, how I got no right to the meaning of the word. My brethren have nothing. And here I sit with all that is '*mine*'. A small sweat break out upon my brow as me remember how this word 'mine', be Miss Lynette's favourite.

'*Orrinda, you know, don't you, how you and all of your kind here are mine?*' *Her voice whines with air about my head, but her eyes is on her wooden spinning toy, she hit it again and again with*

*her stick. It jumps. The both of us watches how each time it tire, the
tip of the head starting to nod, one hit from her can make it spin
again, harder and faster.*

'Yes, missy, me knows it.'

*'Mine, mine, mine, mine, mine! Ha!' With each word she hits
again. She drop her stick, turn, and kick me then, not as hard as she
do sometime, but she got her new boots on, so it's enough to make
me take a heavy stumble back.*

*'Papa says God gave you to us. Did you know that? God. That
means you cannot ever be taken away! Because God himself gave you
to me!' Miss Lynette yawn a little and stretch her arm over her head.
'I get a good many presents, but you are the best of them, Orrinda,
and I love you, with all my heart, I do. Isn't it the most wonderful
thing? To be mine for always? Oh, dearest, your tears are because
you are as joyous at the thought as me!'*

'Mine.' Just a word, but like so many things, it be reserved
for whites. Whites is them ones that's got things they own,
properties, sentimentals, peoples even. Us ain't even got mamas
and babies we can calls our own. Even us own limb don't
belong to us.

Mine. Is this what the true living mean? Possessing the power
to take and the power to own?

Knock, knock.

'Come in,' me say, finally me is used to the privacy of
my own room.

'Hey,' say Jacob. 'Have you got a minute?' Him rub gruffly
against his forearms. 'It's freezing in here, can I close the

window?' Him walk over and close it before me answer.

'Obah. Do you remember what happened before? That girl who was strip-searched at her school by the police and how it made you want to go back to Unity? Well, it's happened again. Not just searched. They hit him too, pretty bad. A boy this time, a black boy.' Jacob voice growl soft. 'There's a rally in town tomorrow. I know it's not much, but I need to be there. I don't expect you to come, it'll be busy, crowded, scary . . . but I wanted to let you know.'

'I'm going too.' Kitty is beside the door. 'Don't try and stop me, Jacob, I'm nearly fifteen, I'm old enough. It's happening to kids my age, I have to do something too!' Before Jacob can protest, a shadow form against the frame of my door.

'Neither of you is going, do you hear?' Miss Dinah complete the audience in my room and me sit and watch the family before me begin to argue. Each of the voices rising above the other as them bicker. Musket and Drummer add to the clamour with their barking.

'You can't stop us! Why do you always try to pretend these things aren't happening?' yell Jacob.

'How dare you! You're still a child and you're still living under my roof, under my rules!' Miss Dinah's voice is shrill as she place her hand upon her hips and her feet widen them stride.

'Mum, we need to show *we* care about stuff like this, it's the only way to make a change!' Kitty plead, softer than me have heard her speak before. Me see the spark of something new in her eyes.

'Look, protest all you want, sign petitions, write to our MP even, but going out onto the streets? You're children yourselves, for goodness' sake – you can't put yourselves in harm's way like that! What if someone sees you? People know us around here.' Miss Dinah look at me, as if for support.

'But, Mum! Can't you see – your way – this old way of doing things, the letters, the petitions – it doesn't *change* anything!' Kitty cross her arms about her chest.

'Tell the truth, Mum, you don't care about the way the world is today, do you? You think everything is perfect just the way it is – you don't want change!' Jacob's voice catch in him throat. 'I don't know what to do.'

'Jacob?' It seem him eye have become red when him turn to me.

'I can't help, can I? I mean . . . I thought by bringing you here, by protecting you and loving . . . I thought . . .' Jacob turn him face away and him shoulder shake as me realize him crying. 'Obah, I'm sorry. It isn't enough.'

All this time, him prop me up, him hold my hand but me cannot see how him is hurting too, hurting with a pain that watch me suffer.

'Jacob, please,' sigh Miss Dinah, 'what you're saying is nonsense, of course I want things to be better. But this isn't the way to go about it.'

'Then why haven't we done anything? Ask Obah, for goodness' sake, she's sitting right there and she can *see* that nothing has changed! The racism? We're nearly two hundred years on from where we found her. It has to stop, Mum!'

'It's her I'm thinking of! It's her I'm trying to protect – I promised her, I promised her mother!' Miss Dinah's voice choke on her word and she bring a hand to her mouth as if to push it back. Jacob try to straight himself but him footing fail him.

'My mother?' I whisper the words into the air and a silence fall around it. 'My mother? You did see her? You did see me? At Unity?'

'Wait, Mum, what? All this time! What did you do?' ask Jacob, him face grey as him look upon Miss Dinah. She walk over to me then and sit beside me on my window seat. She touch me gentle, stroking me cheek with a warmth but me shift away from her. Me don't want coddling, me want the truth.

'I did.' Miss Dinah sigh deep. 'I met your mother. I can't forget her face. It's your face.'

'You telling the truth, Miss Dinah?' I gulp back the tears that are starting to rise. Miss Dinah hold me in her arms then and as we embrace, I bury my head into her chest and it is my turn for weeping. For a moment we stay as this. Then she lean back and stare into my eyes, wiping my tear with her thumb. 'Obah, Obah,' her voice is calm and whispered, revealing all that she has hidden.

'Tell me all of it,' me say.

'I should have told you before, but I was . . . a coward. There's just so much shame . . . Sometimes, sometimes I think this is all destiny and fate. The past, the future, it's all rolled into one, maybe none of us can escape it. None of us can do anything about it.' She place the palms of her hands upon her breeches and the sides of her lips turn down. 'And nothing is within our control.' I breathe in hard and look to Jacob. His eyes are wide, listening to the words from Miss Dinah as if him have never hear them before.

'When I arrived, I heard the sound of water . . . and I followed it. She was the first person I met, singing a soft song to herself, washing clothes, I think, by a gentle brook. It was a quiet spot – a moment away from the true madness there. She saw me too. And even though I'm white, somehow, she knew that I wasn't like the others. She could sense I wasn't from the plantation but from elsewhere.' Miss Dinah wipe back a tear. 'Do you know what she did? She tried to give *you* to *me* then. She untied you from her back and pressed you into my arms and she said words I'll never forget, *"You must love baby Obah."* But I couldn't . . . I *didn't* touch you. I was . . . confused, afraid . . . just everything, I didn't know where I was, I didn't know what she meant . . . But now, now that you're here. I understand it all so clearly. She wanted you to be safe and she knew you would be, with us. And I should have taken you. It should have been the least I could do, given my family's responsibility for the hell you were living in.' Miss Dinah look down at her hands again and wipe away at a piece of lint that is not there.

'That's where you and me differ, Mum! I actually brought Obah here, you had the opportunity but you didn't. And even worse, you did nothing.' Jacob's anger echo through the room and Kitty and I stare at the face of Miss Dinah.

266

'Where did she go? After that, where she went to?' Me want to know all of it, the truth, finally. The rest is as water.

'Obah, you have to believe me, the truth really is I don't know.'

'You did not bring her here? To High Ostium to stay with you?'

'No, I didn't even think of that! She wouldn't have come anyway, I'm convinced of that. She was asking for *you* only. Not for herself.'

I step back and look close at Miss Dinah's eyes and they too are wet. I know she is telling her truth. My mother, she did love me. She did try for me.

'Obah, I'm so sorry. I should have taken you with me then, brought you up here, away from the violence, given you a better life. I didn't understand how to begin. I was scared . . . can you find it in your heart to forgive me?'

Both her eyes are on bended knee, praying for my pardon.

'We can make it up to you now. We'll look after you, just as she wanted.'

'Mum, the pomander.' Jacob look accusingly at Miss Dinah. 'You knew what would happen? When you left it in my room? Tell her! She deserves the full truth. We all do.'

'You're right . . . you both deserve that.' She cannot look upon my eye. 'I thought that, somehow, if *you* were to go, if you were to see what had happened, then somehow, you'd do something I couldn't. That's why I left it with you. You've always been braver than me, Jacob. I admire that in you.' Jacob reach for my hand.

'Obah, I swear I didn't know any of this! I wasn't expecting

267

Mum to believe me when I told her that I'd met you, I mean, what mum would say *"I believe you, I've been there too!"* when you tell her you've been time-travelling!' He turn to Miss Dinah. 'You even warned me not to go back!'

'Only because I knew you would! Don't you see? You have a mind of your own. I knew through you, we could somehow try again to undo the legacy, to put things right! We can make amends for those wrongs.' Miss Dinah grab me by the shoulder. 'We both want that, Obah; Kitty too. We all want to look after you. We want to do some good. I'm sorry that we can't bring everyone here. I don't know why it works the way it does. But we can start with you. We can save one.'

'But there's more than one, Mum. That's the whole point. That's why we're going to the rally, tomorrow. All of us.' Jacob lift me up and place him arm about me waist. 'We're in this together.'

CHAPTER 38

I have locked my door and I lie in my bed. Them has come to the door a few times to ask me if me okay, but I have not given any answer. My face stare up at the lines that walk across the ceiling, I follow their course from left to right, trying to connect the pathway, to make sense of the faded cracks blurred by my tears. Me can see Miss Frida smile, the sneering one that she did give me many times, the one Miss Dinah say she did give her that day. Here I lie, in the house of my master's offspring. Am I at Miss Frida's mercy again? Have I been eating and drinking a false freedom? Must me be bound always to these Cookes? Destined to be their slave, their object, their toy for ever? Can I never be free? My mother wanted me to live free, but is this it? Is this what she wanted for me?

My eyes try to blink again. I swallow the salt of more tears. From my bed I stare into the looking-glass. Everything 'bout the image staring back at me look all wrong, like it don't belong here. I examine my full-of-fear face, the salt-white tear tracks, my red eyes. I am residing in it still; a modern-day Unity residence is where Jacob did bring me to. I know that this is the Cooke family home. I did leave it – but I have not left. I walk to the door and press my palms against it. Me trying to understand if Jacob have lied to me from the very start. Did him never find me through accident? Did Miss Dinah send him to collect me? So much have been revealed this night. My mother did want me safe, she ready and willing to hand me over into kind arms, black or white, she never care about skin colour, she care about love. But me mother never understand the truth of it, she never realize that I am my mother's daughter. Me don't need no one to save me.

'I know you missed dinner – just leaving some snacks.' I hear his movement, feel the heat of him moving away and I call out.

'Jacob!' I open the door and press myself into his arms.

'Hey! Hey, it's all right.' Jacob let me cry into his chest, me feel his hand rub against my back and me fall against him even more. The mango warmth of him fill my nose and make me head feel light.

'It's a lot to take in, I know. But we're here and we . . . we love you.' Jacob gulp and me feel his heart skip.

'You love me?' I speak into the softness of his shirt.

'You know we do . . . All of us.' We pause together, feeling our hearts beat in tune. Jacob cough. 'We'll be at that rally tomorrow, we'll show we want change. Mum's still in pieces, but I don't care what she says . . . we're going.'

'Jacob, I *need* to go. I could not help my brethren back home. I need to be there, I need to voice the cry.'

'Obah? You know that I'd do anything for you!' His eyes

270

are darker, somehow the blue is burning violet. But I feel him tense as he pull away from me so his eye can meet my own. 'Remember, it could get violent, Obah, and from the looks of it, there'll be a storm tomorrow.'

I glance at the window and watch the wisp of dark clouds moving closer, walking towards me as if arm in arm, merging together to form darkness.

'I not afraid of the storm,' I say.

The rally is due to begin at midday. But me cannot rest with the anticipation. Me never get me uprising at Unity and this feel like the summit to the hill that I have climbed, the moment that me have been working towards. Kitty is excited too, but when she hold up the dress that we did buy and raise one eyebrow, me giggle at her and she put it back into the dresser. Like her, me have on me jeans, breeches that feel comfortable and will strengthen up me legs against this winter cold. Jacob ready and waiting in the kitchen, him hand me the hot chocolate him know me love and me gulp it down, enjoying the burn, the fire in me belly.

'Ready?' him ask.

'Ready,' me say.

Miss Dinah will not look at us until we leave and then, as we crunch the gravel with our feet, towards the car she call out, 'Be safe, please. Be safe!' and stay by the door, watching us with pensive eyes as the car shift upon the drive and out, out into the world. Me palms is sweaty with water. Me not sure what me can expect, but me know that there will be an energy there, a people moved. We park the car and head towards the city centre, following the backs of people heading in the same direction, me look up at the sky still dark with the clouds that did break forth last night. Will the storm come now?

When slaves be together in a coffle, them each of them tied up, waist to waist, feet shuffling along like they be too heavy to lift off the ground because of the chains at the ankles. Them is all one body, them have that same angry energy as them move. Here, as we venture in upon this crowd, this rally, the people are the same, expressing that one same energy. Each one stands distinct in colour, age, height and clothing to his neighbour. Them like one tree that have mango, coconut and tamarind all growing on the same branch. Me watch how them rattle chain at the police, how them sing out for justice for the boy that lie injured in hospital. Did them know this boy, him name, what him did love to do in the day-time, what is his favourite flower to sniff, his favourite food? These people don't pay no mind that them is not his friends, these people don't worry that them have never seen this boy in person. Maybe, them don't even know him name, it don't matter. Them come together anyway to protest against him maltreatment. All for one.

These strangers has come together to chastise power, to say how beating and stripping of the innocent is wrong. This boy, him is not just a history but a present. Same as I am not just a history, but also a person.

It is as we are passing the library house that Jacob and me

begin to witness the commotion. Me hear screaming and the people of the one tree rushing in a heaving movement all at once, them pick up the speed with sloganed boards held aloft. *My life, our lives, black lives. We matter!* Me attracted towards this energy, it steer us onwards, deeper into the noise, into the smell and sound of angry souls.

'Obah! Over here!' Me turn to the voice calling my name and there is Dionne and Maya standing together beside a shop with the picture of a white chicken in a red hat.

I wave and the three of us, Jacob, Kitty and me step towards them. Me is glad Dionne called out my name. I would not have known her now with braided hair that shimmer pink and violet.

'You lot shouldn't head into the eye of the storm, it's gonna kick off *big* time. Keep to the back, stay with us,' advise Maya. 'Who's he?' Her pierced eyebrow raise up, the golden ring glinting in the cold sunlight as she squint at Jacob with suspicion.

'This is Jacob, and Kitty. Them is . . . me family,' me tell her. Maya shrug.

'People aren't taking this shit any more. There's rallies going on across the country because of this. It's on all the socials! Manchester, Birmingham, Sheffield – you name it!' Both Dionne and Maya look upon the mobility handsets and hold aloft pictures of moving crowds, shouting, walking.

'Last night, this morning, even, people were angry but it's worse now. You heard, right?'

'Yes, the girl and then the boy. The police did beat him too.'

273

'You mean, you haven't told her?' Maya look at Jacob with eyes dark with anger.

'Tell me? What is there to tell me? Me know that the boy is beaten and in hospital.'

'Tell her?' Jacob shrug, 'I don't know what you mean.'

'It's worse now. That boy died. Joshua, that was his name. Died this morning. Died at the end of a *truncheon*. At fifteen. He was just a kid! And, get this, the policeman who did it has been let out. There's no way a black guy would've been bailed for a crime like this! Apparently he's going to claim it was a moment of insanity or something, that the *kid* provoked him.' Dionne turn herself in a half-circle as she speak, sure to address each of us with her revelations.

'People aren't waiting for him to get off, we're protesting *now*! They need to learn, *finally*, that black kids matter! They can't keep doing this,' add Maya, stopping the chewing of her gum.

'Doing what?'

'Killing black people!' say Jacob and me hear the fury in him voice. The fury have me too, it lift me up, with wings, as if the White Witch herself have cast her spell.

'Me going in,' I say and turn away from Kitty, Dionne and Maya, pushing apart, I follow the throng, the crowd, to where the noise is, but Jacob is on me in two strides. I feel his hand take mine in his and squeeze it hard.

'Don't try to stop me, Jacob, me going into the middle, me want to be with them, me want to have me voice heard too.' I shift and squeeze and push and nudge and he never let go of my hand.

274

'I'm with you, Obah,' Jacob say and Kitty, who have caught up with us, nod her head as well.

Some police mens is there, standing together, faces empty as if them is pencil sketches of themselves, a contrast to faces in the crowd which shout and scream. This day is as most in this season of winter, bitter and callous. The wind bites against my cheek and the darkness in the sky loom above us heads, the threat clear. But even as the winter sun be slipping away, the bodies all around emit a warmth, a heated anger. The man on the right have remove his shirt and written on his chest; marked in black against the pale of his skin is 'protest' one word to call us all. Directly ahead, another man hold a child on his shoulder who wants to see what is happening. A shrill sound fill the air and quickly, I press my palms to my ears against the pain of it. Jacob pull me gently but I shake him loose again and plant my feet hard. I need to see this. I need to understand. The wounded noise comes again and I see that the root of this cry is from a teenage girl, like me, but her voice is warped by the white cone that she press to her lips. Her eye meet mine and I hear the word standing in the cry. *Justice.*

'Racist police! Stop killing black people!' say a blue-haired woman, her white fist pumps the air. I follow her fist down to her eyes. There is venom there, and I know that she too believes the police have killed this boy because of his black skin.

Jacob hand squeeze mine tight and I look down at how our fingers touching together, there is a unity of us standing here in this moment but me have a doubt, me have a question for him.

'Is this unity, Jacob? Is what I see when I looking at you the truth? Or is this *Unity*?' Jacob drop my hand and turn him body round to face me, him eye is troubled, but I press him more.

'I don't . . .' him say.

'Why? Why me must find out this child have die, from Dionne, from Maya? You think you is me protector? But you can't protect me from life, Jacob, you can't protect me by concealment of a truth, you can only make me weaker when you tell me lies. You see?'

Jacob open his mouth to speak, his tone of voice is low, like the quiet hum of the trafficking cars around us.

'Okay, Obah, you're right. I did see that he'd died, but I didn't say anything. You shouldn't have to see stuff like this happening here. You've been through enough!'

'But she's right, Jacob, there's been too much lying. It has to stop.' Kitty place one hand upon her brother's forearm.

'Jacob, if I don't see all the truth, all what is happening here, I will think this place is something it is not, do you see? You must let me have eyes wide open here or I am just as blind as in Unity.'

Jacob's face fall.

'Something's happening,' say Kitty, a tremor in her voice. 'The storm is literally about to break You guys don't move, I'll be back in a sec.' She is away before we can question more.

'You're right, again and I'm sorry, again. Obah, I keep on failing you. I want to make amends, for my family, my history, I just, I just don't know the right way to do it, you know? And, you are so much stronger than you look! That's one of the

276

reasons why I . . .' Jacob thumb brush gentle against the back of my hand.

'Why you what?'

'Jacob!!' Kitty is back and she tug upon me and Jacob with both of her arms.

'It's him!! They've got him,' she say and her fingers tremble as she place them to her lip.

'Him?' Jacob look into her eyes and she nod back at him urgent.

'Who? Who them have?' me ask them both.

'Obah, there's something else I have to tell you . . .' Jacob's voice cut out as the chanting rise louder and louder and the crowd jostle and push so that I cry out as we is separated. Jacob on one side and me on the other, the crowd has parted as though to create space for an important personage like we do for a masser or mistress.

'Pull it down! Pull the bastard down!' Voices in unison are calling out a chanting, louder and louder it rings about us like an urgent bell. *Pull him down! Pull him down!*

The chanting continue and me look at Jacob face to understand what is wrong. Jacob skin is white and his lips too have lost their colour as he look on at the commotion. Jacob try to cross the crowd but him get pushed back. Between us, there is a movement now, a tug-of-war as back and forth, the people sway to and fro with a unity of energy and then me see the rope them holding, joining them together, just as the coffle me remember from the past. There is grunting and wiping of sweat and screeching of women as them pull the rope and pull again. The rain start then, a drop or two at first and then like a bursting dam, the water pour hard and fast and from my side of the crowd I see how it wash Jacob. I blink against the fat drops but me cannot fight them, them making Jacob fainter and fainter before my eyes.

'Watch out! He's coming down!' cry a voice and everyone take frenzied steps to widen the level gap. My knee buckle as I fall and me face hit the dirt. Then, there is a crash and a black object, shaped as a person, lies in the gap they formed between the crowd. I am on the ground and my head lie level with the object, me stare into his eyes and there is a feeling of something lost that start to rise within me as we regard each other. Then Jacob is beside me, pulling me to my feet, asking if I is okay. But me do not answer him, me is pulled as a magnet to observe the figure on the ground. The rain fall hard, but it does not stop the people. Them now have run to the object, they jump upon it, they kick it with their feet they spit upon it. All the while, Jacob stay white and silent beside me.

'Who is that? That statue that they have pulled to the ground? Did you know him, Jacob?' I blink at the rainfall.

'It's Cooke,' he tell me, him voice solemn and grave. 'Cooke from Unity . . . Your Cooke. *My* Cooke.'

CHAPTER 39

The rain is battering, hurting as if to rouse me and I remember where I am. When I am. The wetness is as heavy lead, each droplet hitting hard punches, waking me up from my slumber. Now I see everything as the night owl. I see Cooke, but more than that. All of my senses are afire but me think of nothing, nothing else but Jacob's word.

Cooke. Masser Cooke. Here.

'Jacob?'

'Wait, let me explain, okay? I've been trying to tell you.'

'Masser Cooke? How? I cannot understand it.'

'This is what I was trying to tell you. The truth. It's him. Cooke. It's him they've pulled down. And I'm glad he's down. Finally, he's defeated. The old world and the new, we're meeting in the middle, do you see?'

'Jacob, give me answer. How is Masser Cooke here?'

'They made a statue of him, okay? Years ago. To remember all the "great" things he did for this town, the money he invested in schools, in hospitals, alms-houses for the poor. But he couldn't have done it without the money he got from slaving. That's the truth of it. That's why now they hate him. Why *we all* hate him. Why Mum didn't even want the inheritance, the house, not any of it.'

Slowly, my head twist back to the scene before us.

'Bastard!' A man spits upon Cooke's cold black visage.

'Slaver!' Another strikes a blow at his trunk with a stick.

The persons about me, of all the colours possible for a human, are together as one, kicking, spitting and shouting at the prone figure lying on the ground. It looking up at them helpless, unquestioning, accepting the blows. The statue of Cooke. My master. For a moment I gaze upon his face and there is the likeness there, the shape of the nose, the lift of the chin, the eyes, black hollows, just as his own. For a moment his face glows and the hairs on my arm stand, but I realize the clouds have shifted, making light, a blemish in the sky, as if the sun want to see this toppling for herself. The crowd parts again as three men approach, them faces is covered with masks. Them drag sticks and heavy woods between them placing them atop of the stone edifice of Cooke. As the men pour a foul-smelling liquid over the wooden pieces, the noise swells with cheering and suddenly there is a light, golden, orange, red and blue swimming about Cooke's head and body. Fire.

I am empty as I watch, numb with no knowledge of what I should feel at this, but I see the people, I see how they feel. The people cheer at the burning. Watching the stiff body glowing with flame.

'What did I tell you? I knew they'd get him down. About

time too. I've had to look at his ugly face too long. He's a sign of all that's wrong here today, he had to go.' Dionne have squeeze through the crowd beside us, her phone before her face, waving it from side to side so it can see the scene too. Kitty bring out her phone too and with Dionne and Maya them record the history being made.

A man in denim breeches has brung a babe to bear witness, pushing him in a red-wheeled carriage. The baby's arms are tucked tight under a blue blanket and his eyes are closed to the disturbance. Fleshy pink lips move, sucking an imagined teat as he sleeps, soundly, unaware of the carefree clapping and whistling that circles us all. I fear for him. Fear that he will wake startled at the clamour, crying for his mother. Which is all I want to do.

Me have drive pass the statue every day me come to school, but I never looked close upon his face, never saw who was really looking down at me from this plinth. I watch the flames which will not die. They add more and more fuel, wood, boxes, rubbish, whatever they have, each person bringing them offering and dropping it upon the embers so they cannot expire. The few police men standing about do nothing but watch, as if them too is hypnotized by fire.

This is the present, the world where things are fair, the light to my darkness. How can this be? How can there be fighting and screaming and fire and murder? I see it now. These people *are* the fighting. These are the people who will stand up against the tyrant. This is who I should be.

There is a ringing against my ear and slowly I touch my lobe, inspection of my finger shows red. My blood. I feel myself spinning round and it is Jacob, his hand in mine, pulling me away from the fiery spectacle. The breezing air above me whistles again and I cry out as a bottle lands its smash beside my feet.

'Quick, this way.' Jacob drag me towards the shop with the white cockerel sporting the red hat and we stand beneath the canopy, turning to see the scene again. The noise frightens me more than the fire. Men growl, faces bitter, twisted. Women screech and babies cry. The crowd is a mix of masked youth throwing objects and others trying to run away from the projection of flying articles. Me see now that other things are burning, not just Cooke. The window of a shop is broken and with a cheer a group enter and come out carrying large boxes which they run with. A moment later it too is aflame. The smoke billows about us and I bring my hand to my mouth to catch my cough.

'Are you okay? You're bleeding!' Jacob have taken a small paper from his pocket, him unravel it from its ball and gently touch it to my ear.

'Jacob, can you see what is happening?' I strain away from his hand.

'Yeah – it's getting out of hand, we need to get you away from here.' Him try again to wipe about my ear with his kerchief.

'But it is more! Much more! Them fighting, Jacob, them making people see them.' Me hear me own voice rising.

'Obah, I want the protest, but this is getting violent now.' Jacob voice have a sadness.

'But cannot violence, like this, where none is hurt, be a call for us? Be the voices, be the cries that others will hear? Think, Jacob, think to Unity, the fire there was burning, wasn't it?'

'Yeah . . . and you remember what happened that night?' Jacob lean back and look into my eyes.

'The fire! Can you not see? That is the moment when everything becomes clear. When the old dies away and the new can be born. When the people will hear and awaken. The fire is our moment in Unity, Jacob. We left too soon. *I* left too soon.'

'You're not? Wait – seriously? You cannot even *think* of going back there. I won't let you.'

'Jacob, you don't own me.'

Jacob stagger back as though me have strike him across the face. Him shoulder shiver, but not against the cold that bite us both.

'I *never* wanted that, not ever. I worried about it, you know. Because of who my family are, because of Cooke. But I know I'm nothing like him. I only wanted to help. I only wanted to just . . . try to set things right, you know. And then, you were so amazing and beautiful and kind-spirited and . . . it became more than that, I wanted you to be . . . happy, with me.' Jacob face look upon me and me see the tear start to swim from out his eye.

'Jacob,' I says. 'Cooke is part of you. And I *am* happy. Because of you, there is good come from him at last.' I grab him arm and turn him to face the clamour.

'Just as all of these white standing here with them fist in the air is asking for a black life to matter, the white can stand united

283

with we. Jacob, look upon *your* people, you is a part of them. You can work to help them understand their power over we.' I take him hand into mine and squeeze him fingers so he can feel all my strength. 'You stand with me.'

'But . . . you're saying something else, aren't you?'

'Them is your people, I have mine.'

'You want to go? You want to go back there? If you stay, *I* can stand with you, *always*. What you're thinking, it's suicide!' Him pressing his thumbs upon me person, pressing his words, but them make no imprint.

'Jacob. There's a smell here that me can't stomach no more. It start soft, but with each day pass, it grow, like a dead rat rotting behind a cabin board. I sit here, sipping sweet juice, while that smell spread. I sit here upon cushions while that hiding rat grow maggoty and white. I biting cake while its bones press through the flesh. If me stay here? Me leave a legacy without hope. Hopelessness is passed on, in the blood.'

'I don't understand.'

'This smell, Jacob, it have choke me, make me sick, but it's like this fire have finally let me breathe again. I got to give my Murreat and my Nita some hope. Now. Before them believe them don't got any right to it.' I smile at him, rub his arm.

'Me know misery. Being hit on, being beat, being starved. But there be another kind of suffering. This one more clever than what I knowed, it hide itself here.' I press at his chest. 'Like a spider spinning a web, patient, waiting for prey.

'Here, there be food to eat, but people starving just the same, there be jobs that pays, but not all jobs is open to all of us, there be homes to live in, but some of us don't get the ones with strong roofs and trees in the yard, there be songs to sing but many voices is quiet. Do you understand me? This not just about me, we all of us have to sing.'

And Jacob sob then, his voice break and his body shake and me take him into my arms and hold him so tight. I never want to let go. But I must.

'Hush . . . hush, Jacob. All will be well,' I whisper into his ear.

'It wasn't supposed to be this way. You were supposed to be happy. You deserved that.' Jacob hiccup and me lift his chin up from his chest and gently place my lips upon his. The scent of mangoes and warmth fill me up as him press his lips back against my own. And for that moment it is him and me and nothing else matters. Not that I am slave, not that I am black, not that he is white. It is just us, together.

I push him away gently, feeling the warmth of him still against my mouth and although I want his lips on mine again, I stand firm. We sway a moment, finding warmth together in the cold.

'I can't stop you, can I?' Jacob's voice is a whisper. Him have place his hands in mine and look down upon our fingers, linked in unity. I shake my head.

'And you don't want me to come with you this time . . .' I shake my head again.

'What if they kill you?'

'If them kill me? Me have been dead before.' Me stroke him

face, gentle. 'You did bring me back to life, Jacob, and I will find you again in another world. Just as you found me. You *have* helped me. My eyes see what kindness looks like. My heart feel what love be like. I find it in you, in Miss Dinah, in Kitty and I never saw that before. Me never even dream it. I have to do this on my own, Jacob. You have see it too. Just as you and the people of this world need to fight for them own justice, I must fight in mine.'

Jacob's blue eyes shine at me.

'I have to fight, if I don't, how can I ever live free? I have to try. I won't never forget you, my Jacob. Never. You will always be my duppy.'

'Obah . . .' Jacob eyes crease at the corner with a painful smile. 'You are your mother's daughter after all, aren't you?'

'And like her, in the end, I must go alone.'

He squeeze my hand again and his fingers say what his words cannot, he loves me, I feel it coming from him. A love that wants all good things for me. I know it, because it is as I feel too. Jacob loves me enough to listen to my voice and hear me. He loves me enough to let me go. Slowly, we draw our hands apart, but the energy that Jacob talked about, the *Niagara* between us is standing there still, connecting us in the empty gap between our fingers. I nod my head, and Jacob nods his to mine, pressing against it for a moment. Then the warmth lifts and through my half-closed eyes, I see the silver spin as Jacob pull out the pomander and press it in my hand. And then, he is gone.

PART FIVE

UNITY PLANTATION, BARBADOS, 1834

CHAPTER 40

As I reach the clearing, the air is still and the emptiness of the field echoes about me, there is only the soft sound of my own newness. The want of Jacob is a hole in my person but somehow I smile, stroking the red ribbon that binds us in my pocket. Me know exactly where him be, cornered in time, like me. And the togetherness we have is always with me, even though me will never see him again.

Being born again here, for a third time, be easiest of all. This time, it's like I slip through an opening covered in grease and sweet cream, smooth as mink, like I do the birthing of myself. I's in control now. I have the pomander. And being here is my choice. This be my time.

To my right from within the tall reeds that stretch across the plain, a whistling frog is singing, a music I have almost forgot. Their song of hospitality reach me and I answer back. I's singing again, I hear my voice after so long, my lamb song. Slowly, dark shapes start to sway in the sore light, moving, dancing to the winding melody that tap about my head, the tree limb of Martha, tapping, clapping, welcoming me home. The cold fat moon have a sombre glow. This be me home. For better or for worse.

I smile at my temerity as I stroll along in my shoed feet that cushion as I step over stones and obstacles. Under the night sky my legs is secure from errant roots in my blue jean breeches, the belt at my waist holding in my clean pink shirt, the buckle closed neat. I walk, not run, towards the Big House. Then me feet still. Me smell the fear. The smell of burning wood, the choking thickness of black smoke, the song of panic and dread. The reckoning is here. Me breathe it in.

Me smell how the fire that me did run from is burning still. The smile is gone replaced with the seriousness of what me have done. What me have come to do. All around me is ablaze; fire in Unity and fire in Jacob's world – when will the world stop burning? Me hear a rustling sound and bristle as me turn to find Hector, him eyes squint upon me in the dark, him stagger back and him mouth hang open.

'Obah? How you did? Where?' Him pause and breathe in slow, placing him hands against his knees to catch his breath as him speak. 'Leary's hounds, them almost have you and then . . . you and the white boy is gone! How? How?' Him look up and down upon my person, eyes widen as him note my clothing, my shoe, my hair.

'Why you burn down the house?' Hector squint him eyes at me and scratch his head.

'Hector, where is Leary? Where is the masser?' I ask him, pressing my hand upon his arm.

'Them searching for you! Everyone craning them neck to find where you is this past couple of hour. Where the boy hiding?' Him press a hand upon him hip and bend to look behind me as if Jacob at my back.

'Just a few hour have pass? That is all?' My toes curl up and my feet strain, ready to run. Me have come back too soon. I need more time. When Jacob and me did return together, a day had passed, now, alone, just hours since we ran. Me stomach squeeze in pain and me bite me lip.

'You sure you is ready for this? For when them find you?' ask Hector. His gaze fall upon the ground as him speak.

'We taking Unity,' I answer. 'We do this now. I know me asking a lot, but you must trust in me. This our time now and we must own it.'

'We? How *we* ever own Unity? We negroes! Them just gon' give up all this to us and walk away?' The whites of Hector's eyes is grey.

'We have to try. We will rally together to take this land for us. We fight together or fail, together. But we must not be divided. Together, Uncle, we win.'

'This a game?' Hector widen him lips into a smile but there is no laughter. 'Child, the Big House still red-hot, and you want we to rise up now?' He glance over his shoulder and sniff lamentable at the burning to illustrate our dilemma.

'Uncle. Cooke cannot kill us all! What him have without us? *We* is the treasure, not the house! Please . . . tell the brothers them to get ready, me come soon to the Big House and me will give signal. We move now, before it too late!'

'Obah, me been beat too many times. We placing our trust, all our hope in you. You best to be right 'bout this.'

I swallow the air rising in my throat, feeling the dryness there. The weight of responsibility on me, on what must be done. Hector reach down and squeeze me shoulder before turning towards the house. Him take two limping steps before he turn and although his voice is low, me hear him whispered question.

'Is she be watching over you, child? Your mother? Over your spirit? Is she what make you so strong?'

'She did give me my name, Uncle. Obah – it mean, she have come.'

Me don't have much time. Soon them will know where I is. Me need to make my way to the Big House.

Nita's voice is dark and angered when she see me at the door of her kitchen. 'Them been here. Everyone be working on the fire or looking for you! Miss Frida give me pause on account of my poor breathings. Lord, what kinda garbs you wearing to disguise yourself? Taken to stealing as well as starting fires?'

I move to explain, but Murreat jump up at me like Musket, curious, she stroke me clothing all over and reach up on her fold-up toes to touch my tooth gap. Aunty Nita place her hands upon her hips and bend over me, cutting out the little moonlight that enter the hut.

'What have taken you, Obah? Satan? Starting fires that kill us own? Me never like Mimbah, with her heathen way, but me never wish her burn up and dead!' Nita pause only to wipe the sweat from her top lip.

'Them looking for you and them surely coming back! Girl, me can't hide you no more – me done. Step out and take the punishment, me and Murreat no want your mischief. Go. Now. Or me will call them here meself.' Nita quieten now, her eyes hollow and empty, all love for me lost.

'Mimbah?' Me hear so many words tripping fast from Nita's lips, so me hope me have misheard.

'Murreat, you go on and call the masser, tell him Obah here!' Murreat stare back at Nita and stamp her foot *'no!'*

'What about Mimbah? What you saying, Aunty?' Me choke the words and cannot speak more. I know what she will say next. Me have seen the future already. But I want to stop time. Stop so Aunty Nita cannot say the words. Stop so that I can take the pomander and go back and return again before this moment, stop before she speak again with words I do not want to hear.

'Mimbah dead. When she hear how you disappear, she follow the heat and the smoke to the house and gone in, calling out your name. She never come out.' Nita turn her back on me and play as though to tend to the kettle.

Me belly knot up as she speak. 'My Mimbah? She gone?' This *is* my fault. Me cover up my face with two hand and sob into it, holding back my screaming. She trying to save me. And, like a coward, me have run off with Jacob. I have come too late. My Mimbah, me only true friend here. I press Nita's arm again, my hand gentle and with the sob still in my voice I whisper soft in her ear.

'Aunty, listen to me, now. Me never start no fire. You know me! Me not a callous one, me not without care for me brethren!' The heat rising within me.

'Then, who the culprit? Mad Lizzy telling everyone she seen you do it . . . and then you disappear. Lizzy . . .' Nita go silent and walk away from me, she pace back and forth. Me watch how she take the kettle off the grate and bend to place it upon the iron rack. Her big back ripple like a breeze blowing in the room and me see her reach for the knife she use to slit hen throats. 'Me gon' kill her. Me gon' kill her.'

The knife glint and me step back. Me don't go close to her but whisper from where me standing by the door. 'Mimbah in peace now, Aunty. We don't none of us need to suffer more. Not another life. Come.' Nita shiver, drop the knife and it glisten up from the ground at the three of us in the room. She press her hand upon her stomach.

'Where you going, Obah? Where?' Nita have turn towards me. For the first time, me see her eye shimmer with wet. I open my mouth, ready to tell her everything that have happened, everything that is planned, when a voice speak.

'Well, what a happen here?' Mad Lizzy stoop and growl at the door, one foot in the room, one out as though ready to run. She eye my shoed-up feet, my jeaned legs and my collars with a wrinkled nose, like me have a bad smell and step further into the room for closer inspection.

'Well, well . . . the prodigal daughter has return, in garb as ugly as she. Masser gonna be real pleased you back, him been searching for you these past hours.' Mad Lizzy turn to go but I grab her arm and pull her deeper into the room. Slowly, Nita walk towards us, she bend and pick up the knife from the ground, she pass round Lizzy and stand in the entrance to bar the way out. The knife shine like a star in the smoky musk of the room.

'What? Why you barricade me here, Nita? Me must go tell Masser! Him looking all over!' Lizzy's eye flash emerald with cold.

'You kill Mimbah? Tell we the truth.' Nita hold the knife aloft and me gulp.

'Aunty Nita, no,' me say, me voice low. Lizzy laugh.

'Mimbah? Who crying for she? You? Me know you never like her.' Lizzy place her hand upon her hip and press them forward, haughty and proud.

'*You* have kill Mimbah. And *you* have start up that fire.' Nita's knuckles shine bright as the blade she holding. Her body stand boulder-like against the doorway, Mad Lizzy cannot make her way past with words, but she try just the same.

'Me? Me never kill her! It's she who done it!' She point her shaking finger at me, her eyes squeezed into slits. 'She! With her nonsense! With talk of walking free! Talk of decampment. You did hear what she say before? To the company? All me do is me duty. Me had to do it, to stop her guile! She feeding all with applesauce words and them lap it up, no tasting the poison she

295

lace it with. Is *she* who make a fire burn, a fire inside the people hearts! And for what? What freedom possible here?' Lizzy voice raise up. 'When Mimbah ask me where Obah gone, me tell her no one have seen, she must be in the house. Me never ask her to go inside and search for herself, me just never stop her is all.'

Aunty Nita have a vein in her head that have come alive at Lizzy's words. She reclasp the knife in her hand and step towards Lizzy. Me move between them.

'Aunty, please, she not worthy of you.' Nita stand stiff, her eyes cold upon Lizzy, her chest rise and fall and rise again and her breath come from between her lips, a hissing that tear from her lungs. Finally, her hand lower and the knife clatter upon the floor. Me turn to look down where Lizzy cower on the floor, her beautiful face hideous to me now.

'Lizzy. We want you here no more. When this be over, know you cannot stay with us. You must find your own way.'

'What you mean? What over? What way?'

'Aunty, let she pass now. Let her go, she have something she want to do.' Nita look me long in the eye, but she must see something there that offer up some assurance and she step aside. Lizzy hurry off, howling 'Masser! Masser!' into the night.

Me have to act, now, before she cost more lives. Before me will see Mimbah's duppy rise, angry with me, demanding justice.

CHAPTER 41

When me get to the Big House me feel how the sky about me is hotter than before from all the eating of the walls, boards, furniture and curtains. Almost half of it have gone. The little pail of water the men is splashing at it is useless as dew drops. The fire will not go out, just like the one in me. Cooke pace the ground forward and back, Miss Frida and Miss Lynette sit on stools a little stretch away from the heat and the working men. Them heads is bent, kerchiefs wiping away tears.

Hector turn his head from the line, him eyes meet mine and lift up my arm to raise my fist in signal. Him nod and whisper a word into Mungo's ear, then a whistle tear out from him, high in pitch, rustling the air, mixing into the smoke and raining down into the ears of the men and women until the pail is dropped. As one, the brethren turn and walk away from the house, coming to stand in line, beside me. We fold us arms into each other and together, a wall of defiance, we listen to the hiss, smell the char and watch the house burning.

'Ho! Who there dared to whistle? What's this? Cato? Apollo? Get back here at once, boys! Who told you to drop the pail?'

Masser Cooke take out his gun and shoot up into the night sky, the bang make all of us jump and the scent of gunpowder cause a shiver in the line. Then he train the gun on us, waving it from side to side unsure of who to shoot first. Me know the sound of gunshot will alert Leary – we have very little time. Miss Frida cry out, she lift Miss Lynette's head from her lap and bring herself to standing. She walk across and stand between the path of Cooke's trajectory, facing me.

I step once, then twice, towards Cooke and his family and the line shuffle with me, all of us, moving as one. We are tight, arms linked, we move together, all except one other. Staring down from the top of the stairs, glowing in the firelight, is Lizzy, swinging her arm on the ash-covered pillar, like a solitary pear on a blowing tree.

'There, Masser! There she is, just like me said.' Lizzy stop her swinging and point a single finger at me. Cooke turn, his eyes narrowed, the gun wobble a little but then him raise it again, pointing now solely at me.

'Orrinda! What have you done?' him say. 'Because of you this house has fallen! And, on Leary's return, I will have *all* of you collaborators whipped blue.' Masser Cooke wave the gun around at the company and the people start to step uncomfortable at him words but I raise my hand again and them stop their mutterings.

'Have faith,' I tell them, the fire in my voice now. 'We are together, we are one! Him cannot divide us!' Apollo bend to pick up a stick that stand by the well and him hand it to his son. He take another for himself and tuck it in the crook under his arm.

298

Cooke does not see, him have returned his gaze upon me, eyes pinched in the firelight to understand why I look so changed.

'We have our own destiny, Cooke. That is all we asking for. We are yours no more. The house is gone, the plantation over. We claim our freedom.' My voice has no tremble as the words come out, I know that what I speak is truth.

'*Freedom? Destiny?* This is your final opportunity to step back towards the house and continue putting out the fire! Whatever she has told you is lies. We don't hate you, niggers.' Masser Cooke step forward to line up with his wife, him wave his gun at all in line. 'This action of yours must undoubtedly fail and then the consequences to follow will be your own fault. Why, whites had to teach you how to walk on two legs! You were swinging from the trees like monkeys! This is disorderly, unnatural and it goes against the very word of the Lord! The comforts such as we enjoy are not suited for the negro! You remember that from our Bible readings?' He reach into his pocket and wave the Good Book above his head, weighting his words.

'The beatings stop now,' me say. 'We consent no longer, Cooke, leave us be. Leave us to till this land in freedom.'

'Let us be,' say Cato.

'Let us be,' add Hector.

'Our black lives matter,' I say, my chin pushes out and my legs stand firm.

'Evidently, I have been remiss of late. Spare the lash, and now look! The negro becomes a dissident.' Masser Cooke step back, confused by our strong, unmoving station then him

299

begin to walk the line, peering into every brethren's face. The gun remains in his left hand.

'Hector! Apollo! Now!' me shout, raising me arm and the two men rush towards Cooke, them take him by each arm and wrestle the gun out of him hand. It drop to the floor but there is no accompanying bang. Apollo hold the arms behind him and Hector take the rope from the gate and start to bind his hands.

'Husband!' shout Miss Frida. 'Dear God, what has come over these slaves? Apollo? Hector? This will not end well for you! Orrinda, explain yourself!'

'Hold him, Uncle!' me shout as Cooke curse and kick. Miss Lynette, weakened still from the fire, have now roused herself to sit beside her kneeling father. She hit weak fists at Hector and rock to and fro with tears.

'Frida my dear, step aside,' says Cooke, feebly from his crouched position. 'It is too dangerous. You must allow the men to deal with this.' Him twist his head. 'Hector, you dare to point the pistol at me? Leary will return post-haste and when he comes, we will deal with all of you.' But the growl has gone and there is a finger of doubt in him voice now.

'Miss Frida,' me say pointing at Cooke kneeling on the ground. 'The personage of Cooke, it stands no longer. I seen it fall. We, the people, we have pull it down, have burn it with firewood. Just as we stand now, watching the Big House perish, watching it fall, so it is with Cooke.'

Miss Frida step forward to slap me hard across the face. The stinging make me step back, but me feel Murreat's hand squeeze hard in Mimbah's place and slowly, I turn my face back to my mistress and straighten my shoulder. The weaver women Anna and Rosemary step out of the line and wordlessly, come between Miss Frida and me, a barrier to further abuse, but I brush them aside.

'You attack your master! You have burned down my house! When Leary returns, I will be unable to stop him from taking the most fervent action.' Miss Frida's voice scream her anger at me. 'Orrinda, you have betrayed me. Has it come to this? After all the attentions I have paid you.' She part a fold of her skirts and put her hand to her waist to place a single finger on the pomander that shine there. I see it glimmer and glint, this innocent bauble at her hip, knowing all of its power. Just as does she. She shake her head. 'Yes, you've been there, to that far-off place. You must know that the liberation you saw is not due for another two hundred years!'

Miss Frida turn to look over at Mad Lizzy and she shake her head at her woeful. 'Orrinda *didn't* start the fire, did she, Lizzy?' When them eyes meet, in shame, Lizzy drop her gaze.

I can smell her breath, rosewater and rum, blowing her anger against me and I press forward to speak directly in her ear.

'You are right, madam, I have been there, but our liberation is now. We will not settle for less than justice.'

'Mendacious girl, have you no shame? To think I once cared for you, thought to protect you! You're just like all the worthless others. You wretched, wretched people.'

There is a barking from the trees and then Leary appear atop his horse, the hounds at his feet. He slow the nag to a whinny and step down from the saddle. Walking slowly towards me, me see him reach into his belt and remove his whip.

CHAPTER 42

Miss Frida walk softly back to the crying Lynette and Cooke, the three of them cower together upon the ground. There is a loud snap from within the burning house as the weight of some timber falls. Lynette cry out again and Miss Frida console, rocking her back and forth, brushing at her hair, dabbing at her eye. Lizzy make as if to step towards them but Miss Frida give Lizzy a look that makes her back away, so that she stands alone once more.

'Leary! At last!' Cooke squeal. 'You arrive in good time. As you see before you the girl has returned and ordered my house be burned down. She has some inexorable hold over the others. It seems she alone is present, that miscreant accomplice has not been seen. Put this matter to bed at once,' Cooke croak from his kneeling position.

Leary slash his whip against the ground and the dispersed dust rise up. We in line tremble together and me see Hector step forward, his eyes meet mine asking . . . pleading.

'Step away from your master.'

We have no whips, but we do have the pistol. Me nod and Hector raise it up, training the muzzle on Leary. Will he have the strength to use it if required? Me swallow.

'Husband, before you finish with her, you must attend to this one here. Lizzy started the house fire, of that I'm sure.'

'Oh, madam, no! It not me, madam, you see her there, she the culprit. Madam, me would never . . .' Lizzy is on her knees now, wringing the hem of her skirt in both hands.

'Henry.' Miss Frida turn to her husband and Cooke nod before him turn to Leary.

'Deal with it,' he instruct.

Leary strut towards Lizzy and she run up to the top of the Big House steps, shaking her head to and fro and screaming innocence. She reach the flaming doorway and stand there for a moment, sure that Leary will not come close. The golds and reds bathe her in a glow of hellfire.

'Leary . . . me begging you, please. You know Lizzy! We good! Me never . . . me would never . . .' Lizzy cry.

'Listen here and listen good. Either turn around and walk into that building, what's left of it, or take a step towards me and I will have this hound here tear you limb from limb. You got ten seconds. Make up your mind.'

Mad Lizzy drop to her knees and clap her hands together.

'No! Me begging, please! Look at *her*, she the one to blame. She have changed everything. It not my fault, please, Leary, please.'

'It's Masser to you. And your time is right about up.'

'No!' me cry out and Leary turn his face to me. 'No,' me say again. 'Leave her alone! You have damage her enough!'

'Enough!' say Bertha.

304

'Enough!' say Nita and step forward.

'This be your fault, Obah,' cry Lizzy. 'You have ruin everything! Everything!' She sob and turn this way and that, unable to find peace.

'She is not well, Leary. Let her go.' Me stare at him.

'And pray, Orrinda, why should I listen to you?'

Hector raise the pistol and hold it aloft, him cock the barrel but only I see the tremor in his hand

'Well, well? What have we here? Do you have the resolve, Hector, to take a white man's life? Surely, you know that will be the gallows for you. Are you really going to shoot me?' Hector swallow, but him arm stay straight. Him grip the gun with both hands and keep it trained on Leary.

Lizzy have use this time to get down from the step and she run to the edge of the forest, she sniff a little and then right her shoulder as if to muster up her dignity again. Watching us, she step backward, again and again further into the brush until we can see her no more. The crowd murmur and me thinking them saying same as me, a silent prayer for Mad Lizzy and her tortured soul.

Leary is before me now, the growling black hound is at his foot and me recognize the ready bile in his looks. He put his whip aside, step up, finger my collar, finger my cuffs, his eye confused, then he spit at me, I feel it damp my chest but I don't flinch. Leary, unafraid of Hector's gun, place his hands on his hips, ready for me soon as Cooke give word. The black hound at his feet be looking like a baited trap, 'bout to spring. I thinks of Musket, how sweet and kind hounds can be if them is shown a loving hand, instead of hate.

'Let them stand,' me say nodding to Apollo and him lift Cooke up to his feet.

In the silence, save the soft crackle from the house, Masser Cooke step his way to me too and the both of them stand together in a circle of dust-red emptiness. There's a heated murmuring in the crowd. I close my eyes. Trembling, I wet my dry lips. Murreat stay holding my hand as I move out of the line and stand before my family, the crowd is deep now, barefoot and cautious, all faces I know, facing me, waiting for me. Nita, Murreat, Hector, Cato, Apollo, Mungo, Rosemary, Anna, Bertha, Benjen . . . and, me gasp, me think me see her too, standing, serene, my Mimbah. Me want to tell her how sorry I am it have come to this. How I have fail her, how me will be with her soon. But not yet. Wiping my eye, I glance down at Murreat, she nod at me, squeezing me fingers tight-tight and me know, me have to tell my truth.

'Cookes, Leary – we must part company today. We cannot live together more. You must leave, take the next ship and return to England. The sun will be up soon and it is a day for change. The old is burned away and with it comes the new.' The voices behind me chorus them approval of my words. I turn to my brothers and sisters and raise my voice.

'Brethren, we have our unity, we have our pride, we know right and we know wrong. I is poor, weak, little. But when you stand beside me, I get strong. For our hand tills the land and sows the seed. Our hand picks the beet and grinds the corn! We

306

is us own agents. If we plant a tree of mettle, right now, and we work together on cultivating, in time that tree will be sturdy and strong and no one man can break it down. Our poor black lives, they matters some.'

I turn now to face the Cookes, my voice bellow like thunder.

'We demanding better treatment than the mule. We demanding to make the day through without shedding blood. We demanding clothes enough to keep us warm at night. Food enough to stop our eyes craving hogs' scraps.'

'Say it, Obah, say it!' the weaver women sing low as my words is voiced and I goes on, heart beating fast.

'We demanding ownership of ourselves. To choose who we marries, to unite again with that sold-off child. The freedom soon coming for us all and nothing you do can stop it.'

'Amen,' say Nita, rocking back and forth on her heels.

'Amen,' the crowd echoes.

'Nonsense!' spit Cooke. 'You are chattel – you do not make demands! Do you see how she has misled you? Regard her, in strange attire, speaking like she is no more a negro than I!' Cooke sways in his leathers, desperate to make eyes with one of us, to find a compliant ally, but there is none.

'I have the muzzle here.' Leary steps towards me, the dark leather strap tapping on his leg, but Hector lift the gun again and Cooke, his face level and placid, just as his statue did portray, press Leary back. Miss Frida and Miss Lynette have come closer too, them watch me with eyes wide as if them do not recognize me.

Benjen, the crawling infant, climbs naked up Bertha's ankles.

Swatting a fly from her mouth, she lifts him and begins to rock him to and fro. Both sets of eyes are tight, urging me on, trying to absorb my words before I speak them. Their movement back and forth, it sets a pulse for my words and my voice grows.

'Brethren, listen. What Miss Frida says is true. I *have* been away. But the place me did went to, it was not heaven, it was right here. Its roots start here and they are the roots of us, our blood, our sweat, our lives. We are a people. Right now, I have learn that, not far from us, Frederick Douglass, former enslaved and a black like we, be addressing a conference of white folk, speaking our truth. As I stand here, Sojourner Truth, she have rid herself of slavery and petition for equality. And in our islands, there's more still, hard at work! Toussaint Louverture, have make Haiti free from bondage, and right here, in Barbados, Bussa have start the flame! Let us make it burn!'

'That is quite enough,' Cooke cry. 'These names are meaningless. Such insolence, even now, Orrinda? Have you no shame that you refuse to kneel before me and beg for clemency? Your mother may have got away without fair repercussions for her actions. But that is not to be your fate. Men will come and you will answer for this.'

'Let her speak!' Hector step forward from the line and Cooke blink, as if momently aware of the numbers around him, the potential mob of us, he lowers his lifted hand. Expectation of his menace thickens the air, we is all familiar with its scent.

'Cookes, this is who we are! We are more than black bodies born awry. Your winter is over.'

CHAPTER 43

Without knowing how, the muttering of the crowd has become a music, the song we sing is a melodious spiritual tune, in a foreign tongue from far away. I catch sight of Nita now, in the throng, holding Benjen's hand. I never knew she was there. There is change stirred. A straighter back, a lifted head, hands clasped together, a hoe thrown down to kiss dirt. These are the eyes of a people turned. We have our freedom, we have won! We turn away from the Cookes, from Leary, leaving them to bicker amongst themselves.

I close my eyes brief, enjoying our victory. This is all me have ever wanted, just as my mother, a life without the yoke of bondage. Jacob would be proud, me blink away a tear as me heart pang for the missing of him. As I squeeze my eyes together, I feel a happy pulsing within me. There is a sound of tapping, of drum sticks in rhythm against a hollow skin, I smile, someone have found a drum! We will dance, we will celebrate. But as me look across at Cato, Hector and my friends, me realize this sound does not come from us. The drumming increase and the distinct sound of the marching of boots and bodies draws closer.

Cooke's eyebrows knit together and his head twists to scan for the source of the disturbance by the entrance to the courtyard. Led by the drummer announcing their arrival, a regiment of officers in full naval regalia stand lined in the light of the early dawn. The lead officer straightens his back.

'Wonderful!' announce Cooke, snarling and pointing at me. 'Mark me! I told you men would come! Officers, these slaves are guilty of rebellion, look upon my house, they have burned it to the ground!'

'Why, how now! Tis the King's Men!' Miss Frida's mouth opens and shuts.

'We are the West Africa Squadron. We seek an audience with Henry Reginald Cooke, Esquire.' The seaman's British accent is calm and commanding.

'This is he,' confirms Cooke, him square his shoulder, looking at all the officers in turn as if demanding an explanation from each. 'Your attentions here are most welcome. My house burns. And perhaps you also come with word of the missing miscreant? I sent word to the docks to secure the white rascal, the fellow ringleader of this failed enterprise.'

Jacob. Me gulp back my fear.

Apollo picks up another stick and Hector fondles the gun at his hip, them look upon me, their eyes tell me them will fight. We will not be yoked again!

The lieutenant snaps his heels together, unrolls a parchment and clear him throat in our silence before he reads the document aloud.

'In the name of King William the Fourth. Cooke, Henry Reginald, Esquire, you are under arrest for the crime of transportation of four hundred negro slaves from the Guinea coast to Barbados under the 1810 convention.'

'What in heaven's name is this blackguard entreating? What is the meaning of this prattle?' says Cooke. 'You want *them*, not me!' Him point at me.

'Where is your evidence?' squeal a pale Miss Frida circling the officers, curling and uncurling the folds of her violet pleats. She stop her walk at the head officer, but continue to press at her skirts.

'Papa?' plead Miss Lynette and her body slump against the ground, her tears exhausted.

'The boat was intercepted at sea, some two hundred or so nautical miles from the Guinea coast. You are named on the manifest as the owner and intended recipient of the chattel. You are in no doubt aware of the ending of such trading across waters since 1807, and the significant penalties for breaking these laws.'

'But I, I have done no such thing! I swear it!'

'We have the warrant. We must admit you aboard. You may put your defence to the courts in due course.'

'Give me that here, what are you talking about? What warrant?' Cooke reaches for the paper but him is pushed back firm by the butt of a rifle.

'I must compel you to restrain yourself. This warrant is dispatched under the authority of the King. In the meantime, we have reverted those at sea back to Guinea and we are

311

additionally under instruction to confiscate the ill-gotten stock you have here. You will have the right to a defence at the trial.' Two officers move to take Cooke by the elbows but he shakes them off.

'Don't you know who I am? This is my plantation. I have all the necessary documents, let me produce them!'

'Indeed? That would be a most suitable action. Where are your documents of ownership?'

Cooke look behind him at the flames that continue to snarl and bite the Big House.

'My advocate in London will affirm that all of these slaves belong to me, bought through fair and proper means. Half of them have grown up here! You there, Rosemary, and you there, Anna – answer truthfully now, is this not your home?'

Rosemary and Anna glance up at me before both bend their heads and solemnly shake them. Cooke swears and reaches for his gun, forgetting it is lost to Hector, and the men immediately raise their rifles. Cooke sighs and his hands raise up to remove his hat. He smiles, breathing easy, his tone like treacle.

'Now, surely, officers, this is a matter that we can settle amongst ourselves, as gentlemen. Englishmen. I have several fine kegs of rum that I'm sure you will enjoy. Perhaps, perhaps some have survived the fire – might I fetch them from the outhouse?'

The head squadron officer squares himself against Cooke. 'Sir, we carry out the King's orders. We do not require rum. You hold no valid documents. Those you mention in London are invalid until such time as they have been verified by the courts.

Do not attempt to obstruct the enforcement of our statutes. Come, let us behave like gentlemen or we shall have no choice but to treat you otherwise. You there, your name?'

'That's Leary, my overseer,' announce Cooke.

'We will take your man too, he is listed as accomplice and facilitator.' The officer tap against the parchment.

'Shrew!' Leary spit. 'I told you the risks! Time after time that it wouldn't work! In every one of your damned letters! Now look what you've done?' Leary scream profanity, but he looks not at me with his madness, he looks at Miss Frida. Miss Frida's complexion is bleached at Leary's attack. Two officers' arms press into him and he cries out to escape, his eyes rolling. Black nails fist together to aim punches that land in the air. There is a blow to his crown to stay his movement.

'It appears your abetter in this grave matter prefers to admit responsibility without debate – albeit with a rather discourteous tongue.' The officer beckon to Cooke. 'Come now, be a man.'

Cooke staggers back.

'Leary? Frida What have you done?'

'I only meant to secure our future, Henry – poor Lynette, our only child, we have no sons, what if she were to be an old maid? Stock is everything! And with this we would have secured her match! Don't you see?' Miss Frida press her hands against Cooke's chest but he push her away. He looks around him at all of us, at the eyes – black and white – on him. Finally, him settle a dark gaze upon me.

'This is your doing, is it not?' him snarl and his flying saliva

313

catches my feet as the men move to take him away. 'How is this happening? This is . . . some sort of witchcraft. I saw you disappear, before my very eyes. Leary was on you, right by that tree . . . I know what I saw . . . You were there, and then . . . then you were gone . . .' Cooke's voice fade to a whisper.

'The gentleman is quite mad.' The officer shake his head in disgust.

'What did I ever do to you, Orrinda?' Miss Frida grips her fan through white knuckles and sinks to her knees. I walk to her bending low to look her straight into the eye, the fire aflame in me.

'Madam, my name is Obah,' I tell her, for the first time.

As they lead Cooke away, he strain to look behind himself. His eyes don't rest on Miss Frida as she sobs silently into her handkerchief; his eyes don't rest on Leary, marching with him, or where the dropped muzzle lies. His eyes don't rest on me. His eyes are fixed hard on the crowd, as if counting our number. Branches of the pines in the courtyard moan softly as the breeze whips through, as if to voice the chorus of the silent crowd. As Nita come to stand beside me, I breathe out the air that was trapped within me and press my back against her warm and stout strength and as ever, she prop me up. I watch the white men leaving but one has stayed behind, as if him have remember one more task.

'Slaves, now, listen here. Your master has gone for a time. Perhaps he will return, perhaps not. There will be a full inventory of his possessions so I would advise you to stay put and wait here with Mistress Cooke until it is established whether you are to remain endowed and part of his estate or if you may walk free. There is to be a law announced imminently that will see some further change in your condition. Until then, stay faithful, work hard and God save the King.'

'But how did you know?' I ask the officer. 'How did you know about him crimes?'

'Why, naturally, we received counsel. A dispatch, of course, from a concerned third party. There are many good men today, who would see the law is not violated.'

Even though the Big House is gone and the battle for Unity won, me realize someone have tipped them. Someone who care about law, about justice. It can only be one person. My Jacob.

CHAPTER 44

The sun rise up again, as it ever does. There is always another day.

I is writing with my small knowledge of letters, as best I can, notes in the journal Jacob did give me for Christmas; finally, it is here. One day, in the future, I hopes to read it. The memories of a youngun who ain't so sure of her strengths, I hope it bears me up.

'I'm going to teach you now, Murreat. A power. On this paper is where we put words. This is a potency above all others. Shapes of black on white that decide fate. Words can hold secrets. Words can give life. Words be telling all what's passed and what's to come, all of this, you holding in your hand.'

Murreat's eyes is round moons as me scribble and she blink as the paper come to life as me write down *Jacob*. The both of us is watching how them black shapes seems to float, just above the page, like what be wrote be so important, that even paper can't bind it.

The Big House is blackened and bent, the warmth of the flame still curves about it. Murreat and me, we is huddled, cold, even though the sun shine as we walk the land. Some of us have gone, some have stayed. Some are skipping, some are singing, some are crying. But all of us are free. I turn the events over and over in my mind and finally me understand all. Jacob, him must have travelled here without me, before me make me final return and him did send the correspondence, detailing all the crimes of Cooke. Him was always curious about the letters between Miss Frida and Leary, my one confusion is how him have an opportunity to read them contents? How he did know that Miss Frida and Leary is in cahoots to bring more of us here? And then, me realize, of course, the hole in my pinny. Him must have seen the letters then, each time one did fall from my person. With my inside eye, me trace him brow and stroke him cheek and touch him lips. But *we* did it, Jacob. We didn't need the squadron. We did it ourselves!

We should wait, the officer tell us, with Miss Frida until the confirmation of us freedom. But in the morning, she have gone too. She and Miss Lynette. Not one know where she gone, not one know where she be now.

We have walked a half day behind Cato before we see it. And my eyes cannot believe that this was ever here, so close. It is everywhere, not pond, not brook, but the sea. And there is such a muchness of it! Like a draping sapphire sheet at the haberdasher's bench, it stretch out before us until it meet the sky. Cato did steal away and follow the men who took Cooke. Cato see them place him upon the ship and him come back full of a song of sea, telling us how we all must follow.

*

Murreat let go of my hand and start to run then towards the water's edge, and I feel myself taking off, flying with her, running on air, my feets riding on the breath of our new hope. I reach the edge before her and stop, gasping as the cool water kisses my toes, tickles my ankle, washes me clean. Closing my eyes I let it engulf me, the heady scent of hope. Then I raise my arm up to the heaven above me and throw my hand at the sky.

'What's that?' ask Murreat pointing at something shining in the blue before us and I stare at her.

'Murreat! You speaking? You speaking!' I pull her to me and hold her close, squeezing so hard that she complain.

'Hey, stop, stop!'

I pull away and look at her and she is alive! Her face beam, even the gap between her teeth isn't dark, instead it seem to glow with bright light.

'You never answer me question!' Murreat point and I see what she refer to, a ball of silver, spinning, winding, bobbing further into the waves and far away from us.

ACKNOWLEDGEMENTS

Thank you to my amazing agent Lydia Silver. Your unwavering support, insight and kindness are unparalleled. I am in awe of how wonderful you are and so grateful to have you by my side. I am very, very lucky indeed. Thank you too to all at Darley Anderson Literary Agency.

I am incredibly grateful to the hardworking publishing team at Simon & Schuster and realize how much fortune has blessed me. To my two incredible editors, where can I begin? My huge thanks to Amina Youssef for your sharp editorial eye, insight and direction, you helped me to unlock so many doors. Lucy Pearse, thank you for believing in this book, dedicating your heart to it and making it so much more wonderful than I could ever have managed alone. What a privilege for me to work with you.

Thank you to Mireille Harper, Anna Bowles and Sally Critchlow for your careful, considered and highly skilled close analysis of my words.

Thank you to Neil Arksey for many years of quiet support – I appreciate you so much.

Thank you to Leila Rasheed for working with me on my first draft and providing me with support and feedback.

Thank you to Danielle Jawando, Roi Campbell and Brenda Gray Champion for your wise counsel that kept me going when times were rough – I am so grateful. Mitra and Ed you guys just kept patting me on the back. Rebecca Thompson Teers for always being so lovely. Thank you to the Creative Accountability WhatsApp group for making me keep my promises!

Thank you to Nina Douglas for getting the book out to people and raving about it so well and for all your work behind the scenes.

To my dear sister Ju-hyun Kang – we did it!

To Maria Inzani and her team for providing me with a safe haven to repair and recharge and for championing the book much better than I could do myself! Thank you so much.

To Mum, Lucy, Bridget, Chris, Jamilah, Gary, Aaliyah, Arabella and Sandra – you're all the very best of the best.

Finally, to Ant, Ben and Raps – my lovely boys and the apples of my eye. I love you. Thank you.

AUTHOR BIOGRAPHY

Joyce Efia Harmer was born in London to Ghanaian parents. She has a BA in English Language and Literature from King's College, London, and went on to teach English.

In 2016, Joyce was selected as one of six writers to take part in the Megaphone writer's scheme to support diverse voices in Children's Literature. In 2017, she was selected as a finalist in Penguin's WriteNow scheme. She lives in London with her husband and two sons. *How Far We've Come* is her debut novel.

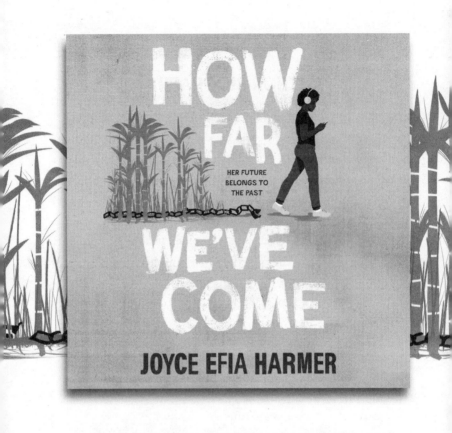

IS ALSO AVAILABLE TO LISTEN TO AS AN AUDIOBOOK READ BY THE AUTHOR!